MARIA LIT

I CHOOSE TO ~~SURVIVE~~ LIVE

ISBN: 978-1-0690216-6-3 (Paperback)
ISBN: 978-1-0690216-3-2 (Hardcover)
ISBN: 978-1-0690216-0-1 (Ebook)

Written by Maria Lit
First Edition (2025)

Table of Contents

Prologue

Maria ran through the forest, her steps frantic and unsteady. She stumbled and fell, but quickly pushed herself back up. Fear, disgust, and a desperate need to get as far from the castle as possible drove her forward. Every nerve in her body was on edge, trembling with unbearable emotions.

Her once elegant shoes, embroidered with golden thread, were now soaked with blood from her raw, blistered feet. She wanted to kick them off, but the sharp stones scattered along the path would be even worse to deal with in bare feet. Branches lashed at her tear-streaked face, catching painfully on the powdered wig with its carefully curled locks. In a surge of fury, she ripped the wig off and hurled it into the bushes.

Her heavy gown, suited for dancing in grand ballrooms, was a nightmare to run in. The tight corset squeezed her chest, making it hard to breathe, while her legs tangled in the torn, once-white hem with its delicate pink frills. Her muscles screamed in protest — Maria wasn't used to running like this. If only she had a horse!

But what good would it do? There was no escaping across the vast stretch of water separating her from her beloved England. How she longed to be back at her family's estate, surrounded by peaceful moorlands and silence. Back to where life was familiar.

But that was impossible now — her father would return her to her husband no matter what. He had sold her.

Behind her, the shouts of men and the pounding of horses' hooves grew louder, accompanied by the snapping of branches and the barking of dogs. The sounds drained the last of her hope. She couldn't run anymore. She had no strength left, no breath to fill her lungs. Black spots danced in her vision, and consciousness slipped away. Maria sank to the ground, burying her face in her hands.

The thudding of hooves drew closer, followed by triumphant cries — they had found her. Rough hands lifted her from the ground — strong, unyielding — and hoisted her onto a horse. She sat limply, swaying like a rag doll, her eyes unfocused, seeing nothing ahead.

The dense forest gradually gave way to a manicured park with fountains, perfectly shaped trees, and paths strewn with fine gravel. In the distance loomed the enormous castle. Elegantly dressed guests, remnants of last night's festivities, strolled the paths under lace parasols, shielding themselves from the sun. Maria's captors guided the horse through the park's most secluded corners, trying to avoid attention. They didn't want anyone to see her like this — no one would recognize the disheveled figure as the newly wedded bride of France's heir to the throne.

***

Maria was born into a wealthy estate in northern England. She barely remembered her mother; death had taken her too soon, leaving the young girl in the care of a devoted, kind-hearted nurse. This round, warm-handed woman gave Maria all the love she could, filling the void her mother's absence left behind.

Her father, a powerful lord, had little time for his daughter. He was always preoccupied with matters of importance, too busy for a girl. Every time her father looked at her, Maria wished she were a boy, a true heir. Maybe then, they could ride horses together across the vast lands, hunt, and marvel at his collection of weaponry.

Though she respected her father, Maria also feared him and didn't feel the warmth of love toward him. Instead, she poured all her affection into her father's advisor. This older man, with laughter often dancing in his eyes, would play with her, tell amusing stories, and bring her bouquets of wildflowers. Sometimes, Maria would catch him gazing at her for long stretches of time, his eyes sorrowful, as if lost in distant memories. He would often stare at her mother's portrait, which hung in the great hall, with the same look.

As the years passed, Maria grew from a girl into a young woman. With each passing day, she noticed more and more of her late mother's features in her reflection. Slowly, she began to understand the source of the advisor's sadness. Her heart had started to flutter with tender feelings — she didn't know when it began, but she noticed she always felt breathless when her father's commander walked into the room.

She had known him since childhood, back when he was just a soldier. Taciturn, serious, and always composed, he rarely smiled, but on occasion, he would gift her with a fleeting grin. Maria would watch, entranced, as his steps were light yet firm, his strong hands gripping his weapons during training. He was old enough to be her father, but that didn't bother her. The pure, gentle love blossoming in her heart grew stronger with each day, filling the cold, echoing halls of the gloomy estate with warmth and light.

One evening, her father gathered the advisor, the commander, and a few other trusted men for dinner. Maria was passing by the closed door of the hall when a loud argument caught her attention. She couldn't make out most of the conversation, except for one word: "war."

Heart pounding, she tiptoed closer, pressing her ear against the door to listen. Was the country in danger?

"My daughter's hand — for victory!" Her father's booming voice made Maria flinch. "It's a fine match, don't you agree?

She's a woman now and I trust that you'd provide a life fitting of her station."

Who was he saying that to? Silence fell over the hall, so deep that Maria was certain they could hear the wild thudding of her heart, beating like a trapped bird. She moved away from the door.

"Only if your daughter agrees..." It was the commander's voice. "But I will do my duty, even if there's no reward for it. May I take my leave?"

Maria stood frozen in place, her legs like stone. The door creaked open, and the commander stepped out. He didn't look surprised to see her outside the hall.

"You heard everything, didn't you?" he whispered, noticing her wide-eyed fear. His voice was soft, trying to soothe her. "Don't worry, I won't tell anyone."

Her heart raced even faster, and finally, Maria could move again. Her cheeks burned with embarrassment as she ran away without a word. She didn't want to return to her room, needing time to understand and dwell on what had been said. Had her father somehow learned of her feelings of affection towards the commander? Was she merely a prize for the commander in order to win the war? What danger was coming to England?

The commander found her in the stables later, her trembling hand stroking the neck of her favorite horse. She still had no answers to any of the questions that flooded her mind, but his presence was a welcome one.

"Maria," he said softly, "you don't have to marry me just because of your father's hasty words. The last thing I want is to see you unhappy."

Maria turned to him. "I will not deny that I'm happy that you are to be my betrothed," she said, watching his face relax, "but what is happening? What war are we facing?"

"One that will have me fighting on the front lines. Our marriage is to be my prize, if I am successful in keeping the enemy at bay."

"Then I'll wait for you," she whispered, barely audible. "Just... return victorious."

* * *

And he did return — alive and unscathed, though he had lost part of his army. Still, he had repelled the attack and made the enemy think twice before venturing onto their lands again.

Maria's father, overjoyed, threw a grand feast and seated the betrothed couple side by side. The hall echoed with raucous laughter and the singing of battle hymns. Tables overflowed with food, and the wine seemed endless, poured from jugs that never emptied. The commander's touches were subtle, as if accidental — a brush of the shoulder here, a fleeting hand against hers there. Maria didn't hide her happiness. They didn't need to exchange words of love; their glances and brief touches said more than any words could. The wedding was set for the following day, and Maria had never looked forward to a day in her life with such eager anticipation.

The only dark cloud over the evening was the constant snide remarks from one of her father's close advisors. He seemed determined to provoke Maria's fiancé into some sort of argument. The commander tried to brush it off with humor, but Maria could tell it was wearing on him.

"Was it really a victory, or a convenient little deal?" The advisor suddenly switched from jest to a serious tone, his gaze boring into the commander. "You could've made a nice arrangement with the enemy — offer them some land in exchange. After all, the bride's a wealthy heiress... Lord, aren't you worried about going to bed tonight?" The advisor turned his attention to Maria's father. "Well, maybe not tonight, but tomorrow, after the wedding..."

Her father only laughed, waving it off, but the commander leapt to his feet, his hand instinctively reaching for the sword that wasn't there — bringing a weapon to a feast was uncouth. Maria placed a hand on his arm; if only to try and calm him down.

"I've endured your mockery long enough. But I will not tolerate a direct accusation of treason against my lord," he said through gritted teeth.

"Come now, no one is accusing you of anything," Maria's father laughed. "Some people just need to sleep off their drink. In fact, it's time we all turned in for the night, or we won't even be able to raise a glass tomorrow."

Everyone laughed, rising unsteadily from the table and staggering off to their rooms. But Maria watched with concern as her fiancé fixed a gaze of pure hatred on the man who had insulted him.

"Go to bed," he whispered to her, giving her hand a quick squeeze. "I'll do the same. By morning, all will be forgotten... I hope."

He was right, at least in part. The next morning, Maria awoke in a brilliant mood, filled with excitement for her wedding day and her life ahead. She flung open the windows, letting the fresh air in that carried with it the sweet scent of roses from the garden.

Her nurse entered the room, eyes downcast, nervously wringing the edge of her apron in her hands. Without looking up, she helped Maria dress and arrange her hair. Then, suddenly, the woman began to sob.

Maria's questions were met with silence as the nurse gestured to follow her out of the room. She led Maria to one of the guest rooms, where her father's knights were gathered. Their faces were etched with sorrow and confusion, and on the bed...

Maria saw her fiancé, lying still. At first glance, it seemed he was only sleeping, but the unnatural pallor of his skin and the dried, dark stain on his shirt told a different story.

"He was killed in a duel last night. They found him on the green hill beyond the estate," one of the knights explained quietly.

Maria's scream of anguish didn't register as her own at first — it was a sound so raw, so filled with pain, that she barely recognized it. Turning sharply, she ran, desperate to find her father and demand justice for the man she loved. Still, deep down, she knew — duels were honorable, fair fights, and every participant knew the risks. Why hadn't he gone to bed as he promised? Had something else happened that she didn't yet understand?

Her father was calmly eating breakfast in the same hall where they had celebrated just hours before, as if he hadn't just lost his most loyal vassal, the best of his warriors. A chilling suspicion crept into Maria's mind: what if her father had planned the killing? Had he orchestrated the duel to avoid marrying her off to a man of lower rank? Why had he been the one to want her to marry the captain, in that case?

She wanted to throw all her accusations at him, to scream, stomp her feet, and tear the tablecloth so that the dishes would shatter on the floor. But she did none of it. She knew that if she showed even an inkling of rage, she'd face her father's own wrath. She had never been more terrified of her outwardly calm father. She was entirely under his control and there was nothing she could do about it.

Her father set down his cup, looking at her with a strange mix of pity and detachment.

"Don't grieve, my child," he said softly. "Consider this a fortuitous circumstance. Just yesterday, I received a better offer for your hand. You will be the queen of France."

* * *

At sixteen, Maria suddenly found herself in a foreign land, a world where it felt like everything was against her. The language, though once familiar, now became a source of constant mockery due to her accent and frequent errors. The unfamiliar dresses, the strange customs, and the bustling palace, forever swarming with servants and guests, made it impossible to ever belong or feel affection for this country or its people.

And the citizens, in turn, seemed determined to never embrace her. To them, she was a clumsy foreigner who spoke awkwardly, dressed oddly, and never quite understood their humor.

Maria's future husband's family met her with a coldness that spoke volumes. To them, she was a naive country girl who had stumbled into their opulent, gilded world by mistake. While she might not have grasped the intricacies of court politics, it was clear that she and her father were insignificant compared to this powerful family.

Perhaps she could have endured it all if her father had given her time to mourn the loss of her former love, or if her future husband had offered her even a fraction of kindness. But neither was granted to her.

On her wedding night, Maria awaited her husband with a heavy heart, resigned to accept whatever fate awaited her. He chose to violate her with force, disregarding her wants and needs completely, using her to satisfy his own. No one seemed to care — no one but the maid, who quietly comforted Maria as she cried into her pillow after her husband stormed out of the room.

When Maria awoke, every movement was a stab of pain. The sunlight streaming through the curtains did little to alleviate her suffering. The maid, roused from dozing in a chair by the window, quickly assisted Maria in dressing — tight corset, frilly gown, and the dreadful wig. Once dressed, Maria opened the double doors leading from her bedroom to her husband's quarters.

The scene that greeted her was a stark reminder of her new reality. The table was littered with wine-stained linens and overturned glasses, the remnants of last night's feast now attracting flies. Further in, the bed's torn canopy hung limply, and there lay her husband — disheveled, drunk, and snoring loudly. He sprawled amid three half-naked women, his sweaty hands, which had recently touched her with revulsion, now resting on the bodies of these strangers.

Tears threatened to spill as Maria fought back the waves of nausea. Maintaining a facade of composure, she walked through the mess, descended the steps into the park, and ventured into its secluded alleys. She found a path that led toward the forest, her only hope now lying in that dark expanse — seeking either salvation or an end, for living in this place was no longer bearable.

***

The images flash before her eyes — year after year passed in a blur of rumors, loneliness, and hatred. There was no respite for her, no way for her to escape her new life except through her dreams as she slept.

A single ray of hope pierces through the darkness: a long-awaited pregnancy. Long-awaited because it means her husband will finally leave her alone and will stop barging into her room at night. Long-awaited because at last, there will be someone in this world who will love Maria simply for being. And oh, how she would love them in return.

The thought is enough to lull her into a light sleep. Maria could feel her mind moving through images of her past, of hopes for her future, and dreams of her present.

The pictures freeze, leaving only one vivid image. A long stone corridor, dimly lit by scattered torches, their weak flames unable to chase away the heavy shadows lurking under the ceiling. The gray columns fade into the darkness above. A woman in a black hooded cloak hurries down the corridor, carrying a candlestick. The sound of her heels echoes against the stone surrounding her. She pauses, glancing in both directions to make sure no one is watching. Then she presses a small stone in the wall, revealing a hidden door.

Beyond the door lies pitch blackness, but the woman quickly dispels it by lighting more candles from her own. Maria follows her in, confused, unsure of where she is or who this woman is — and whether the woman can even see her. She'd never had this type of dream before.

They enter a room with high ceilings, devoid of windows. Despite the oppressive stone walls, the space feels warm and filled with a sense of secrecy. From the floor to the ceiling, shelves overflow with ancient, dust-covered books. It seems as though touching any of them would cause the pages to crumble into dust at her fingertips. Against the far wall stands a simple wooden table, cluttered with more books, melted candles, and jars of powders and liquids. Scattered across the room are peculiar objects: colorful stones, bird feathers, bundles of roots and herbs, small apothecary scales, and a few devices Maria doesn't recognize.

The woman turns toward Maria — she does see her, after all! There's something about her that invites the word *witch*. Her cloak conceals her figure, but her sharp eyes gleam beneath the hood, her face etched with deep lines, and her lips are pressed into a suspicious frown. She begins to extend her hand toward Maria, but then hesitates and pulls it back into the folds of her cloak.

"I am you," the woman says.

Maria isn't surprised, because she feels it too.

"I knew one day you'd come to me. I've been waiting for you. You seek answers — who you are and what your purpose is. And I will tell you. Life forced me to practice magic, or else my son would never have ascended to the French throne. Schemes, intrigues, a hateful husband, and his treacherous family — only through magic was I able to protect myself and my child from all of it."

Maria couldn't help the tears that sprung to her eyes. She was going to have a child, but it seemed his life would be difficult.

"The knowledge I gathered flows in your blood now. Read the ancient books you find, study the runes — they will reveal themselves to you and become your faithful guides. And while I hide my secrets from others in this room and in the depths of my heart, in your world, in your time, there will be no need for that. You will be able to help not only yourself, but others too."

Maria listens, absorbing every word, feeling the weight of the revelation settle inside her. She isn't sure what this power means yet, but she feels it stirring, waiting to awaken. In that moment, the threads of her past, her suffering, and her isolation begin to weave into something greater: a purpose she had never imagined.

* * *

The image of the woman in the dark room flickers, like a ripple in water. Colors blend and swirl, and Maria suddenly finds herself standing in a grand cathedral. Towering columns stretch endlessly upward, supporting a vaulted ceiling that seems to reach the heavens. Sunlight pours through an enormous stained glass window, scattering across the stone floors in a kaleidoscope of colors.

Maria watches from the periphery, as if hovering just above it all, unseen by the crowd filling the cathedral. The solemn notes of the organ swell through the air, joined by the angelic voices of the choir. A wave of awe ripples through the seated congregation as the figure at the front of the room turns to face them.

The man's face looks familiar; his eyes the same shade as hers, his cheeks dimpling just as hers did when she smiled. Her son, her beloved boy, stands tall with a heavy crown resting upon his head. He has ascended to the throne. He is now the King of France.

A weight lifts from Maria's chest, the fear that had gripped her heart for so long finally dissolving. Her son had done it — he had claimed his rightful place. She has nothing to fear.

A woman approaches the newly crowned king. It is the older version of herself Maria had spoken to about magic, the one from the hidden chamber. Her hair is silver, her skin wrinkled, the vibrancy of her youth long faded — but her eyes still shine with an unmistakable light. Perhaps the last time they had shone so brightly was when she had gone out to greet the army of her betrothed after his victory. Yet, it is her. It is Maria.

This is the happiest day of her life. Her husband is gone, her son has become king — Maria's mission in this life is complete. Everything she has endured, every moment of suffering, every triumph, has led to this. She has fulfilled her purpose, and there is nothing left tying her to this world.

At last, she is free.

* * *

"Maria, open your eyes. It's over now. Take your time, don't rush to come up. Here, take this tissue, you were crying."

The gentle voice of the regression therapist feels distant, as if it's filtering through a heavy fog from the past life I'm still trapped in. I'm still mourning the loss of my beloved, still running through the forest, hiding magical books in a secret room, and gazing at my son seated on the throne.

This isn't like waking up from a dream that slowly fades. My heart races, my palms are sweaty, and my face is drenched in tears. My soul feels split in two, unsure of where I currently am.

My name is Maria, and I've been given the chance to understand why I'm surrounded by these particular people and why my relationships with them are the way they are. I can't connect all the dots, not yet, but I hold the thread that will guide me through this maze. I'll need to unravel it carefully, so I can release old grievances, embrace the lessons, and forgive those souls who have journeyed with me through the centuries.

This story will not repeat itself again.

Introduction: Follow Your Truths

Even geniuses make mistakes – sometimes more than the rest of us. It's only through a path filled with trials and errors that we can reach a new level of understanding.

Hello, dear reader! It's me again, Maria, and today I want to share a bit more about myself and the difficult journey I've walked. My life has been full of mistakes, each one piercing me like a dagger. I've stumbled, fallen from the pain, and asked a million questions that went unanswered for far too long. Walking on thin ice, I searched for solid, warm ground. And it was only when I looked deep within myself that I found the way to it.

One day, I finally understood why my path led me through such dark and thorny woods, why I had to scrape my feet bloody, and what awaited me on the other side. I found my purpose, and in doing so, I came to terms with the mistakes of my past.

This revelation can happen to anyone. Every single one of us is a vast whirlpool of energy and knowledge. We all possess the wisdom and experiences that can help others, but not all of us understand what that experience is or how to apply it.

Everyone seeks to know their earthly mission, their purpose in this life. And when a person doesn't realize their importance, they need help.

I believe that each person is unique. Our mission is to find and nurture that uniqueness. Even if you're born with a talent — whether it's as an artist, musician, athlete, or writer — you still have to discover it during your life. Then you must patiently train and develop it in order to find success in that field.

Take, for example, someone born with the potential to be a great violinist. If that person never picks up a violin and never finds themselves in an environment that fosters their talent, they may live their entire life without ever knowing the gift they had. This is why I always say that you have to test your reality, experiment in different areas, and immerse yourself in various situations to see your talents rise to the surface. You have to give yourself the chance to shine.

The most valuable thing in the universe is us: our intelligence, our growth, our worldview, and our inner strength. That inner energy is the framework of our life's structure, onto which everything else is built. When a person finds themselves and strengthens their energy, they attract the right people, events, inspiration, material wealth, and all the other blessings life has to offer.

The inner world is always reflected in the outer one — once you understand yourself, you begin to influence the circumstances around you. There was a time when it felt like my circumstances had overpowered me: moving to a foreign country, giving up my business for my family, facing a life-threatening illness, destructive relationships, my husband leaving during pregnancy, the pandemic, isolation, loneliness, fear, depression, and losing myself... The answers don't come unless you start asking questions, but those questions don't appear out of nowhere. The road, full of obstacles and deep pits, forced me to slow down, stop, turn off the engine, and, in the silence, realize that the path forward was inward — within myself.

To reach this truth, I had to endure a lot, filling myself not only with knowledge and experience, but also with pain.

At 20, I launched my first business. Through hard work and determination, I achieved success and took full control of my life. I didn't know what it meant to lose power over myself until the day I met my future husband. Moving to another continent for him, I slowly lost everything — my business, my independence, the support of loved ones, connection with the outside world, and even myself as an individual. After the birth of our child, my husband vanished — leaving me alone in a cold, bleak world, with almost no means to survive. But I clawed my way back. I climbed out of that pit, grasping onto every ledge I created along the way. Not only did I rebuild myself, but I also saved myself because I believed, I felt, and I knew that a beautiful and happy future awaited me.

I had to piece myself back together. Step by step, stone by stone, I built a new, safer path on which I could walk confidently. I was no longer afraid of sharp stones beneath my feet, walking with confidence on a road I crafted.

I revived my business, launched new projects, healed my body and mind, and eventually created a new, happy family.

"No one wants a woman with baggage," people told me, hinting that I'd never marry someone with my child. But that's just a stigma – rusty chains we shackle ourselves with.

I broke those chains and created a new version of myself – stronger and more self-sufficient than ever before. My child, independent and naturally gifted with leadership qualities, had visited 15 countries by the age of three and a half and had already begun learning four languages.

By the time I turned 30, I had traveled to 40 countries and established four companies across the United States and Canada. I am no longer dependent on anyone and I live exactly the way I want.

The material world must always go hand-in-hand with the spiritual. My earthly journey evolved alongside my sacred one. After all the challenges I faced, I asked myself the ultimate question: Who am I and what is my mission?

I sought answers from various people and through different methods of self-discovery: classical psychoanalysis, hypnosis, regression therapy, the matrix of destiny, astrology, human design...I tried so many things. It was the "matrix of destiny" that helped align everything for me and became my inner compass. But the more answers I got, the more questions surfaced. At one point, I left everything behind and flew to Bali. There, I met a shaman who told me my purpose was to help people.

The greatest task in life is finding your individuality. In this book, I share my own journey and examples of how I achieved this. But you, dear reader, will walk your own path.

I know my mission — through both numbers and life experience, but this knowledge didn't come to me overnight. The place I stand today is the result of a long, difficult journey. This is the journey I want to share in my book. For me, this is stepping outside my comfort zone, but I know that by doing so, I can help others. I'm doing this so that you, dear reader, will know you are not alone. And so that you can gain these insights faster than I did.

Chapter 1: Beyond Other People's Goals

"Maria, you have such a beautiful gymnastics leotard gathering dust on the shelf, along with those white socks, and just look at that perfect figure of yours! You've got all the makings of a top-class gymnast! But instead, you keep running around and never commit to a proper class. You should be at home, studying or going to activities, but you're always out in the yard, like a restless cat," my mother would say.

And so, I've been running my whole life, not chasing after others' goals, just running and reaching my own summits.

I am Maria Litvinenko, as it says in my passport. To my family — Marisha. To my friends, I'm simply Masha. Many names, many roles, and a lifetime packed with experiences that few get to live through have brought me to where I am now.

Desire More

Maria was a 14-year-old girl who lived and worked as a courier. She always wanted more from life: more truth, more justice, more protection for the weak and defenseless. She stood up for others before she ever thought about herself.

It would take years of pain and self-reflection before Maria learned how to listen to herself and to make choices for her own well-being instead of keeping her focus on others. She was quick to jump into a fight and feed every stray cat in the neighborhood. In many ways, Maria was like a cat herself — an animal fiercely independent and hardworking. Even the most pampered housecat, with all its comforts — food, water, a warm spot to sleep — will still hunt at the first chance it gets. That's the spirit of the hunter that lived inside her, and no one could take it away.

I am Maria. I was born and raised in Kyiv, the capital of Ukraine, a fourth generation native. I know the central district like the back of my hand. I could walk its streets blindfolded. Every alley, every cobblestone, every crack in the asphalt is part of the landscape of my beloved city.

At 14, I got my first job. My parents took care of my basic needs, but they did so on their terms, never asking what I truly wanted. I thought having my own money would help me feel more fulfilled, but it was more the independence that I craved rather than the money I made.

From as far back as I can remember, I've always felt that I had to be my own foundation, that I had to rely on myself for everything. No one ever forced me to work, but self-sufficiency bloomed in me from the start. I was left to my own devices as a child, and I made many of my decisions independently.

But more on that later.

Don't Waste Time

I landed my first real job thanks to a classmate when I was in ninth grade. He suggested delivering photographs over the summer break, and I jumped at the opportunity because I had a goal: to buy myself a new model of a mobile phone. At the time, magazines were coming out every week featuring ultra-modern gadgets with steep price tags that seemed utterly out of reach. I stared at those glossy pages like I was under a spell, my eyes lighting up with that hunter's spark.

"Why not? Any job is an opportunity, and opportunities shouldn't be wasted," I told myself. The pay wasn't huge, but it brought me one step closer to checking off a few goals from my wish list.

Yes, any job is an opportunity, but it's also hard work. In the sweltering 30-degree summer heat, public transport in Kyiv turned into a moving sauna. Thousands of hot, sticky bodies crammed together, barely functioning as their minds melted in the heat. But I knew exactly where I was headed: forward toward that brand new phone. It was only the first item on my long list of dreams, but I knew one thing for certain: if I wanted something in life, I had to go out and make it happen myself. No one owed me anything, and I was raised with that mindset. **If you want more, go and do it yourself. If you fail, that's on you. Whether you push through or give up, it's your decision**.

Working as a courier wasn't easy, especially as a young girl. You'd think delivering photographs would be simple enough, but the heavy boxes and bags made my thin arms burn and swell under the weight. The physical exhaustion, combined with the heat and the long walks through endless unfamiliar streets, was dizzying. While I knew the center of Kyiv like the back of my hand, the Left

Bank was a whole different universe and one where nothing made sense to me. The combination of heat and fatigue left my mind a tangled mess.

This was 2007, with no GPS that I could rely on. All I had was a paper map of Kyiv, and I had to figure it out as best I could.

It was a different kind of challenge. Each delivery was a test of patience, resilience, and determination. I'd look at the map, then at the streets around me, sometimes feeling like I'd never get to where I needed to go. But I kept going, step by step, fueled by the thought of that shiny phone and the satisfaction of achieving something on my own terms.

There were days when I felt like giving up, when the heat and the weight of the work seemed too much, but each delivery brought me closer to my goal. I wasn't just earning money; I was proving to myself that I could do it. That mindset, that drive, was what set me apart even at 14. I knew then, as I know now, that the only person who could change my life was me. And I wasn't going to waste any time waiting for someone else to make it happen.

To reach a cherished goal, do not fall into the victim mindset. No one ever promised it would be easy. **When something is truly important to you, you push yourself. If you've chosen your path, move forward and don't stop. Keep going and don't look back.**

Carrying those heavy packages was exhausting. More than once, I wanted to get off the sweltering trolleybus and run home. But my choice was clear, and there was no turning back. Someone else might have quit, retreated to the cool comfort of their room, poured themselves a cold lemonade, and forgotten the whole thing like a bad dream. They may have shrugged off the phone they didn't buy and move onto wanting something else.

Someone else would have, but not Maria. She only moves forward. For me, stepping back is the same as admitting defeat. It feels like losing to yourself and that's not something I accept.

A couple of months later, I had that brand-new phone in my pocket. I still remember opening the box and pulling out the long-awaited Nokia with it's color screen. I remember the smell of the plastic, peeling off the protective film, and turning it on for the first time, the cheerful words 'Nokia: Connecting People' lighting up the screen.

Delivering photographs wasn't actually my first job, at least technically. My first business partner was my dad. We were always the best of friends and allies in any venture. He was both my mentor and my biggest supporter, always encouraging my ambition to work and often finding ways for me to earn my own income.

One day, he called me, laughing, and said, "Maria, you wanted a summer job? Well, I have an open position for you. I'll show you when I get home!"

My dad had a surprise in store for me one that was delivered right to my doorstep. At the time, he owned a transportation company, and one of his trucks had just returned from the south. But why come back empty-handed? When he pulled up to the house, I watched with excitement as he opened the truck, revealing it was packed to the ceiling with watermelons and melons.

"Well, Maria, here's your stock! Let's get this truck empty before the summer is through."

It took us about a week to sell everything. We sold out down to the last slice, the last melon stem. My best friend Anastasia, who I'd roped into this venture, and I sold the watermelons directly from the truck parked right outside our house. Two skinny girls with watermelons so heavy we could barely lift them off the ground would pass them to customers after receiving crisp bills and shiny coins in return.

I was about 12 at the time. The entrepreneurial spirit inside me had found its opportunity and was bursting to break free. I wanted to do more!

But even the watermelon business wasn't my first entrepreneurial endeavor.

It all started, not with melons, but with painted salt dough buttons. When I was about three or four, I learned to make tiny round crafts from salt dough at daycare. We called them buttons — flattened little balls, painted in bright colors, baked in the oven, and turned into decorations. In the tiny mind of a child, I realized these buttons were meant to become someone else's prized possession; not for free, of course.

It's hard to remember whether I came up with the idea to sell the buttons as souvenirs myself or if my mom suggested it. Either way, she helped me bring the idea to life. **Resourcefulness and initiative are the keys to success. Don't be afraid of ideas that come to you, even if they seem silly or impractical at first glance.**

I remember coming home from daycare, full of excitement, and immediately sharing the recipe for the buttons with my mom. We spent hours shaping, painting, and baking them, turning those little dough pieces into bright, colorful buttons.

The idea of selling them came naturally. They looked so vibrant! Who wouldn't have wanted to buy something so pretty? My mother and I set out to sell the buttons for a dollar apiece. The street was always packed, especially with tourists. Whether it was the charm of the buttons or my own childlike appeal, I don't know, but we sold everything in less than half an hour.

A little while later, I decided to embark on another 'business project' involving baked goods. My mom made the most incredible cottage cheese cookies — just looking at them, warm and golden, fresh from the oven, with that scent of vanilla, made your mouth water. And since I already had experience selling buttons, I figured, why not cookies? They were delicious, after all.

Near our house was the National University of Culture and Arts. Imagine a little girl, about five years old, sitting at a tiny table outside her home, wearing a lace dress like a doll. I had a little sign that my mother helped me make, then I shooed her back into the house so I could get to work.

My mom watched over me from our first-floor window while I sat with a plate of freshly baked cookies, still warm. Hungry students devoured them in minutes. Years later, I would walk those same streets as a student at that very university, remembering how I once sold cookies to students like myself.

I've sold so many things since then! In fourth or fifth grade, I even managed to sell a stray cat for thirty cents. That was more of a humanitarian gesture than a business venture, but still, I always loved to experiment. No one thought it was possible to make money from selling a stray animal, but while others were either overthinking or wasting time, I was *doing*. At five, at ten, at fifteen — I was always in motion. The trick is: **don't stop!**

Ice, Fire, and Me

My relationship with my parents was never simple, especially with my mother. All of my early entrepreneurial experiments took place against the backdrop of serious family turbulence. Half of my life was spent watching a drama, with my parents as the main characters. Naturally, this experience left a lasting mark.

Before they were married, my mom and dad lived in the heart of Kyiv, on Arsenalna Street. They met while they were still in school, thanks to their dogs. They both had German Shepherds, and my dad's dog tracked my mom's dog back to her home — just like in the story of *101 Dalmatians*.

She was a model student, a professional major league athlete, and a Master of Sport in rhythmic gymnastics for the Soviet Union.. He was the black alley cat — handsome, but undeniably a troublemaker.

When my mom got into university and my dad didn't, they went their separate ways. My mom met someone else and got married. As the newlyweds drove off in their wedding car, my dad crossed the street in front of them with his friends.

Quite a coincidence.

Three months later, my mom divorced her new husband and went back to my dad. From that point on, there wasn't a single day in their lives, or their children's, without storms and strife.

There were two children, me and my older brother. We both felt the full weight of it, but with 16 years between us, we were raised separately. I didn't have the chance to share the challenges of life with our parents with anyone else. That burden, in all its heaviness, was mine alone to carry.

To say my parents' relationship was unstable is an understatement. My mom was fiery and emotional. My dad was cold rationality, ice. And I was always stuck in the middle, caught between these two extreme forces.

One night, during yet another family crisis, my mother decided to leave home in the middle of a snowy winter night. We had two apartments, both in the center of the city, about two kilometers apart, and she was leaving for one.

I can still picture the scene vividly in my mind, forever etched into my memory: large snowflakes falling on my head, bags hastily packed, sitting in the snow. My mom, her eyes still red from crying, stood there holding onto a suitcase. It was bedtime — the moment to snuggle up in a warm bed, but instead, a long, cold journey to the other apartment lay ahead.

Three-year-old Maria, bundled up in winter clothes so thick it was hard to move, was crying and begging to be picked up. My mom, with calm resolve, told me that she was struggling — not just physically, but emotionally as well. And even at that tender age, I had to learn to understand her. Like a little penguin chick,

I waddled awkwardly behind her, through the wind, the snow, and the freezing curtain of ice. Neither of us had respite until we made it into the other apartment.

When it comes to emotions, my entire childhood felt like a wild rollercoaster, my parents the ones controlling the ride. I wouldn't have the chance get off that ride until I finally grew up and moved out on my own.

It took me years to understand that the real destructive force in my family was resentment. My parents blamed each other for all their misfortunes, harboring this corrosive feeling for years. They didn't know how to forgive, and resentment burned in their hearts, leaving icy scars that never healed. It was as if they had carried this grudge from another life – one where they couldn't be together for reasons I would never know.

That's why, in my life, I refuse to hold onto resentment or hatred. From that struggle, even as a child, I gained invaluable knowledge.

Like waves that shape a stone, my character was sculpted, not only by my parents, but also by my older brother. He played a crucial role in shaping who I am, and for that, I am deeply grateful.

How to Express Anger and Resentment in a Healthy Way

1. Breathe. Take several deep breaths, focusing on breathing through your abdomen. Adding yoga to this can make it even more effective.

2. Scream. Let it out — in the car, into a pillow, in the forest, under the shower, during a thunderstorm, at a sports event, or a rock concert — find a legitimate way to scream and release the tension.

3. Hit. Punch a boxing bag or a couch cushion, go for a run, dance energetically, throw a ball, or swim at full speed.

4. Write. Spill all your emotions onto paper. Don't choose your words carefully — just unload everything that's weighing you down. Later, you can delete, burn, or tear the letter.

5. Cry. It's the simplest and most natural way to release emotions. Crying is the body's natural defense mechanism against stress and can even protect you from a heart attack. Let it happen — your body knows what it needs.

6. Draw. Put your emotions on paper. Even if you're not good at drawing, use shapes, lines, and colors to express what's suffocating you and preventing you from feeling happy.

7. Switch focus. Anger is energy, and you can channel it into something productive. Clean out your closet, throw away unnecessary items, rearrange furniture, or wash the windows — and the world will seem brighter!

My brother was born special. No baby in the maternity ward screamed as piercingly as Anton. If he could hear his own cry, he would have been terrified. But he was born completely deaf.

My parents invested endless amounts of time and effort into my brother. My father complained for most of his life that my mother dragged him all across the Soviet Union, trying to cure Anton's deafness. However, the diagnosis was incurable.

Despite his condition, Anton became a Master of Sport and a European table tennis champion. He followed in our parents' footsteps, as both my mother and father were decorated athletes.

During one of their 'reconciliations,' when they reunited for the thousandth time, my mother became pregnant again. She had planned to have an abortion, but at the very last moment, while already at the doctor's office, she declared, "No, I'm keeping this child." At the time, she was almost 40 years old.

When my 16-year-old brother asked her why she wanted another child, she answered, "Well, you're deaf. One day we won't be here and a sibling will help you." This preordained role was assigned to me even before I was born, shaping how I would be raised and perceived in the family.

A lion's share of my parents' attention and love went to Anton, the child into whom they had poured so much and continued to do so, even when he turned 18, 25, and eventually 40.

My parents remembered everything about their firstborn – his first crib, first steps, first words, and other heartwarming details. I, on the other hand, as the healthy child, always felt like child number two, not just in order but in importance. I grew up on my own, like grass that didn't need watering. It wouldn't be an exaggeration to say that my parents occasionally forgot about me. They tried to find me activities, enrolling me in small, unremarkable clubs in the neighborhood, but I always wanted more.

Since all the emotional and material resources had been drained by my brother, I was left with an empty plate. I spent my childhood largely fending for myself. Spending most of my time outdoors, I quickly learned that in life, I could rely only on myself.

When I needed something, I didn't go to my parents for help. I did it myself. In my mind, I didn't interfere in their lives, and they didn't interfere in mine. But in reality, things were much more complicated.

Any external pressure was a signal for me to resist. And my resistance was always measured and rational. The one thing my mother devoted her energy to, however, was fulfilling her 'pink dream.' Now that she had a daughter, she was thinking about some of the opportunities she had missed or ones she wanted me to have.

When I was six years old, my mother decided to enroll me in gymnastics, hoping I would follow in her footsteps. With my promising physical attributes — grace, flexibility, and energy — she was eager to see me excel. We visited the grand sports hall of the Palace of Sports in Ukraine, where the atmosphere was buzzing with anticipation. Several coaches rushed to my mother, eager to take me under their wing.

At our first class, I was struck by the sight of young gymnasts contorting their bodies. Older girls would sit on top of the younger ones to push them into splits, causing the smaller ones to tremble and cry out in pain. The room was filled with their distressing sobs, and it left me profoundly unsettled.

"Why do I need to do this?" I asked my mother, watching the scene unfold with wide eyes.

"Why? To compete, win medals, and gain recognition!" she replied with enthusiasm.

"What's recognition?"

"It's a certificate — a piece of paper that says your name and your placement."

I couldn't see the value in a piece of paper for all the pain and effort going on around me. Even at that young age, I understood that true respect couldn't be earned through a mere certificate.

Despite earning one certificate for my mother after a few months, I decided to quit gymnastics. The idea of enduring pain for a concept that didn't resonate with me seemed pointless.

I learned a valuable lesson: **follow your true desires not those imposed by others. Real happiness and success come**

from pursuing what genuinely matters to you. Think rationally. Separate your own dreams from others' expectations, and everything will fall into place.

I realized I could have been a remarkable gymnast, but what was the point if it wasn't my dream? Time is too precious to waste on fulfilling others' goals.

Second Time in First Grade

The chaos of my parents' relationship and our constant moving inevitably affected my life. I went through several schools, dozens of teachers, and countless classmates. I was thrown into a whirlwind of events that could have overwhelmed a little girl. But somehow, I came out of it nearly unscathed — the experiences only made me stronger. Every challenge was a lesson and I've always been good at leaving the bad parts in the past.

It all started with kindergarten. My mother became obsessed with the idea of sending me to a Waldorf school. At that time, they were just starting to appear in our country. These schools used a unique teaching method — no grades, with a personal approach to each child. The focus was on creativity: the kids spent their days drawing, playing music in an orchestra (each child with their own instrument), and learning to connect with nature.

When my parents had one of their many breakups, my mom rented out our apartment in the central district of the city and moved us to the Left Bank, where one of the two Waldorf schools, 'Sophia,' was located.

At the time of their split, I wasn't old enough for school, but I was just the right age for kindergarten. So my mom enrolled me in the kindergarten attached to the Waldorf school.

But things didn't go as planned. I was like a wild tiger cub in a cage — headstrong and restless. The only thing harder than getting me to take a nap during quiet time was stopping the sun from rising in the morning. My rebellious streak, which often roped in the other kids, didn't sit well with the teacher. The situation worsened because I didn't get along with her daughter, who was in my group.

The result was surprising and confusing: halfway through the school year, in January, I was moved from kindergarten to the first grade. It felt like winning the lottery, New Year's and my birthday all at once. I turned six in January. But instead of feeling lucky, I was more and more bewildered. My life seemed to be changing by the second.

Despite the odd circumstances of my transition to first grade, things went smoothly. I kept up with the curriculum and felt confident in my abilities. I enjoyed learning, and my relationships with classmates were good. But then summer came. My parents reconciled, and we moved back in with my dad.

He had one condition: I had to attend a regular school. My dad was against any educational experiments and was deeply concerned that in an unknown Waldorf school, which operated without a license, I wouldn't learn anything substantial. Worse, he feared I wouldn't receive a state diploma, which would prevent me from attending university. My mom, on the other hand, believed there was no better place for her child in all of Kyiv, but in the end, she conceded and I was enrolled in a new school.

So, in September, little Maria, with white bows in her braids, went back to first grade in a traditional school.

Regular school turned out to be another challenge for me. After six months in such a different learning environment, I was unprepared for the endless restrictions of the post-Soviet education system. There were grades now, punishments if you were out of line, and the stifling of any creative expression. Even then,

I could sense how harmful it was. I protested loudly, trying to get my parents to understand. But what could a six-year-old do?

Six months later, my parents separated again. And once again, my life turned 180 degrees. My mom sold the apartment and we moved to a different suburb on the opposite end of the city — the last stop on the metro line, a neighborhood of tired, run-down Soviet apartment blocks. My mom made yet another emotional decision, anything to be far away from my dad.

By then, I was seven years old, and drastic changes no longer frightened me. Moving every six months, sometimes even more frequently, had become a regular part of my life. But one thing I couldn't reconcile with was the constant loss of a sense of home and family. I felt like a nomad, being tossed from one end of the city to the other.

I still remember the feeling of being lost during each move, as if I left behind a piece of myself every time. On the other hand, this experience toughened my character in ways that would help me handle everything the future had in store.

Then came second grade, mid-school year. I was back in a Waldorf school, but this time at a different one, called 'Michael.' It was for this school that we had moved from the familiar city center to the outskirts. And it was here that I would spend most of my school years.

Alone in the Field (But Not Alone)

The foundation of Waldorf education is built on comfort, mutual support, and the development of individual abilities. It all sounds quite appealing, to parents at least. But does the reality match the promise? Even in the most carefully crafted environments, there's one unpredictable and all-consuming factor: people.

At first, I was genuinely happy to be back in a creative environment that felt familiar to me. The school was close to home and I quickly made friends with the other kids. Thanks to all the frequent moves and changes in my life, I had developed a knack for connecting with new people. I was good at it — easily making friends, blending into the group, and, almost immediately, trying to assert myself as a leader. That part of me, the need to lead, was strong and undeniable. Whenever someone tried to suppress it, I felt like I couldn't breathe, like there wasn't enough air.

For a brief moment, it felt like things were finally stabilizing. I allowed myself to relax a little, to just be a child again, carefree and happy. But as I would come to learn, stability and my life were incompatible. Happiness, too, was fleeting, as fragile as a snowflake in your palm — just when you think you've caught it and admired its beauty for a moment, it melts away.

My dad couldn't accept that I had returned to what he considered an "illegitimate" school. Unable to influence my mom, he decided to act differently. He used his connections and reported the school's unsatisfactory sanitary conditions to the authorities. That triggered a wave of inspections and checks. The school branch near our home was shut down.. The owners were forced to search for a new location, which turned out to be even further away, in an even more remote part of Kyiv.

What stung the most was that somehow the principal and teachers found out that my family was behind the school's closure and forced relocation. They blamed us and, by extension, me.

The consequences were predictable. People started treating me with thinly veiled judgment. What had once been a source of joy — school and learning — turned into a daily torment. My beloved school had become a torture chamber, and now I had to endure a grueling two-hour commute on public transportation to get there. I'd wake up at six a. m., transfer from the metro to a bus, and finally, I'd arrive.

They say children are the flowers of life. What kind of flower a child becomes — an orchid or a cactus — depends on their surroundings — not just their parents, but also their teachers.

I was still the same active, friendly girl, but I was treated less like a flower and more like a thistle. My homeroom teacher once told my mother, "You're going to have a hard time with your daughter. She's an indigo child. You should read up on how to deal with kids like that. She's going to stray off the right path."

Those words stuck with me. Being labeled as difficult, as someone who didn't fit into the traditional mold, weighed heavily on me. It felt like I was being set up for failure before I even had the chance to prove them wrong. But deep down, I knew the path I was on wasn't crooked — it was simply my own.

For some reason, my teacher was convinced that I, a fourth-grader at the time, would end up as a drug addict or a prostitute. Whether this was because of my father's involvement in the school's relocation or due to a personal dislike for me, I can't say for sure.

Another factor may have been at play — my dyslexia. At the time, I don't think anyone realized it — not my teachers, not my classmates, and certainly not me. It wasn't until after I graduated from university that I finally understood what had been going on. That was also when I discovered that dyslexia hadn't stood in the way of success for some of the most brilliant minds in history: Steve Jobs, Pablo Picasso, Albert Einstein, Charlie Chaplin, Anthony Hopkins, Agatha Christie, Marilyn Monroe, Walt Disney, Nelson Rockefeller, Keira Knightley, and Henry Ford. Dyslexia doesn't mean a lack of intelligence — in fact, it often means processing information in a different way. It hadn't stopped these many creative individuals hfrom achieving greatness in a wide variety of fields.

In school, I could tell I was different from the other kids. The teachers made that very clear. They gave my classmates permission to mock me, seizing on what they saw as my weakness. Every fourth grader knows dozens of ways to tease someone who stands out even slightly, but very few have ever encountered someone with dyslexia.

Whenever I was asked to read aloud in class, my classmates would double over with laughter. I would feel a lump form in my throat, trying to swallow it down. The teacher would correct me on every syllable, the snickering of my classmates in the background only making it worse. My concentration evaporated, and the letters would start jumping from line to line on the page.

The atmosphere at school became hostile, especially from the teachers. It was a form of covert aggression, a veiled form of bullying that hurt just as deeply. I fought to defend myself as best I could, but it wasn't a fair fight. Between me and my teachers stood a metaphorical concrete wall, inching closer and closer, threatening to crush me to the bone.

My homeroom teachers were a married couple. Together, they convinced my mother that if she didn't take drastic measures, her daughter would end up an alcoholic or a prostitute. My math teacher would regularly say, "Maria, you'll end up selling fish at the market if you don't get your act together." While my classmates went out to play after school, I was left behind for extra lessons that did nothing to help, since they were run by the same teachers who made me tremble with fear.

Many students arrived late to class, but I was treated differently. Once, I was about 10 minutes late because the bus I was on got stuck in the snow. I was too scared to offer any explanation. The teacher sent me out of the classroom, saying, "Litvinenko, get out. You can come back after the lesson and rewrite everything during recess!"

This happened during that same fourth grade. For children, teachers represent authority, but in my case, they felt more like prison wardens. Disobeying a teacher seemed unthinkable; it was a blazing line that no one dared to cross.

By that point, I had built up enough hurt and resentment. Holding back tears, I simply turned around, walked out of the school building, and headed straight to my mother's workplace alone, without asking for permission. The injustice, the pain, and my refusal to submit had been screaming inside me like a loud siren for a long time.

After that incident, I returned to school and, summoning all my courage, told my homeroom teacher everything that had been bottled up inside: "In your school, I feel like I'm in prison!"

Years later, at a class reunion, I saw that same teacher. She didn't recognize me at first, but then something seemed to click. She smirked and said, "Ah, you're the one who said this school felt like a prison? Oh, I remember..."

And so do I. To this day, memories of that time in school haunt my nightmares.

By fifth grade, things had lightened up a little. The homeroom teachers had changed.

I still vividly remember the relief I felt when, midway through the year, we were told that the teachers I despised were leaving the school. I could hardly believe it. I might have even counted down the seconds to that moment. The joy was overwhelming. The atmosphere in class eased, and I finally found it easier to get along with my classmates, even forming friendships.

But the daily commute to school and back remained a torment — crossing all of Kyiv every day.

As I've said before, stability was not something my life was known for.

Right before I entered seventh grade, we were informed that the schools, 'Mykhail' and 'Sofia,' were merging. This meant I'd have to travel even farther, from one edge of the city to the other, with three transfers.

One silver lining was that two classes I was familiar with would be combining, and I knew most of the students. However, conflicts quickly arose within the new group, though I managed to stay out of them.

Well, except for one brief spat where I exchanged some harsh words with a classmate. Immediately, I was summoned to the principal's office. It seemed my reputation had preceded me, and they decided to make me the scapegoat. They warned me, "Maria, if this happens again, we'll hand your documents to your parents."

Oh! That's an interesting idea! I thought to myself. *Is that even an option?*

It was the first time the idea of leaving school felt like a real possibility.

Feel It, Act on It

There was a girl in my building who was as old as me. I lived on the fifth floor, she lived on the second. We were friends, and I often stopped by her place for some delicious meat balls when I returned home exhausted after two hours on public transport. She attended a school nearby, waking up just thirty minutes before the bell rang.

One day, as I passed by her apartment, I rang the doorbell. She started telling me about her day at school, her classmates, and how much she needed my help — she was having trouble with some of the kids in her class. Naturally, I was ready to help.

And that's when a lightbulb went off in my head, a thought that flashed and immediately took shape. I couldn't let it go. I grabbed her hand, sat her down on the couch, and said, "Anastasia, what if I transferred to your class and helped you out? How does that sound?"

If you have the strength and the opportunity, always help those in need. Everything in this world is connected. Humanity wouldn't have survived if everyone only thought of themselves.

When it came to standing up for others, I was tough as steel. I grew up on the streets, so I sometimes fought — but only to defend myself or someone else. I always stood up for my rights, whether it was by pulling someone's hair or landing a punch right in the face.

Reflecting on this now, I hold the belief that it's best to defend oneself verbally and in other ways that avoid physical violence. With years of life experience, I've learned to resolve issues constructively without resorting to force. But at that time, as a child in those circumstances, I had to adapt to the surrounding environment. It was, as they say, a situation where 'you have to live like the wolves if you're among them.'

Stand up for yourself. Life will test you in many ways. Don't rely on others – rely only on your own strength. Family and friends won't always be there when you need them. It's important to know how to protect yourself in any situation.

I carefully scouted out the new school. I asked my friend to inform her homeroom teacher about my desire to transfer to her class. I arranged a meeting and, before the official transfer, got to know my future classmates and checked out the school's dynamics. The atmosphere felt right and I was confident I could adapt comfortably.

I realized that my father had as much say in my life as my mother, so I asked him to sign the necessary paperwork.

In the end, I transferred to a regular public school.

I simply informed my mother of the decision, telling her she needed to pick up my records from the Waldorf school.

If something isn't going right, don't be afraid of radical changes. Don't wait for someone else to come and fix the situation. Change your life yourself.

I chose my own school and, for the first time in my years of education, I truly felt happy. Happy and free in my choice, free in making my own decisions, and in living the life I wanted.

This was just the beginning of a series of transformations. Years later, when I became interested in astrology, I learned that during that time in my life, Pluto — ruthless and demanding constant growth — had just entered Capricorn, launching a period of powerful changes in me and my life.

First of all, I made a strong impression right from the start at my new school. One of my classmates even paid a price for testing me.

During the first PE class, the boys, as is often the case in kids' groups, started testing the new girl. One classmate slapped me on the butt. I slapped him back. His finger was broken by the time I was done.

To this day, he still reminds me of that moment. At every class reunion, he asks, "Maria, why did you break my hand?" And I always reply, "It wasn't your hand, it was just a finger!"

Between the ages of 12 and 14, I was friends with football hooligans. These fit, athletic guys were older than me, studying at prestigious universities, dressed in the latest from Stone Island, Fred Perry and Ralph Lauren, and they didn't let just anyone into their group. Many girls didn't last long in the circle. But I was dating the leader of one of Kyiv's most fashionable hooligan groups, who was a respected figure at the time.

Most girls my age wanted to be prettier and attract boys. I wanted to be smarter. At first, I felt self-conscious because I couldn't always keep up with the conversations due to my age, but I worked on myself, and soon enough, I could hold my own in any company.

I was at the heart of all the coolest events of that time — concerts, festivals, fan sections at the biggest football matches, and so on. It was an exciting experience, for a while. One day, I was invited to arranged fight, a kind of brawl where 20 guys from one group would fight 20 from another. Such fights were a regular occurrence among football fans. My inner voice told me not to go, but my boyfriend needed moral support, so I ignored my intuition.

We went to one of the roughest neighborhoods in the city, Borshchahivka — gloomy apartment blocks covered in graffiti, garages filled with profanity, and dark courtyards where anything could happen.

I was also the camera operator that day, filming the fight on the new phone I had earned by delivering photographs. Suddenly, I was grabbed from behind, pulled to the ground, and beaten by a group of girls who stole my phone. By the time the guys rushed over, it was too late.

They got revenge for me later, and I got my phone back, but I was done with that way of life. I broke up with my boyfriend shortly after. Sitting on a bench near my house, I asked him, "What are your dreams?"

He didn't say a word.

After hearing about my own dreams, he told me I needed to come back down to earth. "Working from morning to night, carrying grocery bags and raising hungry kids, that's what your future holds," he said.

I left him there on that bench with his bleak vision of the future. He was wrong about me. I walked away from that crowd much wiser and stronger than before. After that, I never got into another fight. That's when I realized my wild, rebellious days were over. My street-hardened ways didn't align with my mother's desire to control everything around her, filling up all available space like water in a container. Living with her, I'd often sit by the window, waiting for my dad's car to pull up. From a young age, I could recognize the sound of his engine from several blocks away.

My dad was the opposite of my mom. He never gave advice unless asked and always respected my boundaries. For a kid like me, this was the best environment I could've asked for. He gave me the space I needed to breathe, to make mistakes, and to grow into my own person.

At 14, I packed my bags and moved in with him. I beat my brother by two years — he didn't make the same move until he was 16.

I had no idea what the future held for me, but I knew one thing for sure: I wanted freedom and independence. I was ready to leave behind all the emotional baggage and unnecessary weight of the past.

As neuroscientist Joe Dispenza once wrote, "We cannot create a new future while holding onto the emotions of the past." This simple truth resonated deeply with me. It's how I've lived my life ever since.

I'm grateful I learned to listen to myself, to that inner voice guiding me forward. I followed it, even when I was scared or unsure of what might come next. I'm happy that no negative emotion lingers inside me for too long. The hardships I go through are like a rocket shedding its used-up modules – negative feelings fall away, and I carry only the experience and strength they've given me into the future.

And strangely, I'm not afraid. Fear only adds fuel to my curiosity. Ahead of me stretches a vast unknown, sparkling with bright, vibrant colors. Each flickering light beckons me, daring me to dive into the thrilling, terrifying adventure of the future.

Chapter 2: You Always Remember the First Time

The simplest way to extend your life is to travel.

A journey is like an entire lifetime, filled with vivid impressions and intense emotions, a true escape from reality. It gives you more feelings in a few days than some people experience in decades.

My dad was the one who taught me to love traveling, to embrace the world and everything it has to offer. He was always a special person in my life. As soon as I heard the roar of his car, I'd fly down the steps, barely touching them, and race to meet him. The moment he opened his car door, I'd leap into his strong embrace. Yes, I adored my dad, and he adored me. Family is the most important part of life. Spend more time with your loved ones and cherish every second you have with them.

My earliest adventures were with him. We were like two migratory birds, nearly impossible to pin down or keep in one place. Together, we explored all kinds of places: ski resorts, scorching sandy beaches, enchanted forests, and endless lakes. We started with trips around Ukraine, then began venturing abroad.

Whenever you have the chance, travel. It broadens your horizons, stirs deep emotions, and reveals something new, not just about the world, but about yourself. Travel enriches your life with experiences and new perspectives. Use it as a tool to grow.

One of my earliest trips was when I was in elementary school. Dad and I went skiing in the Carpathian Mountains, to a little village called Lumshory. That snowy paradise, aside from the ski resort, seemed untouched by human hands. ature breathed deeply and freely there. The forest, the snow, the mountains, the crisp cold air, and the icy silence — it all made me feel dizzy with wonder.

Learn to marvel at the little things. Find the extraordinary in the simple – whether it's a beautiful landscape, a cup of coffee after a rainy day, or a smile from the neighbor's window. Your happiness depends on your perception of reality.

Those early trips with my dad didn't just introduce me to the world; they shaped the way I see it. Each journey felt like a new discovery — of both the planet and myself.

I was brought back to reality by a rather extreme situation. My dad had ordered a car to take us from the train station to our hotel — a looming building perched like a fortress at the very top of a mountain. As soon as we got into the car, he grabbed my hand and said, "If anything happens, I'll shout, and you jump."

I didn't understand the meaning of his words until a few minutes later. The car's tires were completely bald, and naturally, we got stuck in the snow. In the mountains, one wrong move could send you tumbling into a snowy abyss.

The car was stuck for good, and we had no choice but to get out and walk the rest of the way. So, there we were — facing a kilometer-long uphill trek in wet snow, sharp icy flakes whipping our faces, my dad, me, and a suitcase for each of us. I was in fourth grade at the time, and as I looked from my dad to the enormous suitcase in front of me, I realized this was going to be an adventure. After standing for a moment in a snowdrift taller than me, I was already soaked through.

Halfway up the mountain, I gave up. I collapsed into the snow and yelled, “I’m not going anywhere. I’m done.”

Luckily, there was a group of students climbing the hill with us and they helped me with my suitcase, but their help didn’t increase my enthusiasm. At some point, when my legs refused to take another step, I collapsed again and announced that I wasn’t going any farther. But we had no other option.

“Marisha, the wolves will eat you,” my dad said. His words always carried weight and motivation. So, I gathered what little strength I had left, and trudged on.

We finally made it to the hotel, but to our dismay, there were no available rooms. After that grueling climb, hearing this heartbreaking news made me want to collapse again, this time onto the marble floor. The hotel owner took one look at me, and his face instantly softened. I must’ve looked like a melting snowman, with water practically pouring off of me. Miraculously, he found us a luxury suite — at double the price, of course.

That’s how the journey started, and it set the tone for the whole trip — skiing wasn’t my thing. It’s hard for me to believe, but I somehow managed to break my ski boots. That was when I decided: no more skiing for me — it just wasn’t my sport. I spent the rest of the vacation flying down hills on a sled instead. Still, the memories I have from that trip are incomparable. It wasn’t just fun — it brought me and my dad closer in a special way.

Another unforgettable destination was Egypt — my first trip abroad. Dad and I visited that sun-soaked, scorching country more than once, but that first trip stands out. It was my first time on an airplane. Now, after having flown all over the world and visited more than 40 countries, air travel feels routine, but back then, the experience had my knees shaking with excitement. You never forget your first time.

Dad showed me how everything worked on the plane, explaining how it took off and landed. I was filled with awe, right down to my fingertips. From that moment on, my love for travel was sealed in my heart forever.

Test Reality

My dad always booked our trips through the same travel agency. He knew the staff well, including the director. This same agency had also arranged for my brother's trip to London and even organized his wedding in the Czech Republic. Dad had built strong connections with them over the years.

The curiosity to explore new places, fueled by the trips my dad and I took together, burned brightly within me. By the time I was in high school, I dreamed of working in the travel industry. To me, it seemed like a gateway to a thrilling future, a never-ending kaleidoscope of experiences, filled with movement and ever-changing scenery. In my mind, I pictured myself going on fam trips and free familiarization tours that would take me to new destinations several times a year. I couldn't wait to finish school and enroll in a tourism program. I thought it was the kind of job that wasn't routine, but more like an exciting adventure, one that paid you to explore.

For the time being, while I was still in my final year of school, I had a different, attractive option: Dad offered me a job at the travel agency we used. I expressed my interest, and Dad, being the problem-solver he was, spoke to the director. That's how I, still just a teenager, ended up working there part-time.

Given my experience as a courier, they assigned me similar duties at the travel agency. I already knew the ins and outs of that job, so I adapted quickly, like a chameleon blending into its surroundings. My role was to pick up travel packages from tour operators and deliver them to the office.

Unfortunately, my excitement was short-lived. The work barely inspired a 16-year-old. The pay was low, and the job was unpredictable — I could be called at any time, and I'd have to drop everything and cross the city, no matter the weather. But I knew why I was there. Even then, I was trying to look deeper, to understand the travel business from the inside.

Follow your dream. If you want something, don't wait. Go after it and make it yours. If it's your goal, if it resonates with you deep inside, put in every ounce of effort to make sure that you end up with that goal.

One cold winter day, as Anastasia and I were strolling around after school like we often did, I got a call from the director. It was urgent — I needed to deliver some important documents across town, from one end of Kyiv to the other. Without hesitation, I agreed, and Anastasia came along for the ride. I remember the snowstorm that hit that day. We were like two icicles, shivering in the cold and wind, desperately trying to bury our faces in our hoods. But despite the weather, we completed the task.

Both Anastasia and I ended up getting sick after that. The whole experience felt like a slap in the face, waking me up to my own worth. I realized I wasn't some errand girl to be sent out in a storm.

It was at that moment, sipping hot tea with a thermometer under my arm, that I made an important decision — I quit the travel agency. Almost any resource can be replenished, but not time. Even at 15, I understood that wasting time on work that isn't appreciated is unacceptable. You can't devalue yourself or your efforts — it's like hammering yourself into plywood. Eventually, you won't be able to pull yourself out, and you'll spend your life like a horse pulling a cart, going wherever you're told. But to truly grasp this truth, and to cement it in my consciousness forever, I had to experience it firsthand.

Value yourself, your time, and your work. Don't let people take advantage of you. Your energy and your time are precious resources. Don't waste them on unappreciative jobs or toxic people.

I worked as a courier for the travel agency for a little over six months, and my timing for leaving couldn't have been better. I needed to prepare for my final exams.

When it came time to choose a university, I faced a crossroads: stay in Ukraine or study in Poland. I found an exceptional program at a Polish university that offered subsidies for attending classes and learning the Polish language.

The road is open, so step on the gas, I thought. After all, studying abroad is always a unique experience, offering opportunities you can't find at home. I had always been restless, hungry to fulfill my ambitions, and I jumped at any intriguing option that came my way.

After thoroughly researching the program, I pitched the idea of studying abroad to my classmates. Three of them actually ended up going to Poland to study. Their lives turned upside down — they graduated, found jobs in another country, and have stayed there ever since. Internal energy and enthusiasm aren't just for personal growth; they can change the lives of those around you. Even at a young age, I was brimming with energy and generously shared it with everyone, like a Wi-Fi router sending out signals to idle devices. Once they received that spark, they switched on and started working non-stop.

As for me, I didn't end up going to Poland. Another door opened for me — an opportunity to study for free at Kyiv's Institute of Culture.

A free education was a chance I couldn't pass up, and on top of that, it was the only part-time program offering government funded spots. It was perfect for me — free tuition and the flexibility to work at the same time. It seemed like my dream of becoming a tourism specialist was about to come true. I enrolled in the very university where, years earlier, I had sold my mom's homemade cookies to students.

Once I submitted all my documents, I immediately started looking for a job. From a young age, I was practically programmed to work. I would come home from walks and find new job postings in the hallway — my dad brought them. I never read them, but they left a lasting impression. None of the positions were for someone my age, and I wasn't ready for serious work yet, but the idea that I needed to learn how to make money stuck with me. I made a mental note — I would gain the experience and skills I could use in the future.

I decided to find a job related to my field of study right away. There was a travel agency near my house that specialized in trips to Greece. I knocked on their door, asked if they were hiring, sent in my resume, and voilà — I became a secretary at one of the city's most elite travel agencies. At first, I had no idea that this VIP tour operator, which worked out of a building right next to mine, catered to the entire '95th Quarter' crew. They would often stop by the office to organize their annual 'Fun' tour, entertaining politicians and other high-ranking officials.

But as much as the name of their tour promised fun, my job was anything but.

First of all, I walked into a snake pit. The office was mostly women, and most of them were deeply dissatisfied with their lives. Then I arrived — young, bright-eyed, smiling ear to ear, eager for new experiences. Naturally, their venom was aimed at me. They were willing to step on anyone to get even the smallest of perks, but I wasn't interested in that game.

Second, I had applied for a manager position, but due to strained relations with my colleagues, I was never promoted. I felt like I was dragging myself to work every day, even though the office was practically next door. The atmosphere became unbearable, and when the tension reached its peak, I quit.

Shortly after, I developed appendicitis. I couldn't help but think it was a physical manifestation of all the negativity I had been carrying inside. Sometimes, to move forward, you have to cut away the things poisoning you — just like cutting out a diseased part of your body. It was the first major sign that I needed to start paying attention to my body's reactions and trusting my intuition.

Remember: negativity can manifest physically. Think about that every time you do something against your will or sacrifice your comfort, needs, and desires. These negative feelings can make themselves known in how you see the world.

After I quit, a friend invited me to work at another travel agency, this time as a manager. I was in my second year of university. It didn't take long at the new job for me to realize I felt trapped, like a butterfly caught in a web. My days became a monotonous cycle of endless client calls, emails, paperwork, spreadsheets, and meaningless tasks. It felt like my wings had been clipped.

The reality of the tourism industry didn't match my dreams at all, it was dull and lifeless. My colleagues, instead of traveling and experiencing the world themselves, would read about destinations in brochures. People who had never left the country were telling clients how great it was to vacation in the Canary Islands. The higher-ups were all single, in their 40s, driving beat-up old Renaults and Toyotas around Kyiv's run-down neighborhoods.

I knew that wasn't my future. I refused to accept that kind of life.

My big dreams couldn't fit into that small, suffocating world. I saw no prospects, and my ambitions, like buried treasure, lay dormant, waiting for something more. On top of that, I couldn't lie. In my imagination, I shared real, lived experiences with people, the kind that made their jaws drop. I wasn't about to sell trips by reading off a piece of paper. To pass on an experience, you have to live it. Anything else is just a con. That wasn't a life I was willing to accept.

To get back on my path, I needed to make a sharp turn. **The sooner you start your journey toward change and awareness, the more capable you'll become.** At 17 or 18, I had already lived through experiences that would take most people years to gather. I was moving at full speed and wasn't going to stop because of a bump in the road.

The final push came when the director of the travel agency embezzled from her own company. She collected a hefty sum from clients and then vanished. Even before it happened, my intuition told me something wasn't right — the company didn't keep proper financial records, and the director herself was shady. By the time it all went down, I had already quit and was on vacation with my mom by the sea. I got a message from my former colleagues: the police had come to the office, and I'd gotten out just in time.

Lying on the beach, I thought, *To hell with the tourism business.* That chapter of my life was officially closed forever.

Breaking Out of the Matrix

After leaving the tourism industry, I decided to try my luck working at a bank.

Banks are all about money, about numbers — those won't lie to me, I thought optimistically.

The universe, as if tuned into my every disappointed sigh, wasted no time in lending a hand. Shortly after quitting the travel agency during the summer, I went to a friend's birthday party. There, as if by fate, I met a man who worked at a bank. Without wasting a second, I started asking him all about the job. As it turned out, there was a position available at the bank that didn't require formal schooling, just completing a course within the bank itself and passing an exam.

"Perfect, that's exactly what I need! I'm in!" I decided right then and there the bank was the place, and that summer, I set out to start a new chapter in my life.

Seek out different opportunities and try anything that seems useful and promising. The more active you are, the more likely you'll find what you're looking for. The worst strategy is to sit idle. Act and don't miss a single chance.

To get the job at the bank, I first had to go through an initial screening. I aced the 'casting' process and started the training program, which lasted about a month and a half. The pace was intense — I had to study hard and fast, more than I ever did in university, but since I was genuinely interested, I absorbed the material about loans and financial systems quickly and thoroughly.

Finally, I passed the exam. I had my magic key in hand, ready to unlock the first door to my future. Little Maria had become a bank employee. I was 19 years old.

At my new job, I was assigned to an online retail store's credit department, where I processed loans for customers buying electronics. But salaries were constantly delayed, and morale in the office was low. Eventually, my manager had enough and left for another company, inviting some of the staff, including me, to join him.

Realizing I had nothing to lose, I followed him to a financial company called CreditMarket. They were pioneering the field of online lending, which was just starting to take off.

At this new job, while still in my third year of university, I found myself training the staff.

Days blurred into weeks, and every day felt the same — endless identical offices, routine clients, stacks of paperwork, stamps, and files, spinning me into a vortex that sucked me further down.

One day, my dad bought tickets for a performance at the Kyiv operetta, where his aunt — my great-aunt — had once performed. We were supposed to see a musical where she had starred in her youth, but my boss wouldn't let me take the time off work.

Some abstract figure of authority, at that moment my manager, had blocked me from going to a special family event. I was tied down — no freedom of choice, no say in how I spent my time — not even for something as personal and meaningful as going to the theater. And for what? A measly paycheck of $70–100 a month, just enough for two dinners at a restaurant.

The realization that I had made another mistake, that I had believed in a dream that had shattered into a thousand tiny fragments, hit me hard.

A crushing apathy settled over me. Working for a financial company was considered prestigious at the time, and it did offer some semblance of stability. But my life had become unbearable, like living in *Groundhog Day*. I could feel with every fiber of my being that I wasn't in the right place. The endless hours of sitting in a chair left me physically uncomfortable, while the harsh fluorescent lights and lack of natural daylight gave me headaches and strained my eyes.

It was like being trapped in a hamster wheel: running, but going nowhere.

In between my monotonous workdays, I lived a vibrant life on social media. I joined multiple sites and downloaded numerous apps, if only to see what others had that I was craving.

That's where my future husband found me — though in 2012, I had no idea I'd one day marry this person. Among the thousands of chats on social media, one dialogue — or rather, monologue — stood out. A guy with no profile picture was bombarding me with messages like a machine gun.

Despite my complete indifference, this persistent admirer didn't back down. Eventually, he transitioned from messages to virtual gifts — colorful animals, heart-shaped puppies, little tokens of affection that were trendy back then. These gestures finally caught my attention, and I started responding to him. Every time he asked me to meet for coffee, I declined, too wrapped up in my own affairs.

This online courtship went on for months. Sometimes, I even found it amusing. It was a distraction from my mundane work routine.

Then, one freezing winter day, I needed to get from my dad's place to my mom's, which meant traveling across the entire city. As fate would have it, a phone notification popped up — a message from my persistent Romeo, offering for the thousandth time to meet. I finally gave in and agreed to coffee, but on one condition: he'd have to pick me up and drop me off at my mom's.

Thirty minutes later, a Mercedes SUV pulled up in front of my house. Out stepped a guy in glasses, and, at first glance, I mentally categorized him as a nerd.

He wore a leather jacket by Zilli, neatly pressed trousers, and had a kind, round face paired with a fit, athletic build. He arrived with a friend and was so shy he could barely say a word in my presence. Both of them were from Donetsk. His friend fully embraced the style — Adidas track pants and colorful language —

while my future husband was his complete opposite. Yet, deep down, he longed to be a bad boy. His favorite movie was *Brigada*, and he had an affinity for the '90s gangster culture, and the romanticized world of crime.

But in front of me, he was a silent Kyiv intellectual — a nerd in glasses, missing only a professor's briefcase.

From the start, he handed me flowers — a floral masterpiece. It was an enormous bear made of daisies, weighing nearly 10 kilograms. I could barely hold it in my arms. I'd been given gifts before, but there was something special about this one. Despite his shy demeanor, he was capable of grand gestures. Unfortunately, as I'd come to learn, they weren't always positive.

But more on that later.

For now, I want to share this: who we are today is the sum of the choices we made yesterday. Every second, we choose the life we're living. It's easy to complain, but the hardest part is learning to accept, process, let go, and find the strength to change your life and move forward. Only you are the artist of your life. If your world has become too gray and dull, only you can splash it with color.

Very quickly, I realized that working in finance wasn't for me either, and I needed to get out. That decision solidified in my mind, but I had no clear plan for what would come next. **Life is full of disappointments, and learning to embrace them without losing hope is key. You might have to endure a hundred disappointments before you finally find true happiness.**

One warm spring evening, while walking through the blooming streets of Kyiv's Podil district and watching the pink hues of the sunset, I found myself lost in thoughts about my unfulfilled dreams. I could sense that change was near — almost within reach. And as if on cue, that internal feeling began to take physical shape. When I entered the apartment my father and I shared, a place where no woman other than myself had ever set foot, I spotted a pair of women's shoes.

That discovery would alter the course of my life forever.

Chapter 3: The Shoes That Changed Everything

At that time, I was living with my dad. Walking through the front door, I noticed a pair of expensive, designer women's shoes standing by the entrance. This was unusual — strange women never came to our apartment. From the kitchen, I could hear the confident sound of a woman's voice, occasionally interrupted by my father's deep tones.

It turned out that my dad's goddaughter had come to visit from St. Petersburg. She was his second niece, my third cousin — the kind of distant relative you'd have to trace through a family tree. Unlike my mom, who had cut ties with most of our relatives, leaving it unclear who we were even still connected to, my dad always stayed in touch with every relative, no matter how distant.

He had a great relationship with his goddaughter, but she and I had never crossed paths. Whenever she came to Kyiv, I'd be away, and vice versa. I had heard about her a lot, though — my dad often talked about her. And so, it just so happened that our first meeting, which would go on to change my entire life, took place on that warm, magical spring day.

My cousin was a businesswoman, the owner of a large flower import company. It had been passed down to her after her late husband, who had pioneered bringing the first roses from Colombia to the former Soviet Union. They'd been in the flower business since the '90s, but her husband had been killed — a wrong place, wrong time situation. After his death, the company became fully hers.

For the past 15 years, she had been running a huge international business, commanding respect in the industry. She split her time between two countries: six months in St. Petersburg, six months in Colombia. She was a true powerhouse — a Leo by horoscope, a graceful predator with a fierce grip — a strong, successful woman. Looking at her, many women aspired to be like her — to be powerful and independent, running their own companies, making their own decisions.

As soon as I stepped into the kitchen, we clicked immediately, talking about everything under the sun. It was clear from our conversation that she held the world in her hands, spinning it like a globe, knowing a little bit about every corner. She lived freely, without limitations. She was her own boss, her own authority, not answering to anyone else.

At some point, my cousin casually mentioned that she needed a Russian-speaking manager to handle clients in Colombia. I tried to keep my composure, but speaking to her years later had her giggling that I looked like I wanted to burst from elation. When she saw the spark of excitement in my eyes, she offered me the position.

That's it, I thought, *I'm quitting my job tomorrow.*

It wasn't a spur-of-the-moment impulse. It was a real decision, one I made in an instant. One second was all it took to realize that working in Colombia wasn't going to be like travel agencies or banks. This was something new, exciting, vibrant, and full of promise. It was the dream I thought had been lost, buried under the toxic grayness of routine. The very mention of Colombia set off Latin music in my mind, and I could picture endless jungles and the Caribbean Sea.

Remember – every step you take shapes your future. If you don't muster the courage to change your life today, tomorrow will be just another day of unfulfilled potential and dissatisfaction.

Don't wait. Don't lose a minute. Take action.

At that moment, I knew almost nothing about Colombia – just the occasional mention of Pablo Escobar and the drug cartels. Danger didn't scare me; what terrified me was the dullness that was swallowing me whole; faster and more aggressively each day. Those shoes in the hallway symbolized an escape, a chance to start over, far away from everything I'd ever known.

I didn't yet realize that this was my 22nd energy, or as some call it, the arcana of spiritual freedom. My soul's mission, my true purpose, was to embrace the unknown, to have no fear of starting fresh, and to explore new horizons. **The unfamiliar is always intimidating, but it's far better to risk it all and begin a new chapter than to spend your life stuck in the same place, feeling unfulfilled.**

Right after my conversation with Natasha, I found a tutor and dove headfirst into learning Spanish. A follower from my social media, a final-year student named Zhenya, offered to teach me for free after seeing my post on 'VKontakte.' Instead of payment, I would treat him to coffee or bring some sweets in exchange for lessons. He made learning interactive and fun – instead of memorizing dry grammar tables, we had lively conversations about everything under the sun in Spanish. Thanks to his teaching style, I quickly picked up the basics and conversational topics, leaving only the vocabulary to build upon.

This new goal lit a fire inside me, rekindling hope and excitement. My parents didn't object to my upcoming trip, or at least, they didn't show it. It wasn't until later that I found out my mom had gone to see a psychologist for the first time in her life right before my departure. She didn't know how to handle the fact that her child was leaving for the other side of the world, heading into the unknown. The psychologist advised her that if she held me back, I'd blame her for the rest of my life, feeling like she'd robbed me of such an opportunity.

On the other hand, if I went, I'd probably make plenty of mistakes but would also gain invaluable experience and learn a lot. Though it was hard for her to accept, in the end, my mom let me go peacefully, without any emotional outbursts, even helping me buy the plane tickets to Columbia. Everything in my life seemed to be aligning, guiding me toward this exciting and enlightening journey.

I had three months left of summer to get a decent grasp of Spanish. Those months flew by like an arrow. My teacher drilled in the importance of pronunciation to save me from embarrassing slip-ups and made sure that I knew the words that would be relevant to the business I was joining.

Deep down, I knew I was doing the right thing, but I still felt a constant, throbbing anxiety. As I boarded the plane, my legs were trembling. It was the first time I was flying alone and I was going so far — across the entire Atlantic Ocean. It was thrilling, yet oddly, I wasn't afraid. It was one of those moments where your heart races with excitement, but fear never quite takes hold. That feeling you get in the pit of your stomach just before a roller coaster's first drop. I was exhilarated.

Across the Ocean for Experience

As the plane touched down and I stepped out onto the gangway, I was immediately engulfed by the thick, humid air of Colombia. The sunlight was so blinding that I couldn't even make out the steps in front of me. I felt a rush of pressure building in my chest. This was my introduction to Bogotá, a city that greeted me with a tight embrace that instantly revealed its intense, complex character.

Waiting for me at the airport was my sister, a striking lioness of a woman, dressed elegantly, with perfectly styled hair. The window of the car she drove became my portal — a glimpse into another universe. My wide eyes scanned every stone on the pavement as I absorbed the streets outside, afraid to miss a single detail.

Bogotá wasn't what I'd expected. It was a sprawling, chaotic city of concrete boxes, devoid of the familiar elegance I'd seen in European architecture or the coziness of the old Kyiv neighborhoods. Yet, it wasn't the dreariness of it that intrigued me — it was something entirely different, something raw. The streets buzzed with people dressed in ways I'd never seen, strange and unfamiliar smells filled the air, and the sounds of an alien language echoed around me. I could pick up a few words here and there, but with the speed of people talking, it was hard to even make out one side of a passing conversation.

The city was divided into neighborhoods, laid out in a neat grid like some kind of surreal, geometric puzzle. The poorest lived in the southern districts, while the wealthier resided in the north. It was as if the city itself was a game board, with each block defining the lives of those who lived there.

I'd heard stories about the dangerous southern districts — stories that could make your hair stand on end. They were the kinds of places you'd only see in crime shows like *Narcos*, which chronicled the violent reign of Pablo Escobar. Fortunately, I didn't know much about that before I came, and the series hadn't aired yet. It was probably for the best, otherwise, I might have hesitated to come at all.

We drove north toward my sister's home. The streets and houses were unlike anything I'd seen before. Every inch was taken up by buildings pressed tightly together, lined with high fences, much like the ones you see in American movies. It was nothing like the sprawling yards and gardens I was used to in Ukraine and I couldn't help but marvel at how this world operated on its own set of rules.

At the house, I was greeted by my sister's pets, a wrinkly shar-pei and a ginger cat. They sniffed me suspiciously, as if trying to figure out where this stranger had come from. But within minutes, we became fast friends, and they were nuzzling up against me as though I'd been part of their pack all along.

My sister introduced me to her housekeeper, a kind woman who, to my delight, could cook all sorts of Russian and Ukrainian dishes. She also cared for Natasha's daughter, who had been born in St. Petersburg but was brought to Colombia as a baby.

One day, my sister and I went to a local supermarket. For Colombians, it was just a normal grocery store, but for me, it was like walking into an encyclopedia brought to life. Exotic fruits were piled high, seafood in every imaginable size and shape, and vibrant flowers overflowing from every corner. I couldn't get enough. My sister casually ordered an enormous salmon, easily a meter long, which the fishmonger struggled to pry from the display. Back home, that fish would've cost a small fortune, but here in Colombia, the bounty of the ocean was commonplace and far, far cheaper.

It was in Colombia that I first tasted so many fruits that were only just starting to appear in Ukraine's upscale stores. I was ahead of the curve, enjoying ripe avocados, sweet papayas, and freshly pressed mango and pineapple juices every morning. My favorite fruit became mangosteen, which I savored as a dessert. It felt as though I was living in a paradise, with invisible wings lifting my spirit as I smiled for no reason at all.

Colombia was also where I saw my first hummingbird. Those tiny, vibrantly colored creatures zipped through the air so fast that my eyes could barely keep up. Their wings moved so quickly that they looked like shimmering insects. And then there were the cows: they were cows with tiger stripes! Their brown hides were scorched by the sun into dark, jagged stripes that I'll never forget. They were some of the most beautiful animals I'd ever seen.

Explore the world around you and try to keep your childlike wonder alive no matter your age. The world is vast, and there's always something incredible to discover, even for the most jaded among us. Seek, explore, marvel and enjoy. Our senses and emotions exist to be engaged constantly.

Emotions washed over me like waves, and I looked at this new world with the wonder of a child seeing bright colors for the first time. To experience life with such delight and enthusiasm is something we should carry with us to the end of our days. It's how we give meaning to each moment. The child within us, who loves the world so intensely, reaches out to it and receives everything they desire. Success, wealth, people, and happiness naturally gravitate toward those who manage to keep that sensitivity alive. The goal remains to keep that urge alive and yearning for more, which will expand your experiences.

The world is a giant mirror in which we see reflections of ourselves. The colors and lights we notice are the same that dance inside us. Beauty recognizes beauty and beauty is drawn to beauty. No matter how hard life gets, we must continue to love the world for what it is.

That childlike simplicity and ability to marvel at life is a magnet for all the good things life has to offer. When you stop demanding things and simply observe, appreciate, and delight in what you see, the universe responds by showering you with gifts. Happiness finds those who carry joy and wonder inside them.

Despite the emotional richness of my time in Colombia, life there came with its own set of challenges. I once again found myself in a situation where I had to rely entirely on myself. But this time, I was far from home and family, nearly alone. My sister was busy with her business, and there were no close friends or familiar faces around me. For the first time in my life, I had no one to talk to. My limited grasp of the language made making new friends almost impossible. Even something as simple as walking the streets of Bogotá was dangerous, and I knew those walks could end badly.

So, I turned inward.

At 19, I had already gone through multiple stages of growing up, and this was yet another rung on the ladder that would bring me to a new level of self-discovery. I was far from done, but looking at the progress I made felt good, especially now that I was in a much better headspace than my previous jobs.

After spending just a day in Bogotá, my sister, her business partners, and I headed to Cartagena, a beautiful coastal town on the Caribbean Sea. Unlike the capital, there was plenty here to admire. The picturesque streets of the city center were lined with short, colorful houses, each adorned with vibrant flower arrangements cascading from door canopies and balconies. Climbing plants wrapped around the facades, adding to the city's charm. All of this beauty was framed by gleaming white skyscrapers, a bright welcome for tourists.

Colombia continued to cast its intoxicating spell over me. My childlike wonder at everything was now mixed with a deep exhaustion, one that, unfortunately, wasn't metaphorical.

Bogotá, at over 2,500 meters above sea level, had already given me trouble with my blood pressure. Moving down to the coast made it even worse due to the rapid altitude change. But that was only the beginning: along with the mountainous terrain and tropical climate, I also had to deal with a new time zone. Fighting jet lag[1] was useless, and for the first few days, I wandered around in a daze. My head was a blur of birds, fish, palm trees, people, Latin music, unfamiliar words, and new sounds.

With my head feeling fuzzy as I was guided around, my adventure felt like a dream, one that I never wanted to end.

Bright Colors of Colombia

The time had come to wake up and begin to work.

Nothing clears the head quite like work. I knew my body would fall back into rhythm once I immersed myself in the familiar comfort of a daily grind.

I was eager to begin, expecting something extraordinary, and my intuition didn't fail me. I started urging my sister to take us back to Bogotá so I could finally be introduced to my new responsibilities.

The office was basically at her home, a separate wing on the grounds of her sprawling estate. Aside from my sister, our team consisted of five people: a director who

---

1 Jet lag is a syndrome caused by the disruption of a person's internal circadian rhythm due to rapid travel across multiple time zones during air travel.

ran the company, three Colombian women — one handling paperwork, and two as managers — and myself, acting as the manager responsible for Russian-speaking clients. Most of our conversations with the girls happened through Google Translate, which became my lifeline. Despite having had some bad experiences working with women in the past, I got along with these girls perfectly. Perhaps it was the warmth of the Latin culture; they were as welcoming as their sun-drenched land.

One funny incident happened during my time with them. I kept hearing the girls repeat a word that sounded a lot like my name — always in an exaggerated, emotional tone. Curiosity got the best of me, so I finally asked what it meant. They turned bright red with embarrassment before explaining that *marica* in Spanish is a slang word used to insult. I laughed so hard, especially when I realized this was what my mom affectionately called me back home (Maryka)!

Before long, I went on my first field trip to see the flower plantations — an adventure within an adventure. The view from the car window transformed as dusty roads gave way to vast green fields dotted with thousands of vibrant blooms. I was mesmerized. It was as if I had stepped into a magical world plucked straight from a fairytale.

Once we arrived, I was able to see the flowers up close. They gave me a full tour, and I was left speechless by the beauty around me. I learned how a single rose is nurtured from the tiniest seed, how much care it requires, and the journey it undergoes before it's ready to be sold.

Right in the middle of the plantation stood an enormous aviary filled with colorful cockatoos. They were everywhere in every color of the rainbow — yellow, red, green, and even pure white birds. I couldn't get enough of their beauty, absorbing every flap of their wings and every sharp click of their beaks. My head was spinning with joy, like everything around me was swirling in a dance of impressions.

Colombia astonished me, and I, in turn, fascinated Colombia. As a bright blonde, I attracted curious glances everywhere I went. They didn't even sell blonde hair dye in that country! To avoid drawing too much attention, I would often wear a hood over my head.

Colombians were generally respectful, but the criminal underworld always lurked in the shadows. I had no desire to invite trouble. I just wanted to work and quietly explore this unfamiliar world.

Back in Kyiv, when I was involved in modeling, I had been offered many photoshoots, including some very revealing ones. But I always maintained boundaries. I knew I had to play the long game. Stripping down for the camera might earn attention in the short term, but it also risks turning you into an object of desire, causing people to forget everything about your essence. I never wanted to rely on my appearance for success. It was important to me that people saw something deeper — my experience, my knowledge, and my inner depth.

Work on your spirituality, nurture your inner world. Let people be drawn to more than just the cover; fill yourself with substance and meaning.

In Colombia, I wanted to immerse myself in a new culture, view the world from a different perspective, and enrich my soul. This country became not just a new way to earn money but a wellspring from which I could draw endless spiritual resources.

My workday started at the same time each morning — 5 am — and ended at 2 pm. I would go to bed around nine or ten in the evening, and the hours between work and sleep were fully dedicated to myself.

Social interactions were scarce; there weren't many people around who spoke my native language. Sure, social media existed back then, but it wasn't the same as face-to-face conversation. The internet wasn't always reliable, and there were no video calls or quick updates through apps like Telegram. With most of my communication avenues cut off, I spent almost all my free time engrossed in movies and books.

This was the period when I experienced a boom in self-development: I consumed new knowledge with the same passion and intensity as I explored this new country. I began to explore different areas of art, searching for what resonated with me. My sister, an intelligent and cultured woman from Saint Petersburg, became a great advisor. She introduced me to the works of Dostoevsky, and I watched several films based on his books. Before this trip to Colombia, I hadn't been particularly interested in him, but that changed.

In addition to literature, my sister shared her entrepreneurial knowledge, telling me all about her company, how to interact with people, and how to build a business. I soaked it all up, like soil eagerly absorbing water.

Inside me, a beautiful bud was blooming, ready to open into a full flower, and all of the watering from my time in a new country was helping to make that bloom bigger. I spent only six months in Colombia, but during that time, I gained more experience than I might have in a lifetime.

Dedicate your free time to self-development. If you don't know how to spend a few hours of your life, dive into reading, learning languages, taking courses, working out, watching meaningful films, or try any other enriching activity. Self-development should be a lifelong companion. Invest in yourself and you will never lose those resources.

With a lack of face-to-face interaction, I tried to keep in touch with friends and searched through online groups for Russian-speaking expats in Colombia. Unfortunately, I found none, so I made do with texts and emojis flashing across my phone or laptop screen.

During my time in Colombia, my future husband began writing to me again. He would appear, then disappear, then bombard me with messages on social media, then go silent for weeks, as if he were a spy. But ever since I had arrived in Colombia, our communication had been stable. We often spoke on the phone, sharing long conversations. Our connection became my remedy against loneliness. We helped each other; he was living in Europe at the time, far away from where he grew up, and we both needed support. Yet, even then, I had no idea what the future held for us.

The six months I spent in Colombia flew by, like a flock of wild birds. It was a life full of learning, wonder, love, challenges, and self-reflection. For six months, I hadn't seen my parents and only rarely did I get to speak in my native tongue. I was overjoyed yet completely overwhelmed. At times, things became difficult, but I knew all those struggles would pay off eventually. I'll never forget the velvety, bittersweet aroma of Colombian coffee and the deafening roar of tropical downpours — storms you only encounter in Latin America.

The knowledge I gained during that time changed the course of my life. Those six months in Colombia became an eternity, during which I accomplished more than I had in my 19 years. While my peers were glued to their phones during lectures or chasing party invitations, not a single day of mine went to waste. I worked hard, educated myself, soaked in every drop of information that came my way, and filled my cup to the brim with love and admiration.

Studying doesn't always mean learning and work doesn't always mean success.

Don't waste time on pointless actions. If you feel like your education isn't providing real knowledge or your job has no potential for growth, find something else. Trust your instincts, follow the energy. You only have one life – don't waste it on idleness or emptiness.

All these changes stemmed from the moment I saw those women's shoes and made a firm decision that I only have one life, and there's no time for doubt. The difficult choice I made then bore huge rewards now, and instead of fading away under the harsh light of office lamps, I chose the sun.

Chapter 4: Revolution Inside and Out

The welcoming Colombian warmth had given way to a scorching heat. When I went home to the Ukraine, I arrived in the midst of a revolution[2]. It was late 2013.

"Maria, we're at war here, they're shooting, don't come back," my mother wrote as I boarded the plane. She begged me to land in London instead and avoid Kyiv. Of course, I didn't listen, and within a day, I was back in my hometown.

The atmosphere in the capital was eerie, as if Kyiv was sitting on a powder keg, ready to explode with all its inhabitants above it. While the protests were largely confined to a central street,

2 The Euromaidan Revolution — street protests in Ukraine that began in November 2013 and ended in February 2014, with the main outcome being the overthrow of President Viktor Yanukovych's regime.

the tension rippled through the entire city, affecting everyone, no matter where they were.

Our apartment was not far from the city center. From the epicenter of the chaos, we could hear sirens, gunfire, explosions, the crash of Molotov cocktails against asphalt, and desperate cries for help. When something exploded, the windows in my room would shudder ominously, reminding us that neither I nor my family were truly safe.

A sense of fear hung over us, pricking at the edges of our consciousness, settling like a needle near the solar plexus. The future was becoming more uncertain with every passing day, dissolving into a blur.

I couldn't accept this reality. The uncertainty and panic in my home country felt like shackles, pulling me off course. I had always needed to feel solid ground beneath my feet, to move with purpose and clarity.

In those six months in Colombia, I had undergone an extraordinary transformation. I had left Kyiv as a child, but returned carrying a vast weight of experience, knowledge, skills, and spirituality that yearned to be unleashed and put to use.

I was 20 years old at the time, fueled by the sun and freedom of Colombia, and the thought of returning to the bank I had been working at was unimaginable. For me, that was a prison — cold, bleak, soulless, devoid of any life. Just thinking about it brought to mind the harsh glare of sterile office lighting, which had caused me headaches. I was determined to open something of my own, to work for myself.

I wanted to be free, independent, to create something meaningful. It wasn't just about escaping a dull routine — it was about making use of everything I had learned.

The situation in the country forced doubts to creep into my mind — maybe it was better to wait and put everything off for a while? It was a heavy time for people; business could drown under the pressure. Those were the thoughts swirling in my head. And they weren't unfounded.

One day, Kyiv's metro system shut down. The city was thrown into chaos — thousands of people, like something out of an apocalyptic movie, emerged from the underground and aimlessly wandered, bumping into one another, unsure where to go. They just kept walking and I had no idea there were that many people in the city! Surreal events like these were happening in Ukraine daily — new revolutionary eruptions were everywhere. In such an atmosphere, where you had no idea what disaster might come tomorrow, opening a business felt almost inappropriate. But that was just an illusion.

Time flows like water — you either swim along with it or watch it disappear, leaving nothing but a wet trail on the sand. A wise acquaintance of mine, a seasoned businessman, once shared a truth: "There will never be a perfect time. You have to act now." The world doesn't operate on stability. Revolutions, wars, pandemics, crises... even a slight change in the wind can affect a business. So, the best moment to start is now.

The best time is now. Perfect conditions to start a business, leave a toxic relationship, move, or begin writing a book will never come. You can keep postponing it for your entire life. So, act today.

I made my decision to start my own business with the resolve of a diamond. I dreamed of being like my cousin, someone who was free, without limits or restrictions. The idea of going to work, being led around on a leash, no longer appealed to me. Freedom and personal choice became my guiding principles. I wanted to make decisions on my own, to create something with my mind and my hands, to have room for creative freedom.

The only thing left was to decide on the theme, to find my product. The idea didn't take long — it came to me in a dream. Dreams had always guided me through life's tangled jungles, pointing the way with an unseen hand. In my dreams, I could see the road ahead — someone, invisible in waking life, would give me the answers I sought. That's what happened this time too.

At first, I considered opening a bakery with sweets and croissants. After seeing so many similar places in Colombia, I realized it would be a novelty for Kyiv. But after analyzing the situation, I concluded that it wasn't right for me. I lacked the experience. I decided to focus on something I knew a little more about.

Always analyze the situation. If you can't decide and pick the right option, break each choice down into small pieces. Try to think rationally. Ask yourself: what am I best at? Where does my strength lie? What do I love the most?

Don't forget about your subconscious. It often reveals itself through dreams. Pay attention to the images that visit you in your sleep. Dreams are the key to understanding your inner world.

One magical night, I dreamed of flowers — so many of them, glowing with angelic light, gently wrapping around my body with their petals. When I woke up, I knew this was it.

Startup

At that time, the floral market in Ukraine was a very limited industry. You could only buy flowers in two ways: either at overpriced flower boutiques or from a grandmother selling seasonal blooms in the pedestrian underpasses. There was no middle ground, and the niche was wide open.

Starting a flower delivery service wasn't as simple as just knowing about different types of flowers. While in Colombia, I spent most of my time behind a computer. I was taken to the flower plantations, but I never worked with the flowers myself, so I had a gap in experience that I needed to fill. I also urgently needed a business partner.

In Kyiv, I had a friend, Veronica, who was one of my classmates. She had a creative mind and a great sense of taste; she had an instinctive sense for what worked together and how to present a product in the best light. Ever since our first year of university, we had tried to start a few businesses together, but we never managed to follow through. But this time, I knew deep down that it would work.

Veronica hesitated at first, but eventually, she agreed to join me. At the time, she was working in a travel agency. We met after her workday for our 'business dinner' in a McDonald's.

Veronica had no experience working with flowers, but she took on the responsibility of managing our Instagram. **Always delegate the part of the work that someone else can objectively do better than you.** The rest, meaning the hands-on work — assembling and arranging bouquets — fell to me.

I came up with the name for our shop. It also came to me in a dream: FLORPeople. The name derived from the Spanish word *Flor*, meaning flower. The letter 'L' in our logo was drawn in cursive and subtly disappeared into the design. This created a play on words: instead of 'FLORPeople,' the name read as 'ForPeople,' conveying the message that our flowers were 'for the people.'

I had never worked with flowers and my hands were unfamiliar with the craft. To learn how to arrange bouquets, I decided to get an internship at a flower shop.

I chose UkrFlora, which at the time was a major wholesaler. It was so popular that almost every flower shop in Kyiv sourced their products there. The company was connected to my sister's firm, and I had good relations with them from my time in Colombia.

UkrFlora was housed in a U-shaped building — the right wing contained the shop where I would intern, while the left wing held the flower warehouse. The warehouse itself was like a massive refrigerator, or rather, a set of rooms where the unprocessed flowers were stored. Bunches of roses, peonies, tulips, chrysanthemums, and hydrangeas waited patiently to be sent to their future owners.

During the internship, the florists helped me. They showed me how to best decorate a bouquet, how to package it properly, and how to handle the flowers with care. I was learning directly through hands-on experience, getting used to the sharp thorns, the constantly falling leaves, the tangled ribbons, and all the little details.

After a dozen repetitions, I started to feel more confident with the flowers.

The first steps are never easy for anyone. If you start something new, be prepared for challenges. With time, you'll adapt and things will begin to flow more naturally.

The business model I planned with Veronica was quite simple: she managed orders through Instagram and I would head to the flower warehouse, purchase the necessary blooms, assemble the bouquet, and send it off via taxi. Of course, selling bouquets to outside customers was forbidden during my internship, so I had to create them 'under the table,' quite literally in some cases.

We were the first in Ukraine to use hashtags like 'flower delivery in Kyiv' and later expanded to 'flower delivery across Ukraine.' These clever marketing tactics, paired with our stylish and sleek Instagram design, started paying off. Clients grew in numbers, and each week brought more orders. What began as a tiny seed, FLORpeople blossomed into a thriving business.

After a month of my internship, I felt it was time to take our project to the next level. There was a semi-basement space in my father's house that had been left unused. My older brother had once fixed it up, painting the walls a sunny yellow, installing a faucet, a mini-fridge, blue couches, and a TV. Back in the day, he used it to hang out with his friends, but after he moved to London, the room had become a storage space for winter tires, old items that didn't have a place in the house above, and tools. Despite the clutter, the small space was perfect for us. Our little headquarters was born, and we were ecstatic — this was our first proper workspace.

We also found a new flower supplier, located closer to the center of Kyiv. It was a much easier commute from my father's house.

Our workflow remained roughly the same: we'd receive an order, hop on a bus to the supplier, pick out flowers based on the client's requests, and return to our makeshift studio to assemble the bouquet. After my internship, I taught Veronica the art of bouquet-making, and soon we were working in tandem, a two-person mini-holding, doing everything ourselves without external help.

Since we had no proper storage for flowers (my brother's mini-fridge could only hold drinks), we purchased fresh flowers for each order. The only supplies we had on hand were ribbons, wrapping paper, and small decorative items.

Our business kicked off during a time of not just political revolution, but also a style revolution. Flower shop bouquets back then were often tacky, wrapped in plastic film with garish patterns and tied with mismatched, gaudy ribbons. Minimalism was beginning to gain popularity — restaurants with raw interiors, loft-style apartments, a focus on simplicity with just a touch of deliberate roughness.

That's when Veronica and I had a revelation: instead of using unsightly plastic wrap, why not package our flowers in simple kraft paper? We were among the first to introduce this understated style. The kraft paper, humble as it was, looked elegant and clean, and our customers loved the design. Little did they know that their beautiful flowers were wrapped in the same paper typically used for packaging sausages.

The world always needs fresh ideas and new perspectives. Don't be afraid to propose something no one has thought of before; you might be on the brink of inventing something brilliant.

But if you don't bring your idea to life, it will remain just that – an idea in your head. Don't fear failure. It's better to try and stumble than to hoard ideas and never give any of them a chance to flourish.

Our store was a project born from pure initiative, motivation, meticulous teamwork, and endless creativity, without any sponsors or external funding. It thrived solely on our passion and effort.

Veronica was the creative force behind everything; with her excellent taste and design intuition, she helped us create a truly unique product. I, on the other hand, was the main financier and the worker bee — handling logistics, planning, accounting, and reporting. We made a great team because we complemented each other perfectly. Fueled by our combined energy, we constantly inspired each other, and our little business grew rapidly.

We found our 'office' in the heart of Kyiv near the towering 'Motherland' monument, right on Druzhby Narodov Boulevard. And by 'office,' I don't mean a typical workspace — I mean a designer gas station. More specifically, the Socar station, which felt less like a place to fill up your tank and more like an exclusive lounge.

This wasn't just any gas station; it was a stylish, high-end spot, one of the first locations of the Azerbaijani oil company. With its sleek architecture and upscale café, it became a magnet for Kyiv's elite. Lamborghinis, Porsches, Ferraris, Rolls-Royces — you name it — pulled in constantly, turning the place into an impromptu car show.

Veronica and I thrived in that atmosphere. There was something about being surrounded by ambition and luxury that fueled our own dreams. Sitting there, sketching out our next business move over coffee, I quietly envisioned the day I'd pull up in my own dream car, just like the ones we watched glide in and out.

But my time was yet to come. This was just the beginning. As I sorted through flowers with hands scratched from thorns in that tiny basement, I had no idea how fast and dramatically my life would change.

I loved working in our flower shop, but it was far from easy. Orders rained down like a sudden summer storm, and sometimes the downpour would hit at the worst possible moments.

There were times I'd be on a date in a restaurant when I'd get a call from Veronica, informing me about a rush order that had to be filled in two hours. Dressed in a long gown and heels, I'd dash out, jump into my boyfriend's car, sometimes even onto public transportation, and rush to grab flowers.

I carried my laptop with me everywhere — even to the beach. The guy I was dating at the time would constantly say, "Maria, why are you always on that thing?" But I was always working, never sparing myself. That was my life — quick decisions, on-the-spot problem-solving, all day, every day.

I'd also get genuinely upset if my friends or dates bought flowers for me from anywhere but my shop. So, most of the time,

I received bouquets from FLORPeople. Veronica would put them together for me, and I'd return the favor, crafting bouquets for her whenever she had an admirer send her flowers. That's why our bouquets for each other were always perfect — we put extra care into them.

Then one day, we got our first wedding order. They requested a bridal bouquet and a boutonniere, the small floral accessory that pins to a suit jacket.

That tiny boutonniere became our nightmare. We had no idea how to make one. After scrolling through pictures online and struggling for 40 minutes, we finally finished. We were sure it was a disaster, but to our surprise, the clients were absolutely thrilled.

One thing about our business: we were always our harshest critics. Despite making beautiful products, we often doubted ourselves, always wondering, "Could it have been better?"

The first wedding orders were challenging. We were constantly inventing as we went. We'd take orders with serious faces, only to turn to each other and whisper, "How on earth are we going to pull this off?" We worked on the fly, coming up with new ideas and arrangements as we were making them.

Always set big goals and don't look for easy ways out. If you're presented with a task that seems overwhelming, don't back down. Give it a try – only by overcoming tough challenges can you reach the next level of growth.

With time, our wedding bouquets became more refined, elegant, and flawless. Clients began sending us professional photos of their weddings featuring our flowers, photographers offered to collaborate with us for barter shoots, and we were even invited to exhibitions.

Life among the flowers was like a fairytale, where Veronica and I played the roles of two Cinderellas. We were surrounded by delicate peonies, little doll-like blooms tied with white ribbons. There were blue and white hydrangeas blending into creamy, dreamy compositions. And, of course, roses — endless roses. Their thorns pricked my fingers constantly, but their beauty and freshness never ceased to inspire me.

It would have been easy to give up

After opening my first business, at the age of 22, a monumental event occurred: I bought a car. This moment became one of the most significant in my life. The car symbolized both an achievement and a new starting point, embodying all my hard work and dedication. It represented maturity and financial independence.

I had started learning how to drive even before I turned 18 because it was crucial for me. Sitting behind the wheel, I felt like I was in control of my destiny; this metal beast gave me the sensation of absolute freedom and independence. I chose my own path and moved forward confidently, like a falcon soaring through the sky.

Nothing could stop me.

The story behind buying the car was complicated. Initially, I wanted to buy a used vehicle, but the guy I was dating at the time insisted it wasn't a good idea. He offered to contribute money towards a new car and even took out a loan in his name. Only later did I realize that he had done this because he wanted to keep me tied to him. But his plan failed — we eventually broke up, and the new car left with him.

Some time later, I bought myself the exact same model, a shiny new Nissan Juke. The first time I saw that car on the streets of Kyiv, I thought it was the ugliest thing I'd ever seen. To me, it looked like a giant metal bug slowly crawling along the highway.

But times change, and so do our preferences. In the end, I realized that this car was perfect for me. As they say, there's a fine line between love and hate, and at 22, I ended up with my very own white 'bug.'

I was incredibly proud of myself; it wasn't a Ferrari or a Porsche, but that didn't matter. While my fellow students were busy copying homework, I could take my mom or grandma out for a ride in my very own car. That sense of maturity, freedom, and the ability to help my loved ones brought me immense satisfaction.

From that moment, life began to speed up. I navigated through it with the pace of a race car, even if I was only driving a humble Nissan.

Closer to 2015, I traveled to Saint Petersburg for a couple of weeks. This wasn't just a casual visit to Russia's cultural capital, it was a journey for new knowledge. Knowledge was the lifeblood that fueled both me and my business.

Always invest in your personal development – improve your skills, and broaden your professional expertise. Continuously seek new knowledge and ideas, and observe how other professionals work. The world never stands still, and neither should you.

Our flower shop had grown to the point where it needed to be transplanted into a bigger pot. It was time to scale up. I had brought back another massive dose of knowledge from Saint Petersburg – things that were already in place there but hadn't yet reached Kyiv. I was eager to put everything I had seen into practice. I realized it was time to take the next steps: become a sole proprietor, lease a proper space, hire employees, and start paying taxes to elevate the business.

It was during this crucial time that I received shocking news from Veronica: she was leaving for the United States.

She shared this right after I had signed the lease for a new office and ordered the furniture. The situation was this: her boyfriend lived and worked in the U. S. After three or four failed visa attempts, they decided to get married so she could move there as his wife.

I knew about the process and understood that, eventually, she would leave the country, but I didn't expect it to happen at such a critical moment! Not when we'd made it so close to having a place to call our own.

It was hard to imagine how I would manage everything on my own, especially after the radical scaling of the business. At that time, Veronica was my main support, and I could feel that foundation slowly slipping away. I realized I'd have to go solo again, like a proud bird left to fly alone once more.

Build your life and your business so that you are always your own main support.

People come and go and circumstances change every second. But you are the one thing you'll never lose. Rely on yourself and be ready to stand alone. But being alone with yourself isn't scary at all. Each of us is an entire universe of knowledge, skills, and strength that we must learn to use. Remember that.

The next blow came when Veronica told me she wanted 50% of the business. That demand completely threw me off balance. I had been the sole sponsor of our shop, paying all the expenses and giving every ounce of my time and energy to make it work. Veronica said that for her half, she would manage the social media page from abroad. By that logic, I would be responsible for everything else: running the shop, managing the staff, sourcing flowers, handling documents, meetings, and all the other tasks.

That was not how business was done, at least not with me. I've always stood for fairness and, after having a long talk about the future, we agreed that the shop would remain entirely mine. We parted ways amicably. After a year and a half of working together, and finishing one last International Women's Day rush with me, my first business partner left for good.

A Star Moment at 20

I rented a space in a business center, practically in the heart of Kyiv. It was a prime location — right in the lobby where foot traffic was constant. By that time, I had also managed to take a trip with my dad to Israel and float in the Dead Sea. The sea might have been dead, but I was more alive than ever, with life overflowing in all directions. After returning from the trip, a long-awaited milestone happened on May 1st: I opened my very own shop.

It was the beginning of something fresh and wildly exciting. I could feel, with every fiber of my being, that the world around me was shifting, and with it, I was changing too. Managing it all by myself wasn't easy, but the thrill, running through me like molten lava, kept things moving smoothly and steadily.

One of the most critical steps was buying a refrigerator to store the flowers. My budget was tight since I was financing everything on my own. Amazingly, though, I can't recall a single day when FLORPeople hit zero; we were always making a profit.

To stay afloat, I had to get creative. A good commercial flower fridge back then cost around $3,000. I ended up finding one for only $300, focusing on the 'as long as it works' principle.

That's when my brother flew in from London to help. He gave the fridge a total makeover, transforming it so thoroughly even its manufacturer wouldn't have recognized it. From a dented steel box, we turned it into a beautiful vintage piece. My brother covered it with wooden panels and crafted a decorative finish.

It looked amazing, but making it happen took a lot of effort and energy. That was the nature of things back then, every day required hard work. Yet none of it lessened the joy I felt from doing what I loved.

I felt completely free as if I belonged to no one. The business was entirely in my hands. I made every decision — what furniture to put in the store, how the sign would look, what prices to set, and who to hire.

This was my first experience hiring people. At 22, I had no clue how to conduct interviews, what questions to ask, or how to manage employees. But I knew one thing for sure: I needed people with potential and a strong drive. It didn't matter so much what they could do today — what mattered was who they could become tomorrow. This strategy never failed me. I always had a knack for looking beneath the surface and sensing who was the right fit and who wasn't.

Dasha came to me, a girl who at first glance didn't seem 18. She looked like a child — so delicate and small that I doubted her ability to hold even a small bouquet. But my intuition didn't fail me. Despite her fragile appearance, Dasha was quick, grasping everything I taught her and excelling at her tasks.

Over time, I noticed Dasha adopting the same books I read, mirroring the way I talked to clients, and carrying herself with newfound confidence. I had unknowingly mentored her, watching as this young girl transformed into a skilled professional and strong individual. Eventually, Dasha became the store manager, taking the reins when I was away so I was finally able to have time for myself.

While I remained in Kyiv, FLORPeople flourished like a fern in the wild jungle. I no longer worked directly with the flowers, only helping with bouquets on rare occasions. I had delegated all my responsibilities as the director, but I still kept a firm grip on everything, guiding the business with strong hands.

The fears I'd had before Veronica left proved unfounded. The business didn't overwhelm me; I ran it intuitively, letting my inner voice guide me in the right direction.

I could read people instantly; within seconds, I knew if someone wasn't the right fit and needed to be told "no." Likewise, I recognized my people immediately. Their lives were open books to me, each page revealing their potential and their path.

I always knew who to assign to bouquet-making, who to promote to senior manager, and who to trust with the bookkeeping. I could see the strengths and weaknesses in each person, sensing their potential and guiding them to their true calling. Many of my employees came to me with empty cups and left with their vessels full to the brim.

One day, while sitting in a café, two of my friends were talking about various cultural events in Kyiv — exhibitions, galleries, and performances that I, a lifelong resident, had never even heard of. Their excitement, though, was laced with a kind of sadness — both looked lost, without any direction in their lives. They lacked purpose, unsure of where to direct their energy.

I suggested they start a social media group dedicated to Kyiv's vibrant life. They immediately ran with the idea, and by the end of the evening, The Good was born. Today, that Instagram page has almost 100,000 followers. All it took was pointing their energy in the right direction and it transformed into an unstoppable current.

During this time, dreams became an even greater source of guidance for me. I found answers to nearly all my questions when I closed my eyes and slipped into sleep.

My body thrived as well. I had more free time to focus on fitness, and at 21 and 22 years old, I was in the best shape of my life. Men circled around me, from different walks of life and interests. Even the wealthy ones failed to catch my interest. Why would they, when I was building my own business and could afford anything I desired?

My life sparkled with vibrant lights. I had breakfast in one restaurant, lunch in another, and dinner in a third. I rented the apartment of my dreams: 120 square meters, enormous windows, marble floors; it felt like a fairytale that had stepped off the page.

Opportunities rained down on me, from official events, to exhibitions, to partnerships with hotels and concert venues. I bought a new car and took my first loan, for an Apple computer for the office. Clients would pull up in the latest models of Porsche, Range Rovers and Mercedes S-class, ministers' and deputies' drivers picking up bouquets. Meetings with partners were constant, and I knew I could refuse anyone because I was free to make decisions for my business and my life according to my own will and mind.

This freedom gave me wings which was exactly what I had sought during my entire two decades of life. I could fly off to London for a date and, a few days later, lie under an apple tree at our family country home. Time and distance had dissolved. I had become a whirlwind of energy, moving through space like the wind.

Yet, I was always connected to the store, 24/7. My responsibilities didn't disappear, but they didn't weigh me down either. I enjoyed every part of the process — from riding the bus with Veronica to dining in the most expensive restaurants in Kyiv.

To truly erase all boundaries, I decided to apply for a U. S. visa. I had no immediate plans to leave but wanted the freedom to fly across the world at a moment's notice. While many of my countrymen were being denied, I received my visa on the first try, with the words 'Your visa is approved.'

All the doors of the world were wide open before me.

Chapter 5: Stepping into a New Reality

"If you want what you've never had, you must do what you've never done."

Shortly before my departure from Ukraine, I took on a new project — a factory.

My floral boutique was located in a business center in the capital, which was part of a large knitwear factory. Its owner had renovated most of the space into this business center.

However, the factory was still operating. It was an exceptionally vibrant place — all the equipment was old, yet functional and reliable, which evoked genuine admiration for those who worked there.

The factory's shop sold good quality textiles at prices unheard of in Kyiv for a long time — a T-shirt cost no more than $1. Even more amazing, the cashier still used a Soviet-era cash register. I couldn't begin to imagine how they got it to work.

The factory owners were focused on the business center, which generated more profit for them. Because of that, the factory was almost abandoned, but the enterprise clearly had possibilities; it only needed a little push to unlock its hidden potential.

One day, one of the factory directors came into my flower shop. We started talking and I shared my impressions of the factory. In response, I was graciously invited for a tour.

During the official visit, I became firmly convinced of the factory's promising future. The factory looked amazing and left a lasting impression on me. Walking through its spacious corridors, it felt like stepping into a time machine, transporting me back several decades. Everything was preserved down to the smallest details: the Soviet equipment, the interior design, and even an old elevator operated by a smiling elderly woman.

All of the factory equipment was worth a fortune. They manufactured fabrics from scratch, creating the product from the very beginning. A great deal of labor and considerable resources were invested in this process.

After getting a closer look at the enterprise, I couldn't get it out of my head. It captivated me with its magical antiquity and charisma. My ability to see hidden potential wouldn't let me rest — I wanted to help.

Help selflessly and derive pleasure from it. Life is a boomerang. Today you help someone, tomorrow someone will help you.

After talking with the directors, I offered my consulting services. They were intrigued and open to collaboration. They wanted a fresh, progressive perspective on their business from a younger entrepreneur who hadn't become jaded by excessive information.

I brought my social media specialist to the consultation. Our recommendations turned out to be highly valuable; the factory employees listened to us attentively and with curiosity. It didn't take me long to scan all the details and mentally map out a path forward for the factory. I saw all of its possibilities at first glance and a clear picture immediately formed in my mind of what I needed to do. I just needed to tell the owners how to materialize it.

The employee's thoughts on bringing in new technology were a bit outdated. They wanted to present the factory as it was, even using the same elderly women who operated the elevator and worked the cash registers as a website model. During our brainstorming session, the managers, who had experience placing banners in the metro, suggested printing coupons in newspapers to gather new customers.

"Let's just send carrier pigeons next," I said ironically, and proposed more modern and technological options.

In general, everything needed to be changed at a cellular level, starting with the mindset of the employees and managers themselves. While it was easier with the directors — they were relatively forward-thinking and easily adapted to the new wave of what the future could bring — the rest of the staff needed a profound transformation. But we managed it brilliantly, thanks to our resourcefulness and burgeoning enthusiasm.

Years passed and the results were truly impressive. The owner purchased a new, spacious building outside the city and relocated the factory there. The enterprise embraced active marketing, began developing new collections, and expanded its distribution to international markets. What once seemed like a dying factory was revitalized. With the weeds cleared and a touch of freshness and innovation, the factory came alive, transformed beyond recognition. Today, it has firmly established its niche in the European market.

I didn't earn any profit from this project; I did it purely out of passion and enthusiasm. I wanted to test my abilities in practice and use my skills to unlock someone else's potential. I couldn't wait to see the "before" and "after," and I felt genuine joy when movement finally began where stagnation had prevailed for so long. The warm glow of the factory owners' success spread through me like a comforting bowl of tom yum soup after a chilly walk, and it lingered for a very long time.

I was sincerely happy to have been able to help someone.

Helping others is an invaluable resource: everyone needs it, but not everyone knows how to create or give it freely.

One day, a young man reached out to me on social media — a Ukrainian casino owner living in London. He was planning a trip to Kyiv and invited me to join a gathering with his former classmates. Even before meeting him in person, I could sense his entrepreneurial flair; he had a unique talent for business.

I accepted his invitation and joined him at the restaurant, where I spent time with an enjoyable and lively group. As usual, I left earlier than everyone else, since I don't drink and prefer to go to bed early.

In the morning, I had 20 missed calls. It turned out that the group I had dinner with had been taken to the police station. My friend's classmate had stood up for his wife after some guy had made a couple of unpleasant remarks to her. A fight ensued, which ended in a stabbing. My new friend was being held as a witness.

I immediately started looking for ways to get him out of jail and I succeeded. As soon as he was released, I immediately took him to the airport and bought him tickets for the nearest flight. On the way, his phone received numerous text messages with threats from the local authorities. By that time, my friend already had a British passport and the rescue operation was successful.

"Maria, why are you helping me? We've known each other for one day, and you're getting me out of jail?" he asked, as we sped toward the airport. I couldn't give him a clear answer. It just felt like the right thing to do. My heart simply told me that if a person is innocent, they deserve help.

After that incident, we met in Paris, but purely as friends. We strolled through the city, enjoyed dinner, and laughed as we reminisced about that wild story. He thanked me again, and I smiled modestly in response. Yet deep inside, I felt genuinely happy; who knows, perhaps I had saved his life.

The Guy Who Got His Way

The period when I worked on the factory project was a time of blossoming and inner growth for me. I was overflowing with strength and energy. I saw inspiration in everything; the world around me seemed like an island of opportunities, ripe and ready to be embraced. I loved this active and fulfilling life. I wanted to look good, take care of my appearance, and catch admiring glances. I felt a profound sense of inner purpose and wanted everyone around me to see how happy I was because of it.

While everything was going its course, Michael started writing to me again. He turned out to be the kind of person who could raise the dead — he wouldn't back down regardless of the odds against him. He would disappear for a long time, but when he reappeared, he wouldn't leave me alone, even though he was thousands of miles away from Kyiv.

We had known each other for quite a while, about two years, and had always stayed in touch. Gradually, my future husband began urging me to visit him in Canada, where he had been living for the past few years. I already had a US visa, so getting a Canadian one wouldn't be difficult. But my life in Ukraine was an ocean — in perpetual motion with excitement, and rapid development. I was sailing on my speedboat, fearing nothing and no one, moving along my own vector, confidently and decisively.

My flower business was on the verge of another expansion and I was preparing for changes. And changes in my life did indeed happen, but not at all the ones I expected.

A serious choice awaited me: I had to make one of the most difficult decisions of my life.

My team and I were preparing to take the flower shop to a whole new technological level. I was looking for a space with large windows, high ceilings and I wanted to divide it into zones for the shop, including a refrigerated room, an office, a warehouse, and a meeting room. I had a grand design – an impressive 70-page business plan.

To implement it, I hired the best Ukrainian designers and architects. They developed a cutting-edge interior – something between loft and high-tech styles with backlit counters, pendant lights, elegant decor elements, materials like concrete, wood, iron, and gracefully interwoven greenery. The layout we created was unparalleled and years ahead of its time. The idea was as innovative as possible; similar interiors would only become fashionable in Ukraine years later. A group of recognized specialists worked to realize my project and I am still friends with these amazing people.

The main idea was that all interaction would be electronic: a person comes into the store, punches in their order number on a screen, and their bouquet is brought out to them. Everything would be as simple and technologically advanced as possible. At that time, this kind of business practice didn't exist anywhere and implementing the plan required huge investments.

I had a couple of options for where to get the necessary funds, but I would have to put my head on the line for the money. It's one thing to owe a bank, but quite another to owe private individuals. I always treated other people's money with the utmost responsibility, never letting anyone down or making them wait, so I felt confident that my words could convince them.

The project plan, which was developed with the designers and architects, took about $10,000 of my personal investment. And that was only the first stage. The money was spent rapidly – flowing away like rainwater as the real investments began making themselves known.

At that time, I had already been in a destructive and abusive relationship for five years. Despite the fact that my boyfriend and

I were dating, we lived separate lives — he had his, and I had mine. Formally, the relationship continued, but there was a constant emotional rollercoaster, and I often felt lonely. I never knew what to expect the next day; whether he would write, call, or disappear for several days without explanation.

On Christmas Eve, January 7th, I felt I had reached a breaking point. The window seemed like my only escape. That's how I perceived my loneliness then — against the backdrop of a universal holiday, with friends and family gatherings, I was curled up in a corner, feeling trapped behind ten invisible locks, silently replaying negative thoughts in my head.

And then, in the dead of night, my phone rang. The sound broke through the suffocating silence, and that single call changed the course of my story — it was Michael, reaching out after a long silence.

My future husband kept pleading with me to join him on the other side of the planet. He bombarded me with messages, calls, and gifts. If I wasn't feeling well, he would send flowers, chocolates, or medicine. A constant stream of thoughtful gestures from Michael arrived through his driver, who appeared at my doorstep whenever instructed.

Resisting Michael's persistence was almost impossible. He became omnipresent — like a bird-of-paradise male, dancing before his partner, just so she would notice him. He showed himself to be a real man when he declared that he would take full responsibility for all the arrangements and expenses of our Canadian trip.

"So, will you come to Canada?" Michael wouldn't leave me alone with this question. After some thought, I finally agreed, but on the condition that he would organize a good program for me. I made it clear right away that I wasn't going there just to amuse him. Such trips didn't obligate me to anything — if I didn't like it, I would say no and leave forever.

It's very important for a woman to immediately define her standards, to set the bar accordingly. The first meetings determine how a man will treat her for the rest of her life.

You can take everything from life – everything here is accessible and unlimited. But remember – the cashier will be waiting ahead.

In April 2016, I arrived in Canada as a tourist. My arrival point and starting point was Toronto, the country's largest city. The metropolis, with its numerous glass skyscrapers, is located on the shores of Lake Ontario. Big, cold, gloomy — that's how I remember it. The only greenery in Toronto in April was the Starbucks sign; everything else was gray concrete boxes, sullen and lifeless.

No matter how much I traveled, I never ceased to be amazed by new things. Every city has houses and roads that are made of the same materials, but they look different everywhere. Toronto and other Canadian cities were like going to another planet, another galaxy — they looked so different, seemed so alien to what I was used to.

Canada is a developed country with a good standard of living, but it was quite difficult for me to discern this standard. Most entertainment and shopping centers closed at six in the evening, so finding somewhere to go for dinner was quite problematic. Even the most expensive restaurants had old and very simple furniture. The restrooms resembled those I had seen in ordinary European eateries. No hint of luxury — just a regular white sink and a modest mirror hanging above it. The focus seemed to be on practicality and efficiency — a cultural nuance that took some time for me to appreciate.

Everything was terribly untidy and messy, withchips and scuffs on the walls, as if there were renovations. It was as if the creators of the interior (or rather, its absence) looked at it all and, waving their hand, said: "It'll do. It performs its function — that's the main thing." In general, I was met with a minimum of decor, a minimum of detail. Everything was strictly business.

If you want to enjoy a proper meal in Canada, a bit of Googling is usually required to find the right spot. Many cafes focus on quick and popular options like burgers, pizza, sushi, and other fast foods. However, I have to give credit to the portions — they are incredibly generous, often enough for two or three people. When you do find a place with a good menu, the presentation can be quite surprising. A single, oversized plate might include an omelet, sausages, fries, fruit, and sweet pancakes with jam — all served together with a cheerful smile from the waiter. For me, Canada felt like a completely different universe, with its own customs and culinary traditions that initially didn't align with my usual expectations. It took me a while to fully understand the local culture and mentality.

"Now I'll introduce you to some very important people," Michael would say. These "important people" often turned out to be modestly dressed individuals, very different from what I expected based on European standards. Their views on beauty, lifestyle, and priorities were entirely distinct. What seemed appealing to us might not resonate with them, and vice versa. When I first arrived in Canada, I felt a bit like Alice in Wonderland; familiar things appeared in an entirely new light.

In the small town of Niagara Falls, right on the border with the United States, just a bridge away from another country, Michael booked me a beautiful hotel room with a view of the falls. We spent time with his friends, eagerly anticipating the chance to see this natural wonder illuminated at night. Niagara Falls is a breathtaking spectacle that sends shivers down your spine, with a fine mist of water drifting through the air. It's an experience I would gladly relive someday.

After Toronto, our next destination was Ottawa, the Canadian capital. Unlike Kyiv, which was a capital city with a unique character impossible to confuse with any other, Ottawa presented a very different image. The city felt much more modest and tranquil compared to the bustling European metropolises I was accustomed to. Like Washington in the United States, Ottawa serves as the political center of the nation. Both capitals are relatively small and home to modest populations, reflecting their focus on governance rather than grandeur.

Our next stop was Quebec City and my heart began to warm up. The city felt more refined and captivating to me. I was especially impressed by the Château Frontenac perched high on a hill. Its imposing size and the stern, commanding view it cast over visitors from its small windows are truly mesmerizing. It reminded me of medieval European castles, with their aura of mystery and grandeur.

Our final destination was Montreal, a city whose name evokes softness and elegance, but whose character felt colder and more rugged, much like the rest of Canada. In winter, the city takes on a quiet, almost deserted atmosphere. The streets are empty, and it feels as though only you and a swirling snow storm that frequents the city exist, locked in a cold waltz with the howling wind outside your window.

As soon as summer arrives, Montreal reveals itself as a charming slice of Europe on the North American continent. Crowds of tourists flock to the city to admire its distinctive architecture and enjoy the sound of French being spoken. Gleaming white cruise ships dock at Montreal's port, and the city bursts to life, vibrant and full of energy.

Still, Montreal reminded me more of a metropolis from the 1980s, with its calm atmosphere, quiet streets, and unhurried pace of life. In many ways, these words reflect the character of North America as a whole. It feels as though time slows down in Canada, and when winter comes, people retreat indoors, away from the public eye.

Despite feeling slightly out of sync with Canada at first, I was genuinely happy. Michael had truly gone out of his way to make sure I enjoyed myself. He put in so much effort to keep me entertained and made sure I was never bored.

To make the trip more enjoyable, Michael invited some of his friends and we had a great time together. One of them, a tall brunette named Jonathan, happened to see me video chatting with my best friend Anastasia. He found everything about her fascinating; her appearance, way of speaking, expressions, and cheerful laugh. Jonathan had never met a Ukrainian girl before and she intrigued him. He immediately wanted to meet her.

My best friend Anastasia and I's friendship is a truly special story. We've been through thick and thin, sat at the same desk in school, and then chatted on the phone all the way home. Many years have passed since then and nothing has changed. We still talk on the phone for hours, still confide in each other, and remain very close. Thanks to her, I understand what true friendship is — a bond that cannot be broken by years or distance. You can have many partners in life, but friends stay forever and often even journey with us from lifetime to lifetime. I don't know how my past self would have endured the solitude of a luxurious French castle if it weren't for my faithful friend, who accompanies me from incarnation to incarnation.

Seeing Anastasia on my phone screen, Jonathan immediately took action. Her English was, to put it mildly, not very good, so they communicated through Google Translate. It all started with texting.

Michael and I rolled on the floor laughing at how it all unfolded. Because of the clumsy translations, the phrase 'I have butterflies in my stomach' became 'you make my stomach churn' or 'I have diarrhea.' Memories of this still bring a nostalgic smile and infectious laughter.

Despite the language barrier, their relationship developed romantically. Jonathan sent Anastasia flowers and gifts and patiently waited for her in Canada. She first visited him a couple of months after they met online. They were what people call a 'beautiful couple' — it was a pleasure to see them together.

As for Michael, he was still hesitant to be alone with me, but he had his own methods of capturing my heart. I had never met anyone as attentive as Michael. His attention and care enveloped me from all sides like a warm down comforter. I felt completely comfortable with him. I became the center of his universe, the main goal he strived to achieve.

Michael constantly surprised me — for example, he would ask his friends to pick up flowers to give me at the most unexpected moments. The first time it happened was when we were visiting an observation deck. Michael's friend brought me an incredibly beautiful bouquet which made my already bright day even more colorful and happy.

My companion watched my every glance and sigh. He caught my smiles and gathered information to learn what I liked and disliked. He tried to understand my inner world, my interests. It was important for him to have a dialogue with me, to understand me in a way no one else had.

I was very touched that he cooked for me — for the first time in his life. And this was a man whose family always employed personal chefs. I especially remember one of his first dishes for me: pasta with lobster. Despite the fact that Michael wasn't skilled with kitchen utensils and could barely hold a frying pan, it turned out delicious and looked beautiful. I was pleasantly surprised.

Our vacation in Canada was very active. Michael had prepared an interesting itinerary, never letting me get bored for a second.

Our schedule was packed. We were constantly going somewhere; ice skating, hockey games, horseback riding — everywhere we went, we had a lot of fun and enjoyed each other's company.

I especially remember Cirque du Soleil, which was based in Montreal. It's a mesmerizing show with vibrant holograms, performers in fantastical costumes, and a light show where a herd of horses galloped towards the audience from the ceiling. I was captivated. Thanks to Michael, my stay in Canada turned into a colorful dream, a happy fairy tale. I fed bison and deer in a safari park right from the car window, saw stunning castles, visited great cultural monuments, and enjoyed the magical northern nature.

Know how to savor the moment, especially in relationships. If you can dive headfirst into pleasure, why not do it? Don't hide your feelings and emotions – always experience them to the fullest.

It seemed that Michael was ready to do anything for me. He became a conqueror and I gradually began to succumb. The most important thing for a man is to be a hunter until the very end. Michael pursued me like a predator, but having caught me, he remained gentle and careful. At some point, I finally surrendered.

He had won and I fell in love with him.

Dinner with Tiffany

It was time to return to Ukraine. Thousands of miles once again separated Michael and me. Despite this, our emotional connection only grew stronger. He called me 20 times a day. I would sometimes fall asleep listening to his velvety voice through the phone's speaker. It was important for him to know how I spent my day, what I was thinking about, what mood I was in, how many times I laughed, and who visited me in my dreams.

My future husband had perfectly mastered all five love languages: touch, time, words, gifts, and acts of service. The first was inaccessible to us, but he excelled at the remaining four. Even at a distance, he felt so very close. I received the most beautiful bouquet of flowers in my life from him — he sent me 101 peonies. The lovely buds exuded tenderness and love, touching me with their silky petals. I was completely delighted and would continued to remember that gift forever.

Analyzing the matrices of destiny now, I understand that my relationship with Michael could only be developed abroad. According to all indicators, the compatibility between Michael and I was only possible outside the country where we were born. Back then, I didn't know this and I wasn't concerned with conventions. I was overflowing with feelings and intoxicated with love.

A couple of months later, at the end of June, I flew back to Canada.

The apartment Michael and I shared in Montreal was in a very beautiful location — between the old port and downtown. While walking, we often passed by the 'Combat des Titans' fountain, a unique work of art where all the elements converged. Not only water, but fire also erupted from the fountain — an extraordinary sight to behold, especially in the evenings. And Michael and I were always together and always at the center of these elements.

I was provided with enough gifts and flowers for three lifetimes. Michael tried very hard to find bouquets that suited me, but in Canada, they make them terribly. In the end, he handed me pruning shears so I could arrange the enormous armfuls of flowers he brought me myself. He wanted me to genuinely like them and wanted everything to be perfect.

We went to the gym together — he meticulously watched his figure and always tried to look impeccable. He chose the best restaurants and took me to the most interesting events. Michael's attentiveness and ability to notice details greatly impressed me.

He's a man with a mathematical mind, seeing the world through numbers. Having heard someone's birth date once, my future husband remembered it for life. It was as if a supercomputer worked inside Michael's head, scanning data and filing it away in folders. He very carefully observed which dishes I ordered, which colors I wore most often, how long it took me to fall asleep, and how long it took me to wake up.

Partly due to his unique mindset, partly due to love, Michael accumulated all this data and memorized it. He knew exactly what color roses to give me and which dessert would delight me. Stopping at a gas station, he always bought me a chocolate bar and knew my favorite movies and books by heart.

I didn't need to hint at anything — he anticipated everything in advance. As soon as I thought about a boat trip, we were immediately sailing down the Saint Lawrence River. No sooner had I dreamed of breakfast in bed than it was already prepared. Michael put all his effort into everything he did, putting his soul into his actions, which I noticed and greatly appreciated.

I didn't stand idly by either — I reciprocated. I didn't have his memory, but I could tell what things he liked and how he enjoyed certain dishes over others. If there was an afternoon free, I'd try to plan an activity for the two of us before he could surprise me with something.

It's sometimes useful to have your head in the clouds, but it's important to not get carried away. Don't let your mind become clouded, don't soften. Feel the ground beneath your feet, pay attention to the signals and hints. The universe will always help you find the right path. The main thing is to learn to understand it.

I felt a proposal was brewing onMichael's mind. This feeling hung in the air like a delicate, sweet aroma, the anticipation of something beautiful and grand.

I had a business in Kyiv that I had been growing for over two years. Leaving everything behind and moving seemed unthinkable — it required a compelling reason. Michael understood this well.

One day, as I lay by the pool on the roof of the complex where Michael had rented us an apartment, Anastasia called me. It was a usual occurrence — we called each other every day. During the conversation, she suddenly asked, "Have you even thought about a wedding ring? What kind would you like?" I immediately understood that Michael had put her up to it. He, as always, wanted everything to be perfect, for me to absolutely love it.

It was a special and very eventful day, literally the day before my departure from Canada. A visit to Cirque du Soleil, a boat trip with live music, and a luxurious dinner, which admittedly resulted in an upset stomach for me.

Michael paid the bill, and we returned to our hotel room. "You lie down for a bit, a friend is coming by to bring me something," Michael told me while I was struggling with my stomach.

Half an hour later, I went into the kitchen and saw an amazing scene, which seemed to have been created by several people. Candles stood on the table and plates were arranged with fruits, berries, and my favorite pastries. It turned out that Michael had ordered one of each from different places I had liked — he remembered every croissant, every éclair that had ever brought a sweet smile to my face.

While I was figuring out what all this feast was for, he disappeared for a second. When I turned around, Michael was already down on one knee. A thin and elegant Tiffany ring sparkled in his hand. He even chose a beautiful date — 07.07.16. It was truly a special moment for him.

I was terribly flustered. I literally lost my ability to speak, my thoughts becoming tangled. I felt that some new and very important door had opened in my life.

Despite the excitement from the proposal, I understood that I was facing a serious choice — I had reached a crossroad. I had to decide if I was ready to leave my business in Ukraine and move to Canada indefinitely, to be with my future husband.

I had a strong team in place and I could manage them remotely. Still, it wasn't the same level of involvement I would have had if I was physically there. I understood that I was torn between my work and the prospect of starting a family, and I had to choose.

Someone close to me once said, "You can always build a business. But family is a very delicate matter. A marriage proposal doesn't happen every day." I didn't answer Michael with a "yes" and I didn't answer with a "no." I simply said that I would be his wife because I loved this man and wanted to be with him. I declared to Michael, "I will marry you. But on one condition. You must promise that you will provide everything necessary and safety for me and our children, for our children and I." And he promised.

About a week later, Jonathan proposed to Anastasia. It happened on Michael's birthday. We were celebrating on the shore of a lake, and our sweet couple walked out onto the pier. Anastasia suspected nothing, and when Jonathan knelt down, she almost fell into the water. He gave her a ring very similar to mine — also from Tiffany. We walked around like twins — content, happy, filled with new impressions and joyful expectations. The story was incredibly beautiful — two best friends marrying two friends, and all of this happening in Canada.

My sun had set behind the clouds.

That same day, Michael received a call from his father, whom he hadn't spoken to in a very long time due to his incarceration. Everything changed from that moment on. My future husband retreated deep into himself and his family problems. A veil fell before his eyes, obscuring everything. Physically, Michael remained with me, but mentally, he had flown far away. The proposal was followed by a dead silence, and the question of the wedding was pushed to the back burner.

Michael didn't tell anyone about the upcoming marriage. Interacting with his family was very difficult for me. He became a completely different person — his face, voice, and even gestures changed.

My future husband constantly warned me that there were things "you shouldn't say." I felt constrained. It was as if thick ropes bound my hands and feet, preventing me from making any unnecessary movements or uttering an extra word. After family gatherings, he would declare, "Why did you say that? You shouldn't have said that."

Michael and I started brainstorming ways to increase our income. He had an idea — he owned property in Ukraine and needed my help to rent it out. Michael decided that I would handle all the organizational matters, as he couldn't return to his homeland at the time for reasons beyond his control.

I flew to Kyiv to arrange our future. Instead of focusing on my own business, I was rushing from one apartment to another, ordering trucks to remove old furniture, hiring plumbers, and searching for tenants.

I temporarily turned my back on my business because I chose to prioritize family. In doing so, I sacrificed my present, placing all my hopes on the future Michael and I were building together.

Only later did I come to understand how dangerous it is to focus on one thing at the expense of everything else. This imbalance is wrong. Everything in life should coexist in harmony. You should never underestimate your potential. The universe provides enough room for both work and a personal life. Never abandon your ambitions for the sake of illusory goals. Strive for balance, embrace this harmony, and, above all, always choose yourself.

In Kyiv, I met with one of Michael's family members to hand over the property documents. Upon meeting me, this person looked at me with a blank stare and asked, "I apologize, Maria, but who are you exactly?"

Michael had kept the proposal a secret from all his relatives. This was probably the first sign that something was wrong.

In Kyiv, I was accompanied everywhere by Michael's personal driver. He drove me to meetings where I often crossed paths with my future husband's friends. One of them told me, "Maria, please don't get involved with these people. Walk away. You're a good person. This will only bring you unhappiness."

I dismissed those words without a second thought. I loved my man and was determined to do whatever it took to build our shared future. But the red flags were waving in the wind and I was too blinded by love to see them.

As a result of our efforts, all the profits from renting the property went to his family. From the perspective of building our young family's future, all the work felt meaningless. We didn't even receive so much as a simple "thank you," and it felt like a physical slap in the face.

Meanwhile, my flower shop had gained nationwide recognition. We were invited as sponsors to high-profile events and our bouquets were presented to the winners of 'Miss Ukraine.' I realized that this magnificent palace which I had carefully built, brick by brick over the years, could fade into nothing more than a beautiful memory in an instant.

But I made my choice, reorienting all my energy and focus toward marriage, leaving behind the dream I had nurtured for so long.

By summer, I had finalized the rental of Michael's property and in September, I prepared to return to Canada. While in Kyiv, I managed to complete a mountain of tasks, bought a wedding dress and rings. My phone's photo gallery was filled with wedding collages featuring festive looks and interiors.

At first, they were pastel, delicate tones, exquisite classic styles. Later, I decided I wanted something more unconventional, like a mountain wedding. I was really looking forward to this moment; my head was full of plans, fantasies, and beautiful dreams.

One day, my friends invited me to a cafe before my trip to Canada, but they actually took me to karaoke and threw me a bachelorette party at the Kyiv Passage. The girls put a bridal veil on me, but the celebration still felt flat.

I hadn't expected the surprise, and for me, it was just an ordinary day. I had come back from work very tired, in a black dress and with terrible hair, exhausted by the thought that everything was going wrong. I had no mood or energy to celebrate — I just wanted to go home and collapse on the bed. It was a portent for what the marriage would become.

In Montreal, Michael and I had a small apartment and we did everything we could to make it cozy. The hours spent in that tiny apartment became the happiest of our life together. We were practically starting our life from scratch, building every little detail in that small space together. I was ready for this new beginning because I saw immense potential in Michael and in our relationship.

A woman falls in love not just with a label, but with the promise of what could grow from that small seed. I placed my bet that our union would blossom into a beautiful tree, eventually transforming into a gorgeous garden.

After the proposal, Michael tried to completely separate himself from his family. With their authoritarian ways, this wasn't easy. His relatives declared that since he was creating his own family, he should be on his own. Now he had to take full responsibility for earning his own living.

I always chose people I saw potential in. Those who don't lie on the couch wondering what to do, but immediately take action. In this respect, my future husband showed his best side. The man who had always had everything taken care of for him and served on a silver platter got a job as an Uber driver. The golden boy went to earn money for his family in the way that was available to him. Later, he started working with a friend, renting out spaces on Airbnb. Sometimes, it got to the point where he, a guy from a very wealthy family, was painting stairs himself.

At that moment, I saw a real man before me. With his actions, he continued to prove that he was ready to give up everything for our happy union.

Communicating with Michael's family became increasingly difficult for me. Over time, this led to chronic stress. To them, I was an outsider — unnecessary and out of place. I could sense their undisguised hostility, and it was deeply painful. I tried to justify their behavior by telling myself it was because they were older. But with each passing day, interacting with them became more and more challenging.

Before the wedding, I was asked, "When your child is born, will you baptize him?"

I calmly replied, "My husband and I will decide whether or not to baptize our child." And although these were words spoken into unlistening ears, I was firm in my boundaries. I showed them that these were the internal affairs of our family and nothing they said could make me budge.

Michael's relatives loved to cling to religious issues, trying to provoke me with them. They asked why I, being baptized, didn't go to church. I have my own point of view on this: I'm not a religious person, and like many, I was baptized without my knowledge as a child. But this didn't impose any obligations on me. Why should I blindly follow religion? I believe that people are something more than just highly developed earthly beings, and that the Universe operates according to certain rules. But to unravel them, you have to observe, study, reflect, understand, draw conclusions, and not just go to church and participate in some rituals.

During such clashes, Michael kept quiet. He wore an iron mask, unable to utter a sound. I tried to understand his viewpoint — we were still partially dependent on his family and if I didn't have the best relationship with them, he still needed to.

I was alone on the field, a warrior fighting a battle that I wanted desperately to win. But I couldn't defend myself alone for long; my strength and nerves were at their limit. Meeting his relatives caused me immense stress. I was shaking inside, adrenaline pumping, but I couldn't express my emotions. I had to remain silent.

Exercise for stress relief: 'Balloon'

Imagine that there is a balloon in your chest. Take a deep breath through your nose, filling your lungs with air. Exhale through your mouth, feeling the air leave your lungs.

Take your time, repeat. Imagine a balloon inside you that inflates and deflates with those breaths.

Pause, count to five. Then inhale deeply again, pause, filling your lungs, count to three. Imagine the inflated balloon.

Exhale the air, feeling it pass through your throat and mouth. Repeat several times with a delay.

Stop and feel that you are full of energy and your tension is gone.

The wedding kept getting postponed. First to the spring, then to summer, then to the next year. None of his family members knew that Michael had proposed to me. He forbade me from talking to them about it.

Even before I moved to Canada, he promised to help me open a flower shop there. But this prospect, too, began to look more and more like a fairy tale with each passing day.

Later, I would understand that my former husband simply didn't want to take full responsibility — he wasn't ready for it. He courted me beautifully, gave me the best gifts and stunning bouquets, cooked for me, worked to provide for the family, and was ready for seemingly heroic deeds. He really enjoyed the courtship phase — it was a time of lightness and serenity, when no one owes anyone anything. But as soon as it was time to take real responsibility, he backed down.

Autumn arrived, and Michael worked all day long. This was a very depressing period for me. I had to spend almost all my time alone. I felt like a pet waiting for hours for its owner to return. The feeling of abandonment intensified with each passing day, especially compared to how much time Michael and I had spent together before he proposed. My life ceased to belong to me again — I no longer controlled the situation.

Immersed in reflection and self-analysis, I asked myself: who am I now?

Chapter 6: Out of Range

The walls of my concrete box were growing thicker. The loneliness and monotony of existence pressed down on me with increasing force. With each passing day, I felt them closing in on me, narrowing the space where I had to exist. It felt like a slow descent into a well, where it grew darker and colder over time.

When Michael proposed, he presented me with a choice. The fact is, he led a very private, non-public life. I, on the contrary, enjoyed sharing my thoughts on social media; I was used to constant communication. At that time, I had around 8,000 followers on Instagram, which was considered a very respectable number back then.

Michael gave me an ultimatum: if I wanted to build a family with him, I needed to change my Ukrainian phone numbers, my car registration and driver's license, close my Instagram page, and reduce my audience to only my closest friends and family. Initially, he wanted me to delete my page altogether, but we agreed that I would simply make it private.

Unaware of the impending ordeal of loneliness, I agreed rather quickly. *When in Rome, do as the Romans do*, I thought, not sensing anything terrible or destructive in his request. If giving up my social media audience was the price for our life together, I was prepared to do it.

At that time, I was completely unaware of the consequences.

How to identify an abuser:

The more points that apply, the greater the risk.

1. Prone to addictions.

2. If they don't get what they want, they resort to ultimatums, threats, and physical violence.

3. Restricts the partner's external contacts to deprive them of support from loved ones and friends and gain greater significance.

4. 'Cares' by trying to control all aspects of the partner's life and violating their personal boundaries. Gradually, this turns into total hyper-control.

5. Pressures and coerces the partner into sex.

6. Often reacts with outbursts of anger that are disproportionate to the situation.

7. Blames the partner for their own mistakes and the atmosphere in the family.

8. Applies double standards: others are not allowed to do what they are allowed to do.

9. Devalues the partner's successes, problems, and hobbies.

10. Ignores and punishes with coldness when dissatisfied or during arguments.

11. Behaves sweetly in public, but transforms into a different personality (including a tyrant) in private.

12. After interacting with them, you feel drained and unhappy.

How to understand that your partner is reliable:

1. They are emotionally open, sincere, and honest with you and with other people.

2. They don't play games, behave naturally, and you can be yourself with them, without playing any roles.

3. They speak respectfully about their friends and former partners. They will speak about you in the same tone someday.

4. They invest in the relationship with their attention, time, and resources, showing that they are interested in its development and improvement.

5. They take responsibility for their words and actions and follow through.

6. They don't project their past experiences onto you, but trust you.

7. They keep agreements, and if something goes wrong, they warn you.

8. They are careful with you, accept and listen to you, understand your emotions, needs, and limitations. If something doesn't suit them, they are ready to find a compromise.

9. They expect the same honesty, sincerity, and naturalness from you.

Communication and contact with the outside world are very important resources that fill a person with strength from the outside. If these contacts are severed, a vacuum is created. A person cannot live in a social vacuum, especially if they are an extrovert. You can limit your social circle to a comfortable level, but by destroying it completely, you destroy yourself.

Michael manually purged my Instagram profile, blocking practically all of my followers. This task took him a month, as there are limits on the platform. Some of my acquaintances are still blocked because I still haven't found the time to unblock so many people.

Never become a 'convenient person.' It's the worst thing you can do for yourself and for the world. Don't become a victim. When you are in the victim position, it means that globally something is wrong with the situation.

Living for others is noble if it's about an important mission. In the case of Vanga or Mother Teresa — it was their soul's path, they weren't asked to do it. It was a mission they sacredly honored and fulfilled. If you are asked to sacrifice yourself for someone's whim, assess the situation from the perspective of an observer, a third party.

Give yourself advice as you would if you were speaking to your best friend, to the dearest person to whom you wish happiness. Everything will immediately become clear to you. Remember, not from a position of ego, but from pure love and happiness: you are the most important thing you have.

Until the moment I finally moved to Montreal, the problem didn't feel so acute. I traveled to Ukraine for business and saw my family and friends — the channel was still open for communication. About two years of social isolation awaited me, an almost complete absence of contact with the outside world, any human warmth and support, but I had no clue about it until it hit.

During that period, a terrible melancholy fell upon me — like a thick concrete slab. It pressed down so painfully that sometimes I wanted to moan and cry. The world became gray and cold, time seemed to stop. Each day was indistinguishable from the previous one. Communicating with relatives was problematic due to different time zones and I was forbidden from expressing myself on social media. Michael's friends, whom we occasionally saw, mostly spoke English. I felt like a fish out of water among them, as I didn't know the language and couldn't fully integrate into the company. Michael would disappear at work and I would sit at home completely alone all day.

It was then that I began to understand that I had given up a very important source of energy: communication. I already had experience living abroad, away from my family, which I gained in Colombia. While there, I felt lonely, but it was a completely different kind of loneliness — much healthier and not so destructive. On the warm Latin American continent, everything happened differently. Even in conditions of social isolation, I saw bright colors around me that transformed my reality and healed me from loneliness. Everything there was new: the food, the people, the locations, the climate. The Colombian sun, tropical forests, and green plantations prevented me from falling into despair.

I had things to do in Colombia. I worked a lot and had the opportunity to communicate with colleagues. In my free time, I would open my laptop, and a whole world would unfold before me: a multitude of followers, messages, and a sea of attention. By posting videos on social media, I would instantly receive hundreds of comments. I felt the presence of people in my life, even though some were thousands of kilometers away from me, and others spoke a language I didn't understand.

In Canada, none of that existed. Work and activities were almost non-existent. Sharing photos on Instagram had me receiving dead silence in return. I couldn't get used to it; it was a shock for me, a departure from my usual life. Only years later would I understand that my natural circulation of energy occurs when I share my knowledge and emotions with others, receiving feedback. This is my life resource — to express myself and help other people express themselves, to show the way and lead them along it.

I realized how important community is for people, especially during immigration. **Each person is a carrier of energy and other people are its conductors. The exchange of energy, feelings, emotions, warmth, and love is a basic need. Without it, it is impossible to survive.** I was deprived of this and all the ways to satisfy this need were cut off.

Experiences accumulated inside me, which I couldn't express anywhere, couldn't share with anyone. They grew like a lump in my throat, which I simply swallowed and which ultimately poisoned me from the inside.

You should never live according to someone else's directions.

You are an independent person, not an addition to someone or something. No one has the right to control your actions except you. Give yourself a deadline and, if someone still doesn't start treating you as a person, leave the place where you are not valued.

You are your everything.

By sacrificing yourself, you risk losing the whole world.

Over time, I became as cold and lifeless as the city I lived in. I didn't want anything, I wasn't interested in anything. While in Colombia I watched my figure, ate fish and fruit, and walked a lot. In Canada I couldn't even make it to the gym, which was located on the first floor of our building. Not because I was lazy, but because I had neither the strength, nor was I in the mood.

I chose one good at the expense of another: I accommodated my partner because I believed in our love and family. I sacrificed my comfort so that we could be together.

Giving up everything for an illusory goal is the worst strategy. You should always choose yourself and listen to your desires and needs. A person destroyed from within cannot do anything useful for the world.

With each passing day, I felt more and more lonely. Out of boredom and anguish, I started watching TV series, although I had never done so before Montreal. To kill time, I cooked —more than ever in my life. Our refrigerator was always crammed full and instead of becoming a symbol of family well-being, it became a symbol of my depression. Because of such an immobile and monotonous lifestyle, I started to gain weight. I was rolling into a deep, dark abyss and couldn't stop myself.

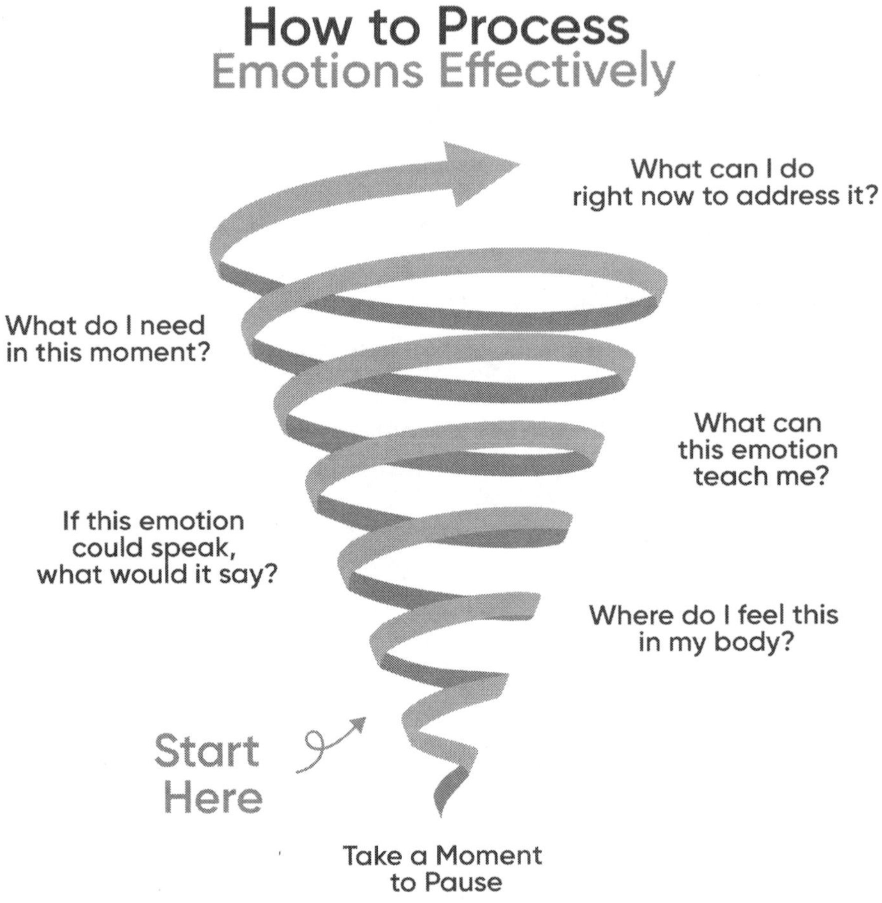

Fig. 1. How to Process Emotions Effectively

Contrasts

To avoid violating the terms of my tourist visa, I had to leave Canada every six months. After about a year of living in confinement, I once again made a short trip to Ukraine. I couldn't return to my homeland permanently — that would have meant giving up and not accepting the challenge the universe had presented me. For me, it would have been a step backward, and I'm used to moving only forward. Especially since I had made a firm decision and chosen my family. I was confident that a door of opportunity had opened before me — life in a developed country and marriage to the man I loved. And every open door, even if darkness lies beyond it, inevitably leads to the next, and this journey never ends.

The state I lived in in Canada could be called survival mode. Of course, physically I had everything — money, a roof over my head, a business that I continued to run online. However, psychologically, I found myself in quicksand, which was slowly but surely pulling me under.

My only consolation was the idea that I just had to endure. Michael kept telling me, "Just hold on a little longer!" He explained that our life in Canada was temporary, and we were about to leave and settle down somewhere else. But the truth was that nothing was changing. And I, having believed the promises, didn't even try to make new acquaintances. Why bother if we were leaving Canada soon anyway?

Only this "soon" never seemed to arrive.

Communication, interaction with other people, is as necessary for us as air. When a person moves abroad for an extended period, it's essential to immediately build a social circle. Clubs, workshops, events, even work can help. Without communication and activities, a person begins to wither, like a flower left alone in a dark room.

I understood this too late and I realized it when I started taking English lessons. There, I met new people of different nationalities and ages. Before that, almost two years of my life took place within four walls; I saw nothing beyond the gray landscape outside the window.

I was very close to the point of no return in that very dark room. It seemed like with one slight push, I would fall into a pit from which I would never escape. And if I had focused only on the negative, that's exactly what would have happened.

During that period, negativity seriously prevailed, but I still tried to stay afloat, so as not to sink into despair, and I believed that everything would work out. It's impossible to get out of a pit by focusing only on falling. What saved me from depression was that I didn't focus on the bad and, despite everything, tried to move forward.

The Hidden Benefits of Playing the Victim:

- You get noticed, receive attention, and are met with sympathy
- People lend you money
- Others do things for you
- No expectations are placed on you
- People patiently listen to your complaints about life, politics, and external circumstances
- Solutions are constantly offered to you, and you find reasons why they won't work

Fig. 2. The Hidden Benefits of Playing the Victim

To get out of the swamp, you need to focus on the lifeline, not the swamp. To get rid of negativity, you need to stop focusing on it. Accept it, process it, forget it, and then leave it forever in the past. Get rid of the burden, and then you can move forward.

Returning home each time felt like teleporting from one universe to another. The contrast was sharp — Canada, where many shops and cafes close earlier than expected, and Kyiv, where life bustles 24/7, were polar opposites of each other. It took me a few days to get used to the change of scenery of my homeland. But when I adjusted, all my life processes easily adapted to the frantic rhythm of the capital, and I felt back in my element.

Time flows differently in the Ukrainian capital — it accommodates a lot of actions and events. On February 14th, my mother celebrated her birthday. The day before, my team and I prepared bouquets for Valentine's Day until late at night and then I arrived at the shop at six in the morning to start sending them out. And a small miracle happened during the night: our dog gave birth—all these events fit into a single day.

During this trip, I expanded the shop and rearranged the premises. I often saw friends and family, went to the beautician, visited the gym, and even managed to fly to my brother in London. Life on the European continent, even though it was a short trip, turned out to be very eventful. This was especially noticeable in contrast to Canada, where the pace of life felt much slower and calmer than what I was used to.

Marseille

Two months later, Michael started getting restless and demanded my return.

He was still waiting for me in our small apartment in Montreal. Still in the status of a common-law husband, without any official stamps in my passport, and still with surprises. During my absence, he had bought me a pile of gifts. His attentiveness and ability to show care hadn't gone anywhere. These pleasant moments smoothed over our difficult conversations about the fact that we still weren't officially married and I was traveling to Canada as a tourist.

Since he had promised that we would open a flower shop in Canada, we visited local flower boutiques so I could see how they operated. My state at that time could be described as 'at the starting block' — I began to draw up a business plan, think about the design, and develop some of my own ideas. While designing a new website, I sketched it on sheets of A4 paper taped together. All the icons, pictures, and inscriptions were drawn in pencil. The dream of expanding the business became a ray of light illuminating the prison I was confined to.

At the same time, I slowly began to transfer the management of the Kyiv shop to my employee, Dasha, whom I had appointed as the manager in my place. We signed a subcontract in order to iron out the details. Dasha got the opportunity to run the shop and make a profit. Most importantly, we agreed that she would maintain my style and concept.

I tried to concentrate on the future with the new branch of my small company. But it was an illusion, a beautiful gift box, inside which, upon looking, I found emptiness. After all the time I spent planning and waiting for the day, no shop ever opened in Canada.

To add some color to my life and compensate for the loneliness, I decided to get a cat. I love those animals very much. I had a dog in my childhood, but my parents forbade cats. With my need for companionship, it was time to fill in this missing puzzle piece. Michael supported the idea and together we chose a breed that suited us. It was a British Golden Chinchilla. When I first saw its picture, I immediately fell in love. We couldn't find a kitten in Canada, so the pet was brought to us from abroad.

Marseille is what we named the cat and he turned out to be perfect. Tame, affectionate and playful, he instantly adapted to the apartment and loved us very much. Nothing foreshadowed trouble. The only thing I noticed was that the cat sometimes coughed. We took him to the veterinary clinic where they checked his lungs and reassured us with confidence that he was perfectly healthy.

At first, everything was fine. Marseille ate well, was active, ran around the apartment, purred like a tractor, and looked very happy. But a month later, he began to wither rapidly. He lost his fur, refused to eat, and almost stopped moving. We went to the vet again. After a lung screening, it turned out that Marseille had pneumonia. The doctor said it wasn't fatal, that he needed an injection and everything would be alright.

A vehicle with flashing lights on rushed him to a veterinary hospital on the other side of the city, while the team tried to resuscitate him during the journey. Half an hour after our arrival, the vet came out to deliver the heartbreaking news: Marseille had passed away.

For me, this was another blow to my already fragile emotional state. Marseille lived with us for a little over a month, but he brought new meaning and an infinite amount of love into our lives, which I lacked so much. I grew very fond of him during this time; he helped me distract myself from the routine and release some of my pent-up emotions.

We buried Marseille by the river. Being close to the water brings healing to the soul and helps to process grief. After Marseille's passing, we got another cat, his brother from the next litter, but chose not to shuttle him between countries. He stayed with my mother in Ukraine and was also named Marseille.

Between Heaven and Earth

Midsummer arrived, bringing Michael's birthday with it. To celebrate, I baked a cake and prepared a surprise for my beloved. He was turning 25. All day, no one had called to wish him a happy birthday and he walked around looking as gloomy as a storm cloud. In the evening, I invited him to a restaurant. When we arrived, he couldn't believe his eyes: a large group of his friends were sitting at the table. He hadn't expected to be greeted by so many people that were dear to him. Michael was as happy as a child, and the birthday surprise was a complete success.

At the restaurant, a couple of our friends, Kate and Philip, were with us. Kate was someone I met by chance, but she left a vivid mark on my life. While I was researching the Canadian flower market, my friends and I visited a flower shop in Montreal's most prestigious district. Unexpectedly, the florist started speaking to me in Russian. Immediately, I thought, "Perfect, I've found my florist."

We exchanged contact information, I found Kate on social media, and we went out to lunch. Back then, I didn't know that Kate would become a very close friend, supporting me during the most challenging period of my life and becoming one of the two friends present at my son's birth.

After the birth of my son, David, our communication with Kate almost faded away as she immersed herself in family matters. Nevertheless, her presence in my life was invaluable and incredibly necessary. This experience showed me that every person we meet plays a specific role. Kate played hers — she provided support when I had no one else. I am very grateful to her for that.

But people come and go; it's important to learn to let them go easily.

My life with Michael drifted along, unchanging in speed or direction. I was still semi-legally living in Canada, and he continued to placate me with empty promises. We still weren't married, and no one knew when, or if, the wedding would happen.

Living in Canada on a tourist visa felt like an ongoing source of discomfort, unsettling my sense of stability. I felt uncomfortable, having to leave every six months. I wasn't in Ukraine anymore, but I wasn't truly in Canada either. I felt suspended between heaven and earth. That feeling of suspension and uncertainty was what I experienced.

For me, a Capricorn, it was simply unbearable. Capricorn is a very grounded sign; it's important for us to feel the earth beneath our feet. I was floating in space, unable to ground myself and put down roots to grow.

Against this backdrop of uncertainty, conflicts constantly arose between Michael and I. I often lashed out at him, snapping in conversations and slamming doors. I always needed to know what to expect from life, to be confident in the future. In a situation where I didn't understand where my real home was, I couldn't make plans. It was very difficult for me to bear. The future became a hypothetical, nearly impossible to predict. All my plans and projects hinged on the idea that I just need to hold on a little longer. Just a little longer and everything would be resolved. But life remained uncertain — there was no progress, only a viscous, foggy unknown.

Time passed, and nothing changed. Only the scenery changed, but the essence remained the same. My few followers saw photos from my travels but didn't see the real me. From the outside, it seemed like I was happy. I was traveling the world, living in the luxurious Île des Sœurs[3] district of Montreal, receiving ex-

[3] Located just a few kilometers from the city center and known for its parks and picturesque views, Île des Sœurs is considered one of the most prestigious suburbs of Greater Montreal.

pensive gifts… but that was just a beautiful wrapper concealing very unpleasant contents.

Preferring not to share my personal pain publicly, I didn't seek sympathy. I was sure I could handle everything myself. I endured difficult moments in proud solitude, not wanting to draw attention to my problems. Instead of sharing my worries and delicate details of my personal life with my followers, I preferred to keep them secret. I thought a mature person shouldn't involve outsiders in their problems — problems that didn't concern them. Everyone finds their own way to cope with painful moments. I, in turn, preferred not to put them on display.

But how wrong I was!

Even when it seems like someone is fine, difficult feelings and emotions can be hidden inside. **It's scientifically proven that suppressed emotions can lead to even greater depression and physical health problems. Keeping your feelings and experiences bottled up may seem like a suitable solution at first glance, but in reality, it only brings temporary relief, which can worsen the situation in the long run.**

Suppressing emotions can lead to severe depression and even more serious illnesses. It's crucial to find healthy ways to let your feelings out so they don't manifest as issues not only for your mental health, but also your physical well-being.

You can be happy living in a wooden hut and unhappy in a royal palace. I gave up everything for the potential I saw in my upcoming marriage. It seemed to me that my loneliness, the feeling of being an outsider, the mockery from my partner's relatives, the uncertainty in the relationship, and separating myself from my business would be emotionally compensated for. I believed that by overcoming this barrier, by making a leap, I would achieve my goal and my life would become better. Much later, I would understand that I was right in many ways — patience and perseverance always bring results.

When difficult times come, many people give up without even starting to fight for their future. The difficulties I faced lasted a very long time, not everyone would have been able to go all the way. But this is the only way to reach a new level — to make an effort, not to give up when the situation seems hopeless.

Life consists of ups and downs. The lower a person falls, the higher they can then soar. Difficulties and obstacles become a springboard leading to a new level. It's important not to give up and to endure each fall to the end.

Every stage of life is a story that needs to be lived. All the good things remain only memories, but all the bad things are transformed into experience. THERE ARE NO EVENTS THAT HAPPEN BY CHANCE. The universe sends us only those obstacles that we are capable of overcoming. To open a new chapter in your life, you need to complete the previous one. And it's only your choice — to give up, or crawl to the finish line. Do whatever it takes to get yourself where you need to be.

Chapter 7:
I Choose to Live

When I visited Ukraine during one of my mandatory visits back, my mother and I went on a vacation to Spain. It was a breath of fresh air after being confined within four walls in Canada. Upon my return, a few days before departing Kyiv for Montreal, I went for a routine medical check-up. Doctor's visits were commonplace for me, each one simply confirming that everything was fine. But this time, things unfolded in a completely unexpected way.

A sign from above was my father's declining health. Just before my appointment, I had started actively managing his healthcare, taking him to various doctors to make sure he was as well as he could be. It was like a message from the future, hinting that soon I would be the one needing medical attention.

After my examination, the doctor thoughtfully placed her medical instruments on the table and sat in silent contemplation for a few seconds.

"You have a cyst. It needs to be removed urgently. Immediately." she emphasized, frowning.

According to her, it had developed rapidly, as only six months prior, during my last check-up, everything had been perfect. There had been no indication of a need for surgery at that time; the cyst was discovered by chance at my current appointment.

If it wasn't for this chance discovery, who knows? Perhaps you wouldn't be reading this book — I simply wouldn't have had the time to write it.

The diagnosis surprised me greatly. I wasn't experiencing any pain and, physically, I felt fine. Years later, through deep introspection, I understood that it was the logical outcome of what had been happening to me over the past year. My emotional state had manifested physically. Suppressed feelings and emotions had found a tangible form. I had been forced to change my usual way of life, placed in unsuitable conditions. My body sensed that something was wrong and sent me a distress signal. The emotional burdens I had been carrying for the past few years couldn't help but affect my health. I had become seriously ill and hadn't even noticed how it happened.

I felt like a wild horse trapped in a narrow pen, forced to conform to an existence that stifled my very nature. I thought that since I was young, I could handle everything and wouldn't break, and that difficulties would be overcome without any consequences. Of course, this was a very naive perspective. None of us are made of iron.

In the eternal race against myself, I stopped hearing my inner voice. I was moving at high speed, trying to keep up with everything, and my sixth sense dulled because of it. I stopped using it, focusing on other things — strength, endurance, resilience, and resistance to all the problems that had fallen upon me.

I had no idea of the true severity of my condition until the very last moment. The doctors initially described it as a minor growth that simply needed removal. I was referred to a prestigious hospital in the heart of Kyiv, and the surgery was ultimately performed at a private medical facility. The doctors emphasized the urgency of the procedure, assuring me it had to be done immediately. "Just two small holes through laparoscopic surgery — that's all that will remain after the procedure," they said with impassive expressions. As the doctor spoke those words, it felt as though the ground beneath me had vanished, leaving me to freefall into an endless abyss.

This unexpected diagnosis led me into a whirlwind of urgent decisions, marking the beginning of a harrowing journey.

I had to change my tickets for my return trip. I had planned to spend a couple of days in Kyiv and return to Canada immediately, but I had to stay longer for the urgent surgery. It wasn't until later that I realized just how dire the situation had been.

How events unfolded further can only be described as a nightmare.

A person can endure a lot, but everything has consequences. Accumulated stress and negativity will inevitably find a way out. For some, it's through panic attacks, and for others, it's through oncology. Listen not only to your soul but also to your body. Pay attention to the signs it gives you.

Before the surgery, I was in a good mood — smiling, laughing, talking to my mother, taking pictures. I couldn't have imagined that I would spend a full 11 hours on the operating table.

When the doctors opened the necessary area, they discovered what they feared. To confirm their suspicions, during the operation, the gynecologist made an urgent call to a renowned cancer research institute. On the other end of the line, a renowned professor said that a biopsy needed to be performed and the tissue sent for an express analysis. While I was under anesthesia, my mother and the driver took a sample of my tumor to the other side of the city.

At the laboratory, my mother was told the phrase that any parent dreads hearing: **"Your daughter has stage two cancer."**

What they did to my body after receiving the diagnosis is not information for the faint of heart. Turning my body almost inside out, cutting through my entire abdominal cavity, the doctors removed the affected area. After the surgery was completed, pumped full of drugs, I was sent to intensive care, where I spent three days. In addition to the usual anesthetic to keep me comfortable, I received a massive dose of intravenous anesthesia that all but switched me off for 11 hours. When I woke up, I felt like I was somewhere between life and death. My medication-saturated body couldn't recover for a long time; I felt terribly ill.

All that time, my mother was by my side. For three days after the surgery, she didn't leave my hospital bed. It was much harder for her than for me. From the shock she experienced, my mother seemed to age instantly — she couldn't sleep, eat, or talk normally. In such difficult moments for ourselves, it's hardest for our loved ones. My mother, like me, went through a very difficult ordeal.

It turned out that I went in for one surgery and woke up after a completely different one. When I regained consciousness, I couldn't understand for a long time what had actually happened. Even when the anesthesia completely wore off, I was still half-asleep. It seemed to me that being in intensive care was normal, as if it had been planned that way. Reality slowly manifested around me, as if emerging from a melting fog, and I came to my senses.

In the end, I learned the shocking truth: the gynecological surgeon, instead of removing the cyst, had removed half of my female reproductive organs. The surgery violated medical guidelines, as only an oncologist is authorized to perform such complex procedures.

Moreover, no one warned me; the organ removal was performed without my consent. Both the surgery and my cancerous tumor came as a terrifying surprise. I went in to have a cyst removed and I woke up after an 11-hour operation, in intensive care, with a cancer diagnosis and a mutilated abdomen. Instead of the promised "two tiny holes," I was left with a huge vertical scar. I was only able to walk normally after the surgery three weeks later. All that time, I endured pain and dreamed of escaping from the hospital room as soon as possible, never to return.

But my nightmare wasn't over yet. As soon as I had more or less recovered, I started going around Kyiv's oncology clinics to understand how to live with my diagnosis.

In a high-end medical center located in one of Kyiv's most affluent districts, known for being home to politicians, they charged me 300 dollars just for a consultation. For a practice in Ukraine, this is an exorbitant amount. For the first time in my life, I saw a bank branch located right inside the clinic. It's not surprising, as people were bringing in money in stacks.

My inner voice told me that staying here would jeopardize my life. y intuition told me to leave. *I won't get out of here alive*, I thought as I tried to find somewhere else to find answers.

Now I knew for sure that I couldn't ignore my feelings and my premonitions. My life was at stake; the situation was critical.

The clinic I had contacted was extorting money from people who were living out their last days. They gave hope to relatives, asking them for sums equal to the cost of an apartment. I realized that this wasn't my path, that they wouldn't save me, but would only suck all the money out of me, and along with it, my life.

It weighed heavily on me that the operation had been performed without my consent, that I hadn't been given any choice. **From now on, I was determined to act, making decisions independently and relying on my inner feelings.**

After contacting another clinic, I underwent tests. The doctors found something resembling metastases and said that a second operation was necessary. I literally ran away from the last scheduled analysis — in the face of danger, my senses were heightened to the limit. I knew that I needed to solve the problem in a different way, in a different place. In Ukraine, I was given several different diagnoses. I still didn't have a clear understanding of what was actually happening to me.

The fight continues

My cousin was living in Germany at the time. He and my close family convinced me to send my test results to a German clinic. Soon, the German doctors informed me that they didn't confirm the diagnosis of their Ukrainian colleagues and suggested I come for an examination. After undergoing further tests and sending the results to Germany, I received the German specialists' conclusion: another surgery was necessary.

Meanwhile, my business in Kyiv was facing trouble. While I was running around to doctors trying to save my life, my flower shop was facing demolition. The business center where it was located had decided to undergo reconstruction. Because of this, my shop needed to relocate urgently. My business was slowly crumbling simultaneously with my health.

To say the problem arose at an inopportune time is an understatement, but trouble never comes alone. It's always like this in life — either complete peace and quiet, or several avalanches descend at once. And each one buries you so deeply that it seems like you'll never get out.

Despite all these hardships, I appeared completely calm. Nothing revealed what was actually happening to me. I continued, as before, posting photos on social media, taking care of my appearance, meeting with friends, and smiling. Many didn't even suspect that a life-threatening diagnosis hid behind my smile. Only my relatives and closest friends knew about my illness. Everyone else remained in the dark.

In Germany, I was met by my cousin Maxim and his girlfriend, Christina. She handled my documents, wrote to clinics in German, and accompanied me to doctor's appointments. I am eternally grateful to Christina for saving my life — she became a true angel for me.

Michael flew to Germany and it was the first time he had left Canada since we started our relationship. This was a step outside of several comfort zones for him — he had been afraid of flying since childhood. Nevertheless, Michael made the effort and we all celebrated New Year's together in Nuremberg.

The clinic where I underwent my examination was located in the small university town of Erlangen, 20 miles from Nuremberg. A highly respected professor, a specialist of international renown, took care of me.

Choose the best. Entrust your body only to true professionals. Health is a resource that is very difficult to replenish. Always take care of your health – both mental and physical.

Once I began the examinations, I felt much calmer, although sometimes this calmness was seriously disrupted.

My mother came to Germany. For the first time in my life, I felt her overprotective nature. And these feelings proved to be extremely destructive. Having heard my diagnosis, my mother couldn't get it out of her head. Her panic, though understandable, was contagious and made it harder for me to stay calm. Being in the same room with her, I felt the air grow heavy and the atmosphere was tense. Instead of support and a positive attitude, the worst-case scenarios played out in her mind and all I received was a frayed nervous system.

For a successful recovery, we needed to distance ourselves from each other. I forbade my mother from talking about my illness and constantly repeated that everything was fine with me.

Thoughts are powerful, they shape your reality. Make plans and never lose heart. Even in situations where the future may not come, it's necessary to believe in it. Without faith and hope, nothing will work out.

I didn't like talking about my illness because I didn't need pity. From the very beginning, as soon as I heard my diagnosis, I refused to take on the role of a victim — to suffer and fall into despair. I wanted to continue living a normal life.

Yes, I had been diagnosed with cancer, but I wasn't going to give up and felt that this was definitely not the end. Instead of fretting over my diagnosis, I tried to distance myself from it. Even if I was destined to die, I would want to spend my last days or years with benefit and pleasure. Therefore, I entertained myself as much as possible — I loaded myself up with activities to the maximum. I went to the cinema, the theater, exhibitions, walked a lot, and enjoyed my stay in Germany. Every ray of sunshine, every dewdrop brought me joy and pleasure. All these distractions helped me stay in a good mood and not give up.

The victim mentality only leads to a person truly becoming a victim. It's a road to nowhere. Avoid falling into the trap of self-pity or allowing others to pity you.

Cultivate within yourself the confidence that the universe has a better plan for you. And even if it's hard and difficult now, this stage of pain is given as a lesson. But the outcome and how the lesson is learned depends solely on you. Will you look at everything from the perspective of a victim and wait for the world to pity you, or will you take responsibility for your life and emerge from the game victorious?

Your mindset is the deciding factor — it will either crown you as the victor or leave you defeated.

Attitude is key — it's important how you set yourself up.

Before waking up, you are in a state of light sleep, on the border between sleep and wakefulness. Are you familiar with this? During this time that your brain sort of boots up its operating system and starts recalling all the tasks that need to be done throughout the day. Something like this: you'll open your eyes, yawn, remember your routine, brush your teeth, drink coffee, etc. The brain also activates the 'problem' programs. And if your mood was spoiled last night, then it will be your decision whether to take it with you into the new day.

Every morning you have the chance to start with a clean slate, a new page, with your good mood. This is the key to everything.

Cancer is a serious diagnosis, but even with it, I continued my business life. In the fall of 2017, alongside examinations and preparations for a second surgery, I was engaged in real estate transactions. Firstly, I sold my mother's apartment in Dorohozhychi and bought two new ones — one completed, the other under construction. Secondly, I needed to resolve issues with Michael's property and lease out all the remaining units. Thirdly, my brother was looking for a house in Kyiv for our parents and we were choosing a suitable option together.

Life was swirling around me. There wasn't even time to catch my breath. This was intentional — I overwhelmed myself with tasks so that I wouldn't have a single second alone with my illness. I managed to shift my focus and even momentarily forget about all the horror I had to endure. My life sparkled with events, enthusiasm, and energy — numerous storylines intertwined into one big, vibrant story.

Try to distract yourself from the problem in every way possible. Make sure you don't have a single free second to think about anything bad. If you have the opportunity, socialize with friends, go for walks, continue living your life. Find joy in the little things. By focusing only on the negative, sooner or later you will slip into depression, and it will be very difficult to escape.

I traveled from place to place, went shopping, chose furniture, met with tenants, realtors, and potential buyers. I looked to the future and made ambitious plans — I was filled with confidence that everything would be alright.

Noticing negativity around is very easy; there's always a reason to complain, and this is the first sign of spiritual laziness and indulgence. Focusing on positive things, finding the good even in the most critical and seemingly terrible conditions — this is significant work on oneself. HAPPINESS IS WORK.

Let's do a test:

How advanced is your situation with your level of happiness? Have you ever met people in your life who are always happy, content with everything, and always find a reason to smile? How do you react to them:

- Do you judge them, thinking, "what a fool"?
- Or does your heart also become filled with joy?

If your reaction is judgmental, it might indicate deeper dissatisfaction with your own life. Recognizing this is the first step toward change.

In modern psychology, we often talk about 'high vibrations,' referring to the state of being where joy, gratitude, and positivity dominate your mindset. To transition to it, you need to change your way and structure of thinking — switch to a positive outcome of the situation. Play out the best-case scenario in your mind, but at the same time, relax and trust the Universe so that you have energy left to realize your plans.

For instance, when faced with uncertainty, I chose to focus on gratitude for small victories, like being able to take a walk in the sunshine. This shift in perspective helped me navigate difficult times with more clarity and hope.

Exercise: Happiness Jar

At the end of each day, I write down one happy moment that happened to me that day on a sticky note. I put the sticky note in my happiness jar. Even the worst day has some happy moments or at least something that was the least bad.

You can collect not sticky notes, but write down a chronicle of happy moments in a notebook.

This way, you'll accumulate a whole jar or book of happiness! You can look through your notes in difficult times. When you are especially sad and lonely. At the end of the year, when you want to summarize. On your birthday, when you want to remember the past year.

Then you will see that after every storm, the sun returns, and even the darkest day will surely have a glimmer of light.

One Avalanche After Another

The upcoming surgery was very expensive. To pay for it, I had to use some of the money from the sale of my mother's apartment. I had nothing left to furnish the two new apartments. Michael provided some additional funds for the treatment.

At the end of December, I went back to Germany. My second surgery was scheduled for the beginning of January.

The German doctors said that the spots that Ukrainian doctors had taken for metastases were a borderline tumor — a growth that could either remain dormant or turn aggressive at any moment, affecting all nearby organs. To understand how serious it was, surgery was necessary.

Before the surgery, Michael and I managed to travel around Europe. We drove to Italy and visited Austria and the Czech Republic. The trip to Prague was his birthday gift to me. He tried very hard to support me emotionally — he encouraged my enthusiasm and desire to live and made sure I didn't lose heart.

I didn't want to go under the knife again, didn't want to plunge back into the atmosphere of anxiety, feel physical pain, or even just be reminded of my diagnosis. Michael, my mother, and my loved ones literally begged me to have the second surgery. I resisted because I wanted to hear what my inner voice was saying, but I couldn't. I didn't understand if it was the right decision or not. In the end, after analyzing all the facts, I agreed and went to the clinic.

We returned to Germany, and the next day I was on the operating table. Finally, I understood that I needed help, and I was ready to accept it. All my life I had helped others, but here everything was the other way around. It was difficult for me to accept my new role. **But reality must be accepted as it is. Learn acceptance and humility. And, of course, allow people to help you when help is needed.**

I felt that I was in safe hands — there were highly qualified specialists working with me. I finally accepted my illness and the reality I found myself in. I realized that the surgery needed to be done very urgently and, regardless of what happened after, I needed to have it done.

My fears were unfounded — everything went quickly and ten times easier than in the Ukrainian clinic. Compared to the previous surgery, I remained almost untouched —

the German doctors did all the work through microscopic incisions.

When I came out of anesthesia, they told me that their Ukrainian colleagues had "forgotten" cotton bandages inside me. If it weren't for the second surgery, it's unknown whether I would have survived being stuffed with foreign objects. Ideally, I should have sued the Ukrainian doctors, but too much time had passed and all the deadlines had expired. But I'm sure that if I had stayed in Ukraine, I would have been treated to an early death.

The situation was very ambiguous. On the one hand, the second surgery was successful — the cancer was stopped. On the other hand, the doctors said that for safety reasons, all other organs within the same system should be removed. With cancer, it's always better to be proactive. This was the case with Angelina Jolie — she made the difficult decision to remove her breasts to prevent the development of cancer.

Since my illness ran in the family on the female side, the German doctors said that if I wanted to have children, I needed to give birth right now. Later, after the removal of all the organs, which might be necessary at any time, I wouldn't be able to carry a child. At 25, I could enter menopause[4].

The entire time I spent in the German hospital, Michael took care of me. He was very sensitive and attentive — his love and care reached unprecedented levels. He gave me flowers, put on my stockings, waited for hours for me to fall asleep and wake up, then walked with me in the park, fulfilling all my requests and whims.

After being discharged, we went to Munich to visit the BMW museum — Michael's favorite brand. The museum was mag-

---

4 Menopause is a stage in a woman's life cycle that marks the end of her reproductive period.

nificent; I took a lot of photos, and couldn't stop looking at the gleaming cars.

While taking another photo, I noticed through my phone screen that Michael's face had changed dramatically, as if he had been struck by lightning. Opening the news, I understood what was the matter. All the news headlines were filled with reports about what had happened to his father.

His family situation had spiraled out of control and it was all over the media. A decision had to be made urgently. Michael himself could be affected. Staying in Germany was unsafe. He booked tickets for the nearest flight to Canada and left.

I went to Kyiv to finalize all of my unresolved issues. After the surgeries, I needed constant medical supervision and regular checkups. Since Michael and I were still not married, I couldn't get the necessary care in Canada due to formalities. The question of our marriage became critical: either Michael takes immediate action, or I stay on the European continent. We couldn't delay any longer — my health and life were at stake.

In the spring, I flew to Canada again. In July 2018, Michael and I got married.

Walking Your Own Path

Life-threatening illnesses come when we least expect them. It always seems like they could happen to anyone, but definitely not to us. And when it does happen, it's very difficult to believe in such a reality, difficult to get used to it, and difficult to accept it.

I gave myself a clear directive: I was as healthy as I could be. What happened to me would forever remain in my past. I needed to go through the process of accepting myself and my diagnosis, work through that problem, and completely eliminate it. Yes, I had cancer, but I beat it, and I didn't want to keep the emotional residue of the illness inside me. I knew that my future was happiness, energy, love, and life, not hospital wards and eternal depression.

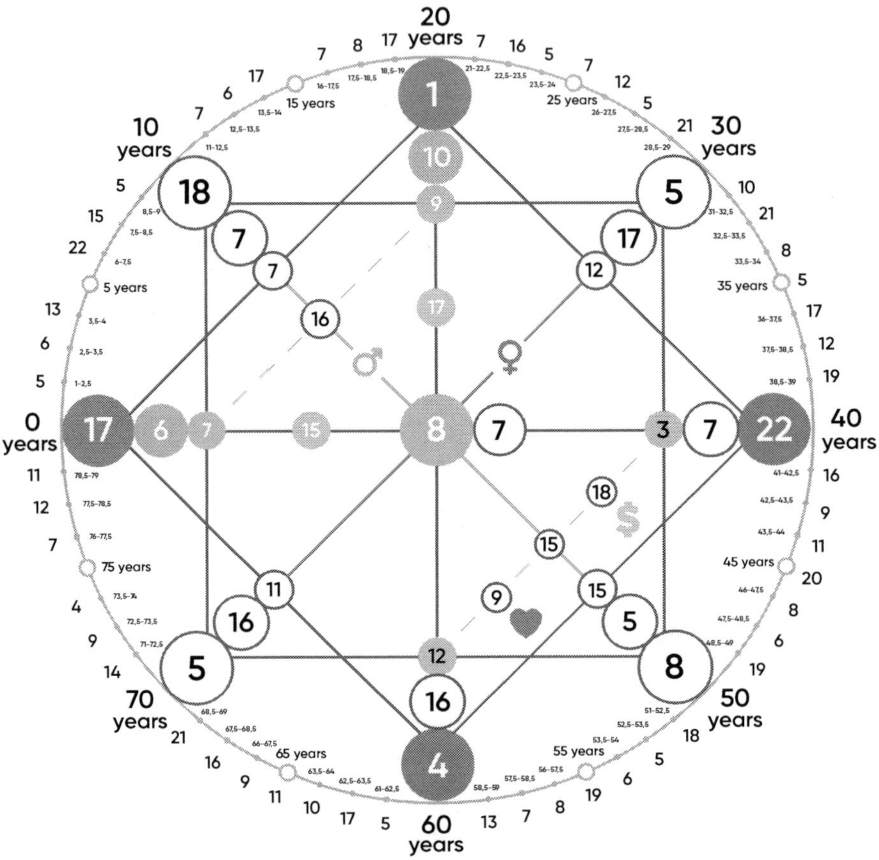

Fig. 3. My Matrix

Of course, the illness shocked me, but deep down I understood its origins. I had regular checkups and tests all my life and always received good results. My health was tragically affected by the last year I spent in social isolation. The cause of my cancer was due to suppressed actions and emotions. I constantly suppressed my feelings, and sooner or later they had to explode somewhere — like a balloon filled with liquid, stepped on by a heavy boot. It turned out that the unrealized resource took the form of a cancerous tumor.

Now I understand that my 17th energy, as reflected in the zone of manifestation in life within my Matrix of Personality, embodies public expression and interaction. It highlights the importance of sharing my gifts and insights with the world.

During the Canadian period of my life, when I broke off almost all social connections, I was deprived of this manifestation. In other words, I was simply robbed of the opportunity to fulfill my life's purpose. Instead of opening up and manifesting myself, I withdrew deep within myself, closed myself off from the outside world, and began to fade.

I'm a future wife, I have to sacrifice for my man since he's in a difficult situation, I thought, lying in bed in complete loneliness. And the result was my cancer diagnosis.

Having moved to Canada, I began to live a life that wasn't mine. I went down the wrong path and I sacrificed myself for imaginary happiness, social norms, and standards set by someone else.

I am ready to repeat this a thousand times: listening to your inner voice and prioritizing your needs is crucial to living authentically. You always need to choose yourself first. Don't strive to be like someone else, don't look for idols and live by other people's rules. Walk your own unique path. Listen to yourself and your soul. You are an individual, you are your own strength and wisdom.

Being yourself is one of the main values in life. And even if you have some flaws, you are still beautiful.

If you already know what your purpose is, fulfill it and don't deviate from it. Follow the call of your inner voice — it will never deceive you. Trust your intuition. One day, your purpose might involve nurturing children, while another, it could mean sharing your story on a stage to inspire others. Today you are a hairdresser by vocation, and tomorrow you are an artist. In both cases, there is a mission, a role.

Throughout life, there can be many such roles or just one. It all depends on the task of your soul. When others say that changing jobs so often is abnormal and that you need to settle down, most likely they simply haven't delved into your individual personality traits. So, my dear friend, I have good news for you. Perhaps the task of your soul is precisely to engage in project work, and not to drown in a boring routine. The most important thing in this case is TO UNDERSTAND YOURSELF.

Chapter 8: The Bridal Bouquet and the "Men in Black"

Michael and I spent my entire post-operative recovery period in Germany. At a follow-up appointment, the doctor suddenly said, "Well, it's time to address reproductive matters if you ever want to have children."

Of course, we knew we would have a child someday, but to have it presented as such an urgent necessity felt rushed.

"I'm giving you one year to try. If it doesn't work out, come back to us," the doctor said as he smiled, handing us a brochure featuring a photo of a happy mother holding a baby. I already knew that this clinic had a reproductive medicine department.

Only after returning to Canada did Michael and I finally talk about it. I tried to explain that with my health problems, if I got pregnant tomorrow, he risked being left alone with the child. Michael nodded and it seemed to me that he was prepared and understood the gravity of the situation.

Talking to your partner about your fears is very important. If you keep them to yourself, they won't disappear, and sooner or later they will play a role in what happens. You shouldn't silently agree with each other just because you can't talk. True partnership leaves no room for silent sacrifice.

I saw that Michael was scared about the financial side of things too, and I kept saying that we would figure it out together and deal with issues as they arose. It was what I was used to doing.

But this didn't help him cope with the wild fear that we couldn't handle a baby, especially in the way he would like — with nannies and other conveniences. He probably had a better idea of this than I did because he already had a child. A heavy burden of responsibility could fall on us, but I believed that if we shared it equally, we could manage.

My mother, friends, and all my loved ones unanimously insisted, "Everything will be fine, you have a wonderful man by your side. It's worth having a child with him." No one objected to my pregnancy, and this encouraged me. If only someone had told me then how difficult it would be... If only all those who supported me with words had also supported me with actions later...

Later, sitting alone in this boat, tossed back and forth by the storm, I often remembered those who said, "Everything will be fine!" In the end, they abandoned me, without even trying to throw me a life preserver. This is the perspective of a mother who has already gone through it all, realizing that you take all the responsibility upon yourself. In the end, you have a child for yourself alone, and you must be prepared to take full responsibility.

And if you want to have more than one child, you must realize how you will cope with them alone. Because at any moment, life circumstances can change, but the children will always be yours.

Words of encouragement, like 'everything will be fine,' fall flat without real actions to back them up.

In the periods between ovulations, I dealt with practical matters. I had to close the store and look for a new apartment; there was no room to turn around in ours. Finding something more spacious on our budget seemed like trying to light a fire in a downpour, but I didn't stop hoping.

Talk of the wedding resumed. I didn't know when and where it would be, but I didn't know whether we were getting married at all. At that point, it was the seventh time we had set a date. Once, Michael even paid for a mobile registrar, but we had a fight and everything was canceled. This time, we contacted the same person, but I didn't know the date until the last minute. A surprise wedding, Michael called it.

I immediately told Michael that I would only handle the bridal bouquet and wouldn't deal with anything else. He informed me that he had managed to book the same restaurant where we celebrated our anniversary. I liked this place, and most importantly, it seemed we had finally settled on a date! The wedding was to be held the next day!

In the morning, I loaded all the necessary things into the car, including my wedding dress. It had been waiting for its moment for two years — minimalist, form-fitting, with a neckline embroidered with delicate lace, it still shone with luxurious whiteness.

With everything packed, I rushed to my friend Katy, the florist. Michael had only managed to book an appointment for the morning, leaving me just an hour to get ready. Katy had given birth two weeks earlier and was home alone with her son, Leo. She probably didn't think that day was when I would show up on her doorstep with a request.

"Katy, I need a bouquet like this," I showed her a picture on my phone. "I'll go to the store next door now and if they have the flowers for it, I'll buy them, and we'll make it. And if not, we'll come up with something else. You get ready while I shop — you're my maid of honor."

I didn't find the flowers for my dream bouquet. All they had were dreary carnations and a lone orchid in a pot. We cut the flowers and hastily arranged them in a makeshift bouquet within five frantic minutes. We spent the remaining time trying to get dressed and do our hair while simultaneously getting sleepy Leo ready, who just frowned sternly and fidgeted with his tiny hands. I helped Katy fasten her dress in the car. And finally, the three of us drove to the restaurant where Michael was waiting.

Walking into the room, I felt the suffocating tension — a sharp, unspoken disapproval hung in the air, making it clear that this was no joyous occasion. I was five minutes late and felt disapproval directed at me, as if I couldn't even be on time for my own wedding. Some of the guests were dressed in black as though they had come not to a wedding, but to a funeral.

Throughout the ceremony, I was stressed; the same sticky feeling seemed to hang between the guests. There was enough tension in the room that I thought the windows would shatter or all the lights in the room would blow. I saw that Michael was also nervous and worried and very uncomfortable. This wedding was nothing like the one I had imagined two years ago. It felt like I was watching a play where the wrong actors had accidentally shown up to perform.

While the registrar recited all the required phrases, I glanced sideways at Michael. He remained aloof and didn't even look in my direction. He had been warned not to post any photos on social media or leave any other 'evidence' by his family.

We went to celebrate with a small circle of friends. Leo was with us and it was he who unexpectedly brought Michael out of his trance. My husband started fussing over him like he was made of glass, offered to take him for a walk in the stroller around the city, and constantly checked to see if Leo needed his nose wiped or his sweater adjusted.

"He'll be a super dad," Katy whispered to me, "If you have a girl, he'll be completely smitten."

It was strange for me even to just hold Leo. I hadn't had anyone to babysit before, just pushed my nephew's stroller a couple of times. Children seemed like little aliens to me; I saw them from afar and had no idea how to handle them.

"Masha, look, this is how you do it, learn," Michael laughingly showed me how to hold Leo correctly. And all I could do was hope that I would somehow manage with our own child.

Finding Myself

A week after the wedding, Michael's birthday arrived. I wanted to give him a symbolic painting. I even knew what I wanted: a lion and a lioness, two noble big cats with gold-tinged fur, gazing devotedly at each other with shining eyes. I needed this specific image and nothing else, but I couldn't find anything like it anywhere.

So, I went to a dollar store and bought some paints. Back home, I spread them out in front of me and stared intently. But what next? I had never painted a picture in my life; neither my hands nor my eyes knew where to begin. The idea came to me to call Artem, as I didn't know anyone more artistic at the time. Artem readily agreed to help. We found a suitable image online, and he explained how I could easily and quickly copy it by dividing the canvas into squares.

For the rest of the week, I painted the lions in secret, losing myself completely in the flow of inspiration as if diving into a bottomless ocean. The process was complicated by the 46°C heat and our kitten, Bunya, whom we had bought right after the wedding. Still tiny, she became very anxious if she lost sight of me. As soon as I went around the corner, Bunya would start meowing loudly. I had to constantly make sure she used her litter box. As a result, I painted most of the picture in the bathroom, sitting on the closed toilet seat while Bunya was engrossed in digging in her litter.

If you truly strive for a result and carefully observe how others do it, you can learn a lot along the way, even how to paint lions.

I was pleased with the result of my efforts and proudly presented the painting to Michael. At that time, everything was still good between us...

Immediately after we got married, I applied for a residence permit, and the two-and-a-half-year immigration process began.

We became friends with a woman named Lily and her husband. She was Armenian, and he was from St. Petersburg. They lived a floor above us, and Lily, being an immigration lawyer, took me under her wing. She said it would take four to twelve months, but no one could have known then that things would go so differently. I quickly received my medical documents and a work permit, hoping the rest of the process would go just as smoothly.

Gradually, I got used to my new role and the idea that Michael was no longer just my boyfriend, but my husband — the same brave lion from the painting, responsible for his family. At least, that's how it seemed to me. The 'getting married' goal had been achieved, and it was time to think about what else I wanted.

It turned out that I wanted personal development because being a housewife wasn't my story. I was too active for that, besides, I always wanted to be useful to people, even if I wasn't paid for it. So, I decided to grasp at any straw that could lead me into society.

After a year and a half in Canada, I started to grasp how things worked here and how to pull myself out of the initial confusion and disorientation. Generally, this period of time is enough to adapt to a new country, but your environment plays a crucial role in this process — it's like a liquid that determines the color of litmus paper.

If you're surrounded by a community of people who speak your language and make you feel at home, it's easy to stay in that bubble. But to truly adapt to a new country, you have to push yourself beyond it, stepping into discomfort and embracing the unfamiliar.

At that time, we had a second car, and I started driving more often. The car became my sanctuary on wheels — a personal space where I could escape, reflect, and spend time with my thoughts in peace. In moments of doubt and deep contemplation, it was the one place where no one could reach me. That's why the interior mattered to me so much more than the exterior. It needed to be light and open, creating mental space for reflection and creativity, rather than weighing me down.

After painting my first picture, I felt a spark — a new sense of purpose I hadn't experienced in a long time. This drove me to dive deeper into the world of art. I began visiting exhibitions, not just as a casual observer, but with an insatiable curiosity. I studied brushstrokes, color palettes, and the way artists brought life to their subjects. Animals became my ultimate inspiration; nature, with its flawless creations, felt like the perfect teacher. Each painting became an attempt to capture that beauty and the emotions it evoked within me.

One day, I came across an ad in a local Russian-language newspaper offering summer journalism courses for the community. The idea of meeting other Russian-speaking people and possibly building new connections intrigued me, so I signed up. The courses were simple but engaging, providing us with a solid foundation.

Soon, my first article, 'Let's Embark on a Real Intellectual Journey,' was published. It was a report on an IQ battle. Holding a printed copy of my work was exhilarating, but that feeling didn't last long. I began to notice how little value they placed on our efforts, treating us like free labor. Slowly, my enthusiasm faded, leaving me questioning whether this was the path I wanted to pursue.

My journey with painting had its ups and downs. While I managed to sell one of my first pieces for a respectable sum, the overall experience was disheartening. The market was oversaturated and I wasn't getting the feedback I wanted. After all, I put so much effort and time into my paintings, but I couldn't sell them. It's not a hobby you can hang everywhere at home either, so my work went into storage, which, from my perspective, felt like a disrespect to my time and creativity. It was demotivating.

Even with the greatest enthusiasm, it's impossible to carry a business if no one believes in it and they don't give you feedback.

I had the idea to open a coworking space. Back then, this concept was just starting to gain traction in Montreal, with the first WeWork locations making waves. I enjoyed driving around the city, scouting potential locations, imagining what could be done with each space. But when we sat down to calculate the budget, the final number frightened Michael. There was so much work ahead, along with immense responsibility, and he wasn't convinced it was worth the risk.

We considered taking out a bank loan, but when we shared the idea with Michael's relatives, their reaction crushed my motivation entirely.

“It’s not profitable. Where’s the income here?” they asked dismissively. I tried to present a well-thought-out business plan, but they didn’t take me seriously.

Women in Michael’s family weren’t viewed as serious professionals, regardless of their education or potential. Despite their degrees from prestigious universities, including some overseas, they were all confined to housework. My own entrepreneurial experience wasn’t acknowledged either; it didn’t bring in millions, so to them, it wasn’t a ‘real’ business.

Soon we went back to Germany again. The doctor examined me, confirmed that everything was fine, and advised me to focus on pregnancy. Since a year of trying had been unsuccessful, we decided to consult fertility specialists.

In the car in the clinic parking lot, I tried again to have a serious conversation.

"Listen, we’re taking a serious step now. You have to understand that."

Michael replied, "You’re my wife, and you have these health issues. How could I not understand otherwise?"

His words didn’t give me confidence. They sounded as if Michael had just been crucified with no choice, no chance to say "no." To be fair, I wasn’t given a choice either. I was presented with a fait accompli, something already decided before I had the chance to choose and I could only accept it as my reality.

The fertility specialist, having reviewed my medical records and learned that we had been trying for a year, frowned.

"It’s already been a long period without results; we’ll take action." What followed were four sperm analyses, a million tests, endless doctor’s appointments, and hormone injections in my stomach. Michael had learned to give them after my surgery. He was fully involved in the process and I felt that I had a partner and his support, which meant that everything would really be alright.

The test that divided life into "before" and "after"

Almost ten months had passed, and I had started gaining weight from the hormones, fluid was building up in my body. Yet, according to the doctors, there was no alternative.

Now that Michael and I were married, we qualified for a government-funded program in Canada that covered intrauterine insemination (IUI). The programs provide vital access to fertility treatments for families, significantly reducing the financial burden often associated with such procedures. After three unsuccessful attempts, I reached my limit.

"No more hormones," I declared firmly, "Come what may."

If I wasn't destined to get pregnant, then so be it — I wasn't willing to sacrifice my health any further by subjecting myself to such strong medications.

In July, during another routine ultrasound, the doctor delivered disheartening news: this cycle was unlikely to succeed because the egg hadn't fully matured. I had anticipated as much, having stopped taking hormones by then. Despite this, the insemination was carried out, but I felt no hope. It seemed like a formality at best and I stopped dwelling on the outcome.

Instead, I decided to refocus my energy. I started going to the gym regularly, throwing myself into exercise with determination. Letting go of cautiousness and self-pity, I found a new rhythm. Whether or not pregnancy was on the cards for me, I wanted to regain control over my life, my body, and my perspective.

Some time later, right before Michael's birthday, my friends from New York came to visit. We took them sightseeing, even though I had started a new cycle. In the humid 40-degree heat, we heroically climbed Mount Royal, located in the heart of the city that bears its name. I was drenched in sweat, but the view of Montreal was worth it. A green sea of a dense park stretched out before us, behind it, skyscrapers glittered with glass, and further on, a wide river shimmered in the sun, spanned by bridges. Distant mountains appeared as a ghostly blue on the horizon.

We crisscrossed almost the entire city until evening and finally settled down in a small restaurant. For some reason, I desperately wanted a cocktail, even though I didn't drink much. I chose a Kir Royale, but when the glass arrived, one glance was all it took to understand that I wouldn't be able to take a single sip. In the end, I didn't touch the drink.

Arriving home and catching a glimpse of myself in the mirror, I sighed sadly. I was so puffy! My nose was swollen, my eyelids were heavy, and my legs! My legs were so swollen and I wasn't even injecting hormones anymore. How much longer would the changes to my body continue? On the other hand, how else could one look after an endless walk in such heat?

On Michael's birthday, before going to the restaurant, I had a strange feeling. I asked him to stop at a pharmacy on the way for a pregnancy test.

At the restaurant, everything was normal; everyone ate in strained silence. I was used to it by now and didn't worry about it anymore. Michael, however, had other things on his mind because his best friend's wife had recently been taken to the hospital and was about to give birth. He sat beside me, on edge, constantly glancing at his phone.

"Shall we step outside?" I suggested in a whisper. We went to separate restrooms. I took out the test, still thinking it was all nonsense, while Michael, behind the next door, called his friend.

"Well?" he asked when we met in the hallway. I didn't know what to say — the test showed one clear line and another so faint that it could hardly be considered a line at all.

"Your praised test turned out to be defective," I texted my friend Katy and sent her a photo.

"I don't know, I see two lines," she replied.

I didn't know either, and I couldn't find out until Monday. It was Friday, and I wouldn't be able to get any lab tests done.

If I found out I was pregnant today, it would be wonderful to announce it on my husband's birthday, I thought. We returned home, but I couldn't relax. Waiting until Monday seemed impossible, so I sent Michael to the pharmacy for a more expensive test to take, otherwise I wouldn't have been able to sleep at all that weekend.

I remember that moment perfectly. I was standing in the kitchen of our studio apartment with the test in my hands, unable to comprehend how this was even possible. Michael was sitting on the couch, wrapping some box with tape. Finally, I pulled myself together and showed him the positive result.

Michael muttered, "I knew it," barely glancing at the test before resuming his task with the box.

That was it?!

It seemed like a second ago, the man sitting in front of me was someone I shared a life with, and everything was good between us. Now, I saw someone completely different, someone who was utterly alien and unfamiliar. Michael's face remained stony and indifferent; he was lost in his own thoughts.

A pregnancy test reveals not only what it's supposed to, but also how a couple truly feels about each other.

That moment marked the beginning of an unraveling I could never have anticipated.

Chapter 9: New Family Secrets

From the moment I saw those two life-changing lines on the pregnancy test, my world split into a 'before' and an 'after.'

Michael became cold, completely withdrawn, and retreated into his shell. I tried to draw him out, suggesting we go look at baby strollers, brainstorm baby names, or simply take a walk together. But the walls of his shell grew thicker and stronger with each passing day — it was simply impossible to break through to him.

If he did agree to a walk, I would again try to initiate a conversation about my pregnancy and our future child, but he'd ask, "Please, can we talk about something else? I don't want to discuss this right now; there's plenty of time."

But when, if not now? Apparently, to avoid these uncomfortable conversations, Michael started leaving the house to wander alone in the park.

There were other strange things happening. My husband began to frighten me. He would suddenly jump out from around a corner with a childish yell of "Boo!" which would make my knees buckle and I'd have to grab onto the furniture to avoid falling from the shock. Michael had never done this before and I hoped he wasn't doing it deliberately to cause me to lose the baby.

No, that couldn't be true.

We hadn't told anyone else about my pregnancy; my husband insisted on hiding it from his family, fearing his mother's reaction.

If we had to appear together with family, he would hiss in my ear, "Your belly is showing. Can't you suck it in?" Of course it was showing, and I couldn't — I was three months along.

Despite Michael's best efforts, our relatives began to suspect something. It was because of my changed food preferences; they were always asking why I wasn't eating this or why I wouldn't try that. Michael was asked at least three times if I was pregnant, but he categorically denied it every time. It was a two-person play that I really didn't want to participate in, but I had to.

Honestly, I didn't understand the point of all the secrecy — we couldn't hide my pregnancy forever. Or were we going to hide the baby too, once it was born? When I asked these logical questions, my husband would reply that his mother couldn't find out, or she would disown him. At the time, it seemed like utter nonsense, but now I understand. Michael's first child had been unplanned, and he'd faced repercussions for it. So, telling his mother about my pregnancy meant reliving that stress, especially since Michael's mother still didn't even know we were married. He kept saying she had enough problems of her own and didn't need this on top of everything else.

Was our marriage a problem?

About six months after our wedding, we spent a week together at a chalet in the mountains. I kept asking my husband to tell his mother everything, and he promised he would, but he never found the right time. Because of this, throughout the trip, I didn't feel like a member of the family; I was just a random girl he'd brought along on vacation. A decorative object with absolutely no rights. When Michael's mother left, he supposedly told her everything at the airport, but I doubt that was true.

At five weeks pregnant, I made a long-awaited trip to Kyiv — a place where I hoped to find the support and care I so desperately needed. I'd had the tickets for a long time and I didn't cancel the trip. There, I finally received the reaction I had been desperately waiting for from my husband. When my mother heard she was going to be a grandmother, her spoon clattered to the floor as she threw her arms around me, tears of joy welling in her eyes.

"You're kidding! What wonderful news!" she exclaimed and rushed to hug me so tightly I almost suffocated.

As soon as I arrived, I immediately scheduled my first ultrasound. In Canada, pregnant women don't receive any checkups or monitoring until 12 weeks. If something goes wrong, they don't try to save the pregnancy, considering it natural selection. I was lucky to be in Ukraine.

After the ultrasound, I decided to go to the premiere of The Lion King, where I sobbed from beginning to end. Even though I knew the story from childhood, it's impossible not to empathize with Simba and his father. Leaving the cinema, I felt something was wrong; a strange heaviness in my lower abdomen made me hurry. An ambulance picked me up from the cinema and I was hospitalized for observation.

Michael sent huge bouquets of roses to my hospital room. For the first time in those three months, I felt the same attention he used to give me back when he was trying to woo me. I so wanted to believe that he now understood everything and that our relationship would return to normal — that he would once again envelop me with his leonine love and affection. I tried not to think about it too much, focusing as much as possible on my health.

Besides my mother, I hadn't told anyone else about the pregnancy yet, not even my friend, whom I went to the beach with shortly after being discharged from the hospital. I didn't swim, of course, just watched the sun glinting on the waters of the Dnieper from under a beach umbrella.

"Masha, your breasts look like you've nursed three children," my friend remarked suspiciously, scrutinizing me.

"Well, I'm home with my parents, eating well, as one should," I joked.

I returned to Montreal with a sliver of hope that Michael would behave differently now that I had almost lost our child. But at home (if you could call it that), everything was the same.

There are men who aren't ready to fully accept responsibility for a family. They court beautifully, and the honeymoon period is simply amazing. But when they get married, they remain in a state of maximum inner freedom. Such men need to be tested with actions and asked direct questions – you shouldn't be shy about having a dialogue so that there are no unpleasant surprises later on for anyone. Everyone can have their own beautiful story inside.

Michael Leaves

After some time, my husband informed me that his situation in Ukraine was resolving and the possibility of returning had emerged. Honestly, this possibility had always existed for him — risks remained, but they weren't direct or obvious.

Suddenly, he decided, as if the prospect of returning frightened him less than living with me and our child under the same roof. Apparently, the situation was pressing down on him so much that he was ready to flee anywhere, under any conditions. It seems that at that moment, even prison would have seemed a more comfortable option than the company of me and the baby.

"Please understand, I need to think about how to provide for you both, because you and I don't have enough money to properly support a child," Michael tried to convince me, "I'll go, get back on my feet in Kyiv, set up our life, do everything so that you and the baby feel comfortable. And then you'll come."

He reminded me that he had a mother and three sisters there and there was no one to take care of them.

He spoke so honestly, so sincerely, that I believed him — what else could I do? Sometimes I tried to object, asking how he could leave me here alone, pregnant, but Michael quickly came up with a solution: I was to go and visit America to see Veronica, with whom I had once started a flower business.

"And please, still don't tell my relatives anything," he added.

While Michael was preparing for his trip to Kyiv, I became completely convinced that our relationship would never be the same. I wondered if he understood this? And did he understand that Kyiv was no longer the same city he had left at 18? Back then, Michael lived in an atmosphere of permissiveness and accessibility, but now he was returning in a completely different position, without the opportunities he once had. Life from scratch — a blank, untouched canvas.

Stressed by the whole situation, I managed to get sick, and Michael took me to the doctor. I irritated him.

"Don't sniffle, please! Can you not cough?" he grumbled endlessly.

Maybe I shouldn't breathe either? There was no longer any care in his accompanying me, only necessity, obligation.

On our last evening before Michael's departure, I decided to say aloud, "I want to remember our relationship as it is now, because it will never be like this again."

He brushed me off — "What are you making up? Don't start!"

He bent down to gently say goodbye... to the cat. He stroked her, saying something tender and funny. He didn't say another word to me, grabbed his suitcase handle, and went downstairs where his relatives were already waiting in the car to take him to the airport.

With my already very noticeable belly, I was forbidden to be seen by his family. I couldn't even see my husband off at the airport — the husband I was parting with for an unknown amount of time. We said goodbye at the entrance to the building.

The door slammed shut, and I pressed the elevator button, which opened invitingly. With a quiet hum, I went upstairs, to the empty, silent apartment, now completely alien without my husband.

At that moment, I felt as if an unstoppable avalanche of chaos was barreling toward me, crushing every sense of stability and hope in its path at tremendous speed. This turned out to be scarier and more difficult than surviving cancer. Back then, it was only about my life, but now I was responsible for another.

I stood at the threshold of the apartment and thought that this is my reality — a lump in my throat, an echo in the room, and a cat joyfully rubbing against my legs. And no one else.

The world became heavy, the air dry and bitter. verything darkened and faded at once, and reality squeezed my temples and buckled my weakened legs. I was completely exhausted, mentally drained. I sat down on the sofa and felt how wet my eyes had become. A nervous spasm twisted my organs in my chest. I realized that I was completely alone.

Me, the Baby, and the Cat

Michael had been gone for three days.

I was completely alone, as if locked within the four walls of the apartment for an indefinite period. Somewhere on another continent, my husband was socializing with friends and finding only 10 minutes a day to talk to me on the phone. Could that even be called a conversation? A dry, formal report of the day's events, while I had nothing to say in return because absolutely nothing was happening in my life. This wasn't how I wanted to live and it wasn't how I imagined my relationship with Michael to be or my pregnancy to progress.

"He who loves must share the fate of the one he loves." – *Bulgakov, The Master and Margarita.*

There was absolutely no one to talk to about how I felt. I didn't want to upset my mother and my friends couldn't help. I didn't know what to do next or why I needed all of this. There was no way out, only to wait until everything somehow resolved itself or until the situation escalated to the point where it would force its own resolution.

The trip to America comforted me a little. Finally, I could distract myself, see something interesting, and experience new pleasant emotions, leaving all my problems in the cramped Montreal apartment and forgetting them for a couple of days.

Unfortunately, the problems were so all-encompassing that I couldn't hide from them, even in another country. Veronica and I walked around, admired the sights, and at night I cried because Michael had now deprived me of even those 10 minutes a day and might not call at all.

Not receiving a message from someone is also a message. If a man doesn't call, it means he doesn't want to talk to you.

He did take enough time to share with me that he was spending a lot of time with his best friend. Michael even bought gifts for his friend's children; this is the man who didn't want to choose a stroller for his own child with me! When he didn't call, I mentally went through the options of where he might be: sitting in a sauna with friends, playing with other people's children, or something worse.

When Veronica and I walked around the city, I asked her to take pictures of me in a way that my belly wouldn't be visible, which is why I have so few beautiful photos showing my pregnancy.

"Masha, did you get lip fillers? Did you get a boob job?" people wrote in the comments, while I kept swelling and swelling.

Veronica traveled back to Canada with me and helped me a lot. We even chose a stroller together. Michael left me money, but I still didn't feel secure. My composure saved me, allowing me to experience everything that was happening to me without falling into hysterics. I had to keep all my feelings in a fist, which, although swollen and bruised, continued to grip its contents tight.

At that time, I started talking to my baby. Michael continued to spend time with friends, doing business, and not understanding how unfairly he was treating me. And he entrusted his friend to accompany me to doctor's appointments.

People around us gradually began to understand what was happening and were shocked. Especially those who had seen our relationship from the very beginning.

Sometimes I was even asked, "What's wrong with you? Why is Michael behaving like this? It's not like him at all." I didn't know the answer.

During those times, it's important to create a positive environment that prevents stagnation. The music you listen to, the movies you watch, everything you immerse yourself in is very important.

There's a high probability of not getting distracted, but instead driving yourself even deeper into depression and completely falling apart. This is the recipe I recommend to my clients, and this is what helped me stay afloat in a difficult situation. Instead of sad songs and tearful melodramas hugging a pillow, you need something motivating. Something that will benefit you, not just distract you for a couple of hours.

The neural connections that are formed during those periods of life are very important. You can either believe that you are stronger than all of this or continue to feel sorry for yourself, getting even more deeply stuck in the trap. There's no need to beat yourself up over anything — no one will pay you for it.

Back then, I was often reminded of my brother, who had long and meticulously prepared for competitions, but didn't make the team. Athletes know how to pull themselves out of such situations, to fall and rise.

Never give up. If you don't help yourself, no one will.

If you rely only on yourself, you'll stop being disappointed in people, and your mood will be much better. When you're feeling bad, imagine that you're drowning. Drowning people don't wait to be rescued, they try to swim out themselves. Don't wait for help, support, or rescue. Save yourself.

I felt like packing up and leaving with the cat to a remote, quiet village. It would be my own little escape from reality: me, my baby, and Bunya. Sometimes, a sense of humor is the only thing that helps you stay afloat. Like a boat that rocks you gently, and with every jolt and splash of water in your face, you feel a little bit more cheerful.

Endless analysis of the situation led me to the thought that Michael hadn't just snapped and left. Most likely, the same thing had happened with his first girlfriend's pregnancy. Maybe he had someone else that he was seeing on the side and decided to run to her.

I wanted to throw a tantrum, but the rational part of me prevailed. If we quarreled to the point of stopping communication, Michael would completely stop helping me. Who would I be hurting in that case? Of course, I told him that I didn't like all of this. I even cried on the phone, but I never brought the situation to a breaking point where he threatened to leave for good.

That would have meant making his life easier. Then Michael could tell everyone, "Masha stopped communicating with me because I went away to earn money for us. She's the one to blame."

I wanted to make him see what he had done. I wanted life's boomerang to hit him!

I knew the consequences in advance; when the child grew up, I wouldn't hide all the details from him. He would definitely learn how his father behaved with us. By that time, I would be doing well, I would be able to provide for both of us. A wonderful man would appear, whom my child would accept as a father. And Michael would have to regain the trust he had lost.

Such long-term thoughts motivated me. I thought it was foolish to forbid a biological father from seeing his child. I'd let my son choose for himself, having analyzed the past. And when the choice is not in favor of the biological father, it wouldn't be me punishing him, but life itself.

Anticipating how events would unfold, I repeatedly told Michael, "You're behaving badly. You'll regret this greatly later."

I tried not to succumb to emotions but to focus on myself because I wanted the baby inside me to be healthy. Nothing is more important than the physical and mental state of the expectant mother — she carries life within her, and it largely depends on her whether this life will be healthy and happy or not.

The Baby Shower

Veronica organized a baby shower for me where my close friends and I were to discover the baby's gender. It was all so lovely! A small group of friends gathered at a cafe. The table was decorated with balloons and a specially baked cake, and the girls brought gifts. I felt like a pink cloud, surrounded by light, floating and twirling. My friends rejoiced for me, hugged me, and we laughed together. It was exactly what I had been missing for so long.

When I saw the bouquet, a sad arrangement of nine half-wilted roses wrapped in cheap cellophane, I couldn't hold back the tears. It felt like a metaphor for the relationship Michael and I had: once vibrant and full of promise, now fading and brittle.

"This is a funeral bouquet for our relationship," I wrote to Michael, "This is the worst moment of my life."

He apologized, replied that no other flowers were available, and that he had already ordered a beautiful bouquet for tomorrow.

"Save it for your next girlfriend. Maybe next time this moment will be happier for you. It's over between us."

I truly felt that it was the end. Tears streamed down my face and I couldn't stop — everything I had been trying to suppress came pouring out. So much negative energy had accumulated that it overflowed. I mentally urged myself to stop crying; I wanted to take beautiful photos to remember this day, to have something fond to look back on.

I only managed to distract myself with the cake, which needed to be cut to reveal the color inside... and there it was, a piece of blue cake on my plate! I was genuinely surprised — after all, for the past few months, I had been talking to the baby as if it were a girl.

The next day, I decided to tell Michael's relatives about the baby. Michael, of course, wanted me to stop communicating with them altogether, but how did he imagine that was possible? I had given them a cat and regularly visited to trim its claws. We interacted, drank tea together, it was impossible to just cut ties suddenly.

What kind of person would I appear to be in their eyes? Someone who turned up their nose at them the moment their husband stepped out the door?

Honestly, it was difficult to reveal the truth to the people who had previously been extremely critical of our relationship. I knew they wouldn't accept it, and I felt like I was walking to my doom. They had no idea about anything; not about the doctor's words in Germany, nor about how long Michael and I had been planning for a pregnancy. The difficult path I had traveled remained hidden from them.

The first thing they said in response was, "You can't put it back now. Good luck then. You and Michael probably made this decision together and he'll be back soon."

But I didn't know when he would return, or where he was, or with whom, or why I was going through all of this. Then I told them how we had been trying to conceive for a whole year.

"So, Michael was even paying for everything?" they asked in astonishment. But even hearing that was much easier than hiding the obvious.

Then my mother, who knew about my situation with Michael, came to Canada for the first time. I felt some relief — my mother, Veronica, and my friends were with me and they supported me. I still understood that they couldn't help me simply by being present, and sooner or later, they would leave. The baby was constantly kicking, and I kept telling myself that I needed to hold on until the birth so the baby would have Canadian citizenship. Then I could leave this lonely, gloomy world behind and try to forget everything.

My mother would sometimes ask, "So, has Michael called you?"

And sometimes I couldn't even remember the last time we had spoken. I had already gotten used to not focusing on it, but my mother's questions forced me to think about everything again. Every time we discussed the situation, I only became more and more agitated. Michael's actions didn't align with his words about us being a family. I understood that this page in my life had been folded in half, and the crease in the paper was impossible to smooth out — it was permanent.

I had made such significant life changes for my husband and he stabbed me in the back – it was a true betrayal.

Time to Make a Decision

I was shopping when I realized I had almost no money left.

What's more, it wouldn't be long before I wouldn't be able to travel anywhere. If I wanted to make one last attempt to save my marriage, it was time to make a decision. I needed to go to Kyiv; otherwise, I would blame myself for the rest of my life for not taking a risky but necessary step to try and get things back to how they were. I needed either proof that everything was over between Michael and I, or proof that it wasn't.

With my remaining savings, I bought plane tickets for myself, my mother, and Bunya, my cat, as I had no one to leave her with. I told Michael about it at the last minute, right before the flight.

The flight had a layover in Germany and arrived in Kyiv early in the morning. With a cat and a very pregnant belly, I figured such a passenger wasn't a common sight. My fellow travelers were probably reminded of a scene from a comedy film, although in reality, it was a drama. I hoped until the very last moment that Michael would meet us at the airport, but not even his driver was there; instead, a taxi driver waited with a sign.

My husband showed up in the evening when we were already relaxing at home.

"Are you out of your mind?" he whispered, pulling me into a room so no one could hear, "Why did you come? It's dangerous here, dangerous for the baby!"

He was, of course, exaggerating the situation, and I was hurt that he didn't appreciate my feat: I crossed the ocean, pregnant, with a cat, to be near him. And in the end, I was showered with reproaches.

We didn't break up, but we didn't see each other very often. When we did arrange to meet somewhere, Michael chose places where none of our acquaintances would see us. We hid in suburban cafes and he refused to take pictures with me. He also said that he didn't have the means to send me back to Canada and that his mother shouldn't find out about anything.

He drove me to hysterics, making me feel guilty for everything, because I had spent the last of the money he had left me for the baby on tickets to Kyiv. Every time we met, I sobbed.

Veronica, who was also in Kyiv at the time, unexpectedly added fuel to the fire. We were eating sushi at a restaurant: Me, Veronica, Michael, and his driver.

"Michael, what are your plans for New Year's?" my friend asked unexpectedly cheerfully.

"I'll be home, with my mother and sisters," he said, shrugging.

Veronica's eyebrows shot up in surprise and I was also shocked, more by her question than his answer. "Maybe you'll come to us?" Veronica continued. "There's going to be a trendy party, I'm sure you know a lot of people there. It'll be fun."

I couldn't stand it anymore and asked, "Veronica, don't you want to invite me? I'm sitting right here, too."

Her eyes widened as she replied, "There's going to be loud music until morning. And you're pregnant."

Later, I found out that even before this, Veronica had been flirting with Michael and constantly provoking him, despite the fact that she was also married at the time. Despite the fact that she came to visit me, supported me and knew the whole situation from the inside. She had been a friend, and the betrayal from a person I didn't expect made my world slowly turn upside down inside me. I began to realize the bitter truth that even the closest people can betray you.

Another ultrasound helped me distract myself from the situation. They made a mold of the baby and I saw him for the first time. My close friends gave me a photoshoot and those are the only pictures where my pregnancy is beautifully captured.

Michael didn't come to the photoshoot, although I really wanted him to.

"Maybe. I don't know. I'll try," he replied, but he never showed up.

I celebrated New Year's with my parents. My husband had completely broken away from me and there was no point in trying to glue that piece back on. Although I still tried.

I wanted to start the new year renewed, so I stopped being a blonde and dyed my hair light brown.

"The color is kind of like a herring," Michael smirked when we met.

I tried not to react to this stupid joke and changed the subject to pregnancy classes. I really wanted Michael to go there with me — I didn't know how else to include him in the process.

He did join me a couple of times, but he sat with such an expression that it would have been better if he hadn't come at all. Everything annoyed him: uncomfortable, not cozy, having to sit for a long time, he didn't like the smells... Not all the girls were with their husbands, but the few men who attended the classes behaved completely differently. This once again confirmed that Michael and I had become strangers.

Due to stress, I developed gestational diabetes and had to inject insulin. It was clear that all that was left was to leave — there was no chance of reconciling with Michael, and I didn't want to anymore. I had a return ticket, but I had no money left to live on.

"There's no money for your support in Canada, nor for the birth," Michael said. "I can only offer a state maternity hospital in Kyiv." This sounded terrifying to me because the conditions there were very spartan.

Realizing that our relationship was coming to an end, I consulted with a lawyer who specialized in divorce proceedings. He was a former investigator from Donetsk. During the conversation, I found out that he conducted research on the political situation in our country and knew many intricacies: how the hierarchy of the top echelons of power is formed, how the political system works from the inside, what shadow flows exist within it.

And then I said my husband's first and last name.

The lawyer frowned, gave me a long look, and said, "You're as deep as you possibly could be in our country."

I didn't understand what he meant. Of course, I had read a lot of nasty things about Michael's family online, but he always gently took my hands, looked into my eyes, and explained that it was all untrue, the machinations of competitors, and that I should divide any information I found by 20.

Now I became very scared, but for some reason, the lawyer inspired confidence in me, and I asked him to explain what he meant. Everything I heard didn't sound like online gossip. Clear facts with detailed specifics, reliably hidden from society and accessible only to those immersed in the inner workings. A black box opened after a crash.

Being eight months pregnant, I listened and broke out in a cold sweat, and everything swam and blurred into colored spots before my eyes. It turned out that I had no idea who I had gotten involved with and whom I had married. Joining the Italian mafia would have been safer. When the lawyer finished, clutching my stomach, I briefly thanked him and rushed out of the office, forgetting that I had come there to talk about divorce. But whether it was possible to get out of all this now — I didn't know...

After celebrating my birthday with the girls and borrowing money from my dad for three months' rent, I returned to Montreal. My friends met me at the airport, in a wheelchair, with a huge belly and a cat in my arms. Complete uncertainty lay ahead.

Me Then and Me Now

When all of this was happening, I was a person who knew neither herself nor her potential. I believed that I could be taken advantage of, that I had enough energy, enough resources, and that I could endure it all. I allowed myself to be treated this way and was sure that I wouldn't break.

Now, I've drawn firm boundaries, unshakable and clear. I refuse to let anyone diminish me again. I am no longer the naive girl who believed love meant self-sacrifice. I stand tall, knowing my worth and protecting my peace. My family can't be kept in the dark about my pregnancy. I can't be hidden away and asked to not be included in shared photos on social media. Disappearing, not writing to me, escaping to another country — these things are no longer acceptable. Now I have established certain boundaries regarding what I will not tolerate in relation to myself.

I am a strong person, and I do what I think is necessary, first and foremost for myself, then for my child, and only then for someone else. Now I build my hierarchy differently; I don't try to please everyone. People may call me whatever they want, but no one can say it to my face. I am no longer convenient. I am no longer a malleable figurine that easily takes any suitable shape from the slightest pressure — I have my own solid inner core.

If only I had met someone like the person I am now back then! If only someone had explained to me how I should and shouldn't be treated. If only I had listened to my intuition, which loudly warned me when Michael first proposed. Back then, the phrase

"He's good for me as a first husband" popped into my head out of nowhere.

It means that even then, I couldn't imagine us growing old together. He felt it too, because when he dreamed aloud about a car or a house, he always said "mine," not "ours." Michael never dreamed of our family, our house, or how he would raise our child. He presented one image, but inside, there was always a different person living, a different personality that I apparently didn't want to notice. Back then, my attention could be bought with gifts. Now, a person's attitude towards me and my son is paramount.

But I don't shift the responsibility for everything I had to go through onto anyone else — not even Michael. What happened was a consequence of my decisions. I am to blame because I allowed myself to be treated that way and trusted when I shouldn't have.

To avoid this, you need to start by understanding yourself and your potential: your inner qualities, strengths and weaknesses, and personal boundaries. This should be taught in school, instilled from early childhood!

Now, I understand my path, I understand myself, I have tested my reality, and I clearly know where my boundaries are — what I can handle, and what can be delegated. And how grateful I am that I came to this realization at 30, not 60.

In consultations, I often see clients with suppressed potential. People who should be public figures but work in regular jobs and don't even look in another direction. Talented women who have dedicated their entire lives to their homes and are burdened by alcoholic husbands — their lives are passing them by; they don't hear themselves or their desires. For example, I recently met a woman who was on maternity leave, tied to her child, fulfilling all her husband's whims, and not developing herself. She was in a terrible state — depressed — but her matrix showed such powerful potential — as if a thoroughbred, strong steed was locked in a stable.

Many people can't create a vision board, and I understand them perfectly because, as a lost girl, it seemed impossible to me at first too. I pasted everything on the board, just to add something, not understanding if my soul truly desired it.

Now, I have a crystal-clear vision of my path, firm boundaries, and an unshakable belief in my ability to face any challenge life throws at me.

"What a beautiful story you have, simply perfect!" People sometimes tell me. No, my story is not beautiful and not perfect. Few people can imagine how scary it was for me to share it and unpack my personality. I had to force myself each time, publishing new details.

Writing about this pain and letting others read it is stepping outside my comfort zone — a painful birth of a new me, but I know that it will benefit people. Only because of this, I overcame myself, remembered everything again, and wrote it down. **Only so that the person reading this knows that they are not alone.**

I'm often asked how I manage to do everything, and where I get the ideas and energy to implement them, especially considering that I have a small child and so many responsibilities.

The answer is simple: the 'Think — Do' method helps me effectively manage my affairs, and find inspiration and energy to achieve my goals, despite being busy and having responsibilities.

That is, as soon as a thought or impulse arises to do something specific, it's important to act immediately. This helps build a connection between thoughts and actions, and also allows you to use the present moment to achieve success. After all, every immediate reaction to our thoughts and desires brings us closer to our goals and helps us become successful in what we desire.

Wealth Colors: Purple, Violet, Green Money, real estate, cars, any material desires	**Self-Realization and Fame** Colors: Red Fame, recognition	**Love, marriage** Colors: Pink, Red, Earth tones Love, relationships, marriage
Family Colors: Green, Brown, Blue Family, pets	**I** Colors: Yellow, Orange, White Your photo, your health and well-being	**Children, creativity** Colors: White, Gray, Silver, Yellow Children and creativity
Knowledge Colors: Yellow, Orange, Beige, Brown Knowledge, wisdom, education	**Career** Colors: Yellow, Orange, White Career, profession, desired job, field of work	**Travel** Colors: White, Gold, Silver Travel, trips

Fig. 4. Vision Board

Chapter 10:
No Chance of Being Helpless

"What now?" I found myself staring at the walls of my rented Canadian apartment, a place that felt less like home and more like a temporary shelter from the storm unraveling around me. My rent was paid for the next three months, and I had money for groceries, but I would have to be frugal. I had to pull myself together and figure out what I could provide for my child.

Let come what may — that was the principle I clung to in this situation. For the sake of my child, I had to take this leap into the unknown and summon every ounce of strength I had left. Back then, I didn't yet know that things could get worse, but a few months later, the whole world would see that for themselves.

In the meantime, I was dealing with pressing matters, and the first task was to find someone to be present at the birth. I had no one to turn to — all my friends were tied down with their own small children and couldn't leave them, no matter how much I needed help. Realizing that I wouldn't have any support, I assembled the crib, the stroller, and prepared all the things for my son myself. A woman can do anything, and a pregnant woman who has been abandoned can do even more. It was physically demanding, and to get myself into some kind of shape, I started going to the gym in the basement of our building. It felt like otherwise, the blood would stop circulating in my swollen body with its edematous legs, and I still needed to recover after giving birth, and the baby would require a lot of physical strength, which I currently lacked. Despite my swollen legs and enormous belly, I forced myself to work out slowly in the tiny gym downstairs, knowing that every small effort would help me prepare for the challenges ahead.

Fate brought me closer to a girl I had met through mutual friends just before my pregnancy. Amazingly, we were both expecting at the same time, and our shared journeys forged a bond that felt like a lifeline amidst my struggles. Amazingly, we were at the same stage of pregnancy. We started going everywhere together, and sometimes she helped me with translations. When we went to a cafe for lunch, we would share one dish because I was saving every dollar.

The situation was critical. I couldn't rely on anyone and was completely alone. I longed for someone — anyone — to say, "Masha, let me help you. Take what you need, and pay me back whenever you can." But all I heard were words of sympathy, empty and fleeting.

One of the hardest days for me was Valentine's Day. It had been a long time since I had spent this holiday alone at home, without flowers, gifts, or male attention. Apparently, all I had to do was get married. I sat in the kitchen, looked out the window, and thought that I was only a month and a half away from meeting my little son, and his father had come up with a brilliant solution for us — to sell my car, which I had bought with my own money. Only one question remained: what was the point of a husband then? What role did he play in our destiny?

Over time, it became painfully clear to me that life in Canada was simply too expensive — a reality I could no longer afford to ignore. Even if I got a job, the money wouldn't be enough, especially since I would then have to bring my mother here or hire a nanny — which meant more expenses. And how much could I earn without knowing the language? Just enough for rent. I didn't see the point in such a job.

If only I could find a stable income and receive government assistance! Even $500 would make a difference in my case; it would be enough for diapers. Michael, as far as I understood, wasn't planning on participating in our lives. I could file for divorce and force him to pay child support, but that would require a good lawyer, whom I couldn't afford. It was a vicious circle.

The Strategy

Several options remained. The most obvious was to return to Ukraine, but I wanted my child to grow up in a place with a more stable political, economic, and ecological environment.

The image of Bali suddenly appeared in my mind, like a shimmering oasis in a desert of despair. I clung to the thought of this magical island, believing it might hold the key to saving me. I started researching this intriguing island. People in blogs shared details about life in Bali. They were living there somehow, so I could too. But what would I do there with a newborn baby? I only had enough money for a one-way ticket, and what would I live on? I never thought that at eight months pregnant, I would have to make such life-altering decisions alone.

I felt completely helpless, but there was no time to wallow. Instead of giving up completely, I accepted the situation. Pushing my worries and regrets to the back burner, I focused on finding a way out.

First, I took out a pen and paper and listed the pros and cons of all three options: Canada, Ukraine, Bali. Anything, just to move forward, otherwise, my path led to a shelter. Canada still seemed like the most suitable place for now; now I needed to solve the income problem.

There's a way out of any situation, and not just one. If a situation seems hopeless, it just means you're not satisfied with any of the available solutions. In that case, all that's left is to choose the option closest to what you desire. What if that's where your potential lies?

And I came up with an idea. To support myself, I needed to draw on my strengths, experience, and skills. At nine months pregnant, desperate to find a way to survive, I returned to selling flowers — a small but vital step to keep myself and my baby afloat. I developed a social media page that I had had for a while and offered home delivery of bouquets. I couldn't buy flowers from wholesale markets — they were all far away, and I was saving money on gas.

I found a solution for this too: large supermarkets sold flowers. I bought them, arranged bouquets, delivered them to customers myself, earning about $20 per bouquet. This type of business might seem ridiculous to some, but for me, it meant a couple more cartons of milk. And that was important. These were my attempts to survive and prepare myself for the birth of my child because as long as we're alive, we can always change something.

My Son Chooses Himself

By the end of my pregnancy, thanks to hormones, I had gained 48 pounds above my usual weight. Considering my short stature, this made me practically square. My mother arrived to help after the birth, and it was good that she hurried because things didn't go according to plan.

At my next checkup, they told me the baby was very large, and since I was also injecting insulin, it would be better to induce labor a week early. I really didn't want this, especially since the initial due date coincided with my friend Lily's birthday — I liked that, and it would have made her happy too.

Lily's circumstances were far from rosy. The previous year, while I was still in Kyiv, she had spent the night at her parents' house. Returning home in the morning, she discovered her husband dead in their bed — a heart attack. She loved him very much. She was left with an eight-month-old baby.

Sometimes it seemed like I was losing my friend — Lily had fallen into such a deep depression that she was teetering on the edge. "How I wish I could leave all this in the past year," she wrote to me at the end of December, and I painted a talisman picture for her as a gift. We had both lost our husbands, both left with sons, but thankfully, Lily had a close-knit Armenian family, and she immediately moved in with her parents.

The doctors presented me with the facts: if the baby wasn't born soon, they would have to induce labor. Despite the external circumstances, I was sure I could program both my body and my baby differently. When a difficult pregnancy is blamed for problems with the baby, I believe the mother's state of mind is of paramount importance — it's what influences the development of the fetus.

It's incredibly important for a woman to understand what she herself is creating, who she is carrying inside her, how and when she will give birth. At this moment, she is like an engineer, programming the basic settings of the growing human within.

A friend of a friend had an interesting experience. When she was carrying her first child, she often thought and said aloud, "I wish he were special." Her son was indeed born special, with attention deficit disorder — he couldn't concentrate on anything and destroyed everything around him. It's good that she recognized the connection. When she became pregnant a second time, she programmed herself to want a completely ordinary child. And that's what happened.

I wanted an intelligent boy, a leader, a child who could cope with any life situation and withstand all the hardships in this complex and cruel world. If it weren't for the current circumstances, perhaps I would have imagined my son differently, but with my health condition, he could be left alone at any moment, and his father was unlikely to help. No, he definitely needed to have leadership qualities, the ability to survive in any conditions, move forward, and not depend on anyone.

On Sunday, March 16th, two days before they planned to induce labor, news outlets announced that due to the pandemic, a complete lockdown of unknown duration would be imposed in Canada starting the next day. Not fully understanding what this all meant, people rushed to clear the shelves of stores as if the Apocalypse was coming. Anxiety spread through the city like a rain puddle — very quickly and rapidly.

That evening, overwhelmed by the news, I stood under the warm streams of the shower and softly spoke to my baby, stroking my belly: "Son, I'm asking you, please. If you want to be born naturally, you have only one chance left — tomorrow. You are strong, you can do it, and I will help you. Please, hurry." I wasn't even focusing on what day tomorrow was.

At five in the morning, my water broke, and I called Kate to take me to the hospital. "Well, you certainly picked a time," my awakened friend sighed into the phone. "I don't know how we'll get there, maybe by teleportation, but I'll try." It was completely unclear whether it was even permissible to move around the city, even in a private car.

That morning, I desperately craved cottage cheese pancakes, and I asked my mother to make them for breakfast before I went to the hospital. While she was frying them, I entered the active phase of labor. Without eating a single pancake, I left for the hospital.

The Magic of Numbers

Not a single car was on the roads. The absolute silence of the city, frozen in the fear of the unknown and seemingly extinct, was broken only by the sirens of ambulances and police cars. Perhaps on another day, such an atmosphere would have unnerved me, but now I was focused on something else.

Anastasia was supposed to accompany me to the delivery, but under pandemic restrictions, it was impossible. In fact, there was a risk of being stopped on the road. But, fortunately, contrary to Kate's and my fears, the police didn't stop us and didn't force us to return to our apartments. I felt like the heroine of a post-apocalyptic film — cinematic realities had spilled over into real life.

When we arrived at the maternity hospital, they told us everything was closed. I showed them my belly, and they realized I might give birth right on their doorstep. Only humor saved me. Strong people are capable of joking in the most difficult situations. In the end, they let us in and even provided a nice single room with a private bathroom. I had just stepped out of the bathroom when I felt such pain that everything went dark. I gasped and bent over, holding my stomach. "Just in case, ask them to give me an epidural," I said to Kate, who rushed to my side.

They administered the epidural, but at the peak of the contractions, I didn't feel any effect. The pain was a 10 out of 10, it was driving me crazy, and I stopped thinking clearly. "Guys, I'm going to sleep!" I announced to all the staff who were actively working on my delivery at that moment, despite the intense contractions. They gave me a second epidural.

My heavy eyelids closed on their own, and I fell into a deep sleep. Then an amazing scene unfolded in my mind. In the dream, my grown-up son and I were running along a beach, laughing merrily. There were rocky mountains, palm trees, and a blue ocean all around. I playfully ran away from him, and he caught up with me. Our feet sank into the warm, white sand, and turquoise ocean waves rolled onto the shore, spraying us with salty mist. I had never felt so good in my life.

And how I didn't want to return to the delivery room, but it was as if someone pulled me out of my dream. I only had time to think, "Is this Bali?" It seemed like three hours had passed, especially since when I opened my eyes, Lily had replaced Kate. "Did I sleep long?" I asked, finally feeling the effect of the painkillers. It turned out to be no more than 15 minutes.

As I glanced at the calendar, a shiver ran through me — March 17th. The date felt almost mystical, woven into the fabric of my life — my birthday, Michael's birthday, the day I learned I was pregnant. Could it be mere coincidence, or was this the universe speaking to me in numbers?

During intense contractions, I turned my head to look at the clock: it was 17:11. I just realized that I wouldn't make it to the beautiful time of 17:17 when, after another push and a second's delay, I heard a loud baby's cry.

Everything happens at the right time because the world is governed by the magic of numbers.

My wonderful boy, David, was born on March 17th 2020. It turned out he wasn't large at all, as they had frightened me. I would even say he was thin, but tall, and my weight gain was due to a large amount of amniotic fluid.

When they placed David on me, skin to skin, I didn't understand what to do with him at first. It was like a little fish was lying on me: weightless and soft. My first thought was: is this my son? Now he will be with me always? My heart swelled with emotions I had never experienced before — love, awe, and a sense of profound responsibility for this new life.

If a woman isn't particularly interested in children and doesn't know how to handle them, it doesn't mean at all that she won't love her child and won't find an approach to him.

David and I found common ground that same evening, but I couldn't shake an unusual feeling: I was no longer alone and was now responsible for another life besides my own. It turned out that this wasn't like a sacrifice at all. I am David's mother; I am his help in this new world. A mother's role is to be her child's main helper. The role of guide, teacher, protector, and defender is the most important role.

Amidst the joyful thoughts, a few unpleasant ones crept in: I wonder what Michael is doing right now? Did he feel anything unusual today?

And so, on the day the world seemed to pause and hold its breath, my son David entered it, bringing with him a new chapter of life, love, and endless possibilities.

The day the whole world went on maternity leave with me for a long two years.

Chapter 11: Welcome Home

And there I was, alone in a foreign country with a newborn baby in my arms. I was standing on the brink of an abyss, its depths swirling with unresolved questions and overwhelming problems.

On the day I gave birth, Canada closed all cafes and other public places. Montreal was in complete isolation, and I felt like I was locked in an isolating concrete prison, completely cut off from the world. I understood that it would be very difficult and

I would have to try a hundred times harder because now I wasn't alone, but with a child.

David's and my discharge from the maternity hospital was like something out of a horror movie. No bouquets or balloons — only gloves, masks, and antiseptics. The baby was swaddled in layers of protective coverings, shielding him from the outside world. Doctors moved through the hospital in hazmat suits, their presence amplifying the fear and unease that hung in the air.

It was a frightening picture. Literally everything was forbidden — you couldn't even touch the elevator button. Because of the pandemic, the city was deserted; people, cars, sounds, lights — absolutely everything had disappeared. The air was thick with the sharp, stinging smell of alcohol-based sanitizers, a constant reminder of the invisible threat.

Covid restrictions were in place everywhere.

And again, the situation seemed hopeless. But this is only an illusion because every problem has a solution. It's just that the solution might not suit us. Many people make the mistake of burying themselves deeper into depression instead of trying to get out of it. Dwelling on how terrible everything is is a useless waste of time and resources.

Despite this nightmare, I tried to keep my chin up, largely for the sake of the child. A friend came to pick me up — in my car. The way home became a real challenge for us. Empty roads were patrolled by police; sirens wailed somewhere in the distance. There wasn't a soul outside; people were locked in their homes. While discharge from the maternity hospital is usually a celebration, David and I were released from the hospital into a kind of Silent Hill[5].

5 Silent Hill is a fictional town in the Canadian horror franchise

When we arrived home from the hospital, our cat met us at the door. Seeing the baby, she arched her back, her eyes flashing with terror and incomprehension. Sniffing him cautiously, barely touching his skin with her wet nose, she couldn't understand what this creature was. The presence of a new life in the apartment drove her crazy. After meeting the baby, the cat raced around the house like a mad thing. Later, she got used to him, and after a few days, she realized that the child posed no danger, and on the contrary — filled the house with new, bright energy.

From the moment I opened the door to my small Canadian apartment, I found myself in a cage. An iron bolt clicked shut behind me. I wasn't physically locked up, but mentally. I was alone with obligations, difficulties, and accumulated problems.

The main warden of my little prison turned out to be... my mother. From the moment the baby was born, she became a different person. Immediately after our arrival, my mother literally snatched David from my arms. I thought that after the hospital I would finally be able to breathe a little, but I was very much mistaken.

My mother swiftly imposed her strict rules and household regulations. She thought I was too inexperienced to care for a baby, so she immediately established her patronage over him. Not allowing me to even touch the child, she assigned me the role of an older sister. I felt that my mother was preventing me from fully realizing myself as a mother — she constantly reproached me and accused me of ignorance.

All this pressure and constant reproaches that I was doing everything wrong took place in a confined space. Our apartment was very small. I couldn't spend time alone with myself or with my son — my mother, like a stern warden, always watched me closely.

Freedom is one of life's most sacred values – the foundation of our choices, actions, and self-expression. Sometimes

our freedom is restricted, and we must fight against such situations. A person is not created to live in a cage. A person is created to be free and do what they want.

It was very difficult for me to tolerate her dictatorial ways, but I understood their nature. My mother couldn't fully realize herself as the mother of a boy, as my older brother was born with special needs. She constantly felt that she had somehow failed him, hadn't done enough, and had missed something. And now she was trying to compensate for all of this with her grandson.

From the outside, it might seem that having a mother help with the baby makes life easier. However, in our situation, the opposite was true. My mother constantly nagged me, found fault with everything, and didn't give me a moment to breathe. From her point of view, since I was a mother, I should be engaged in maternal duties 24 hours a day.

I, on the other hand, was driven by maternal instinct. My anxiety level went through the roof; I felt constant worry for the baby, all my senses heightened. Like mother cats who throw themselves at large dogs, I was ready to pounce on anyone who contradicted me. Going to the store, I walked on eggshells, thinking only of one thing — how my child was doing.

I wanted to always be near my son, to feel his breathing, his pulse, to read his emotions and needs. Tactile contact with the mother is very important for a baby — the so-called kangaroo method, which involves skin-to-skin contact. A third person in this chain is superfluous, needed only when help is required. A special bond should form between mother and baby, and this happens in the first months of a baby's life. Our bond was very strong, but a third person interfered. It felt like an invisible barrier separating me from fully embracing my role as a mother.

This is how the days of our life together in the small apartment passed. My mother instructed me on how to properly bathe, dress, and care for my son, and I, terribly exhausted, constantly asked myself how I had managed to end up in such a situation. It felt like I was sinking to the bottom.

In addition to the domestic totalitarianism, I was pressured by the economic factor. The money was barely enough to cover basic needs — food, baby care products, gas. At first, neither Michael himself nor his relatives helped us. Subsequently, Michael did start covering our basic needs — in exchange for my silence and keeping the birth of our child a secret.

I couldn't give up — too much had been endured, too much responsibility rested on me. Despite the loneliness, financial struggles, and my husband's abandonment, I knew one thing: **I will survive – because I choose to live!**

This awareness lived deep within me. My mindset was rather pessimistic. I was incredibly tired and didn't understand how to proceed. I couldn't see the light at the end of the tunnel.

Run and Don't Look Back

The first important step towards a normal life was learning English. Mastering a new skill helped me to distract myself and cleared my head. The baby needed documents, and naturally, I was the one handling it all. At that time, my vocabulary was limited to a dozen of the simplest, most basic words. Despite this, I had to communicate on complex topics, learn to construct sentences, and understand what people were saying.

Calling the insurance company, I typed text into Google Translate, recited it to the employee, and anxiously awaited a response. What I heard left me dumbfounded — typing the words I managed to make out back into the translator, I tried to answer. So, step by step, I gradually memorized new language constructions and learned to understand spoken English.

Only by experiencing immense stress and stepping outside my comfort zone was I able to solve all the tasks before me. To learn something, you have to sacrifice some brain cells; there's no way around it.

English alone wasn't enough. The days passed in a state of fatigue, irritation, and anxiety. Communicating with my mother was like a taut string about to snap. I was bombarded with criticisms and remarks; the pressure created terrible stress. Against the backdrop of raging hormones, such a hostile environment hit me ten times harder.

My appearance also seriously undermined my morale — looking at myself in the mirror, I didn't recognize my own reflection. During pregnancy, my natural light brown roots grew out, and the radiant blonde faded away.

Before me stood a different person: a girl with tired eyes, frowning eyebrows, and downturned corners of her mouth. The light in those eyes had long since gone out, and the person in the reflection was left in complete darkness.

As I grappled with the overwhelming weight of my emotions, I knew I had to regain control, even in the smallest way. It started with a simple experiment — an attempt to change something, anything, about myself.

I was broken, depressed; my life had become Groundhog Day. Every day I woke up in a terrible emotional state. The perpetual sleep deprivation, the psychological pressure from my mother, my failing marriage, the lack of money, the rejection of my body, the pandemic — I was on the verge of a breakdown. The problems that had fallen on me were so heavy that I wanted to scream and cry from the pain. But there was simply nowhere to do so.

Sometimes difficulties fall on us like a huge avalanche. In these moments, it's important to maintain faith in a better future and understand that this is just a dark streak. Life will definitely get better; the main thing is to do something about it.

Giving in to depression might seem like the easiest way out, but it only pulls you deeper into the darkness. Self-pity leads to nothing good. The deeper you sink, the harder it will be to climb out. This state drags you down like quicksand. And to start climbing up, grasping at every opportunity, requires a lot of effort.

Maintaining the right mindset is crucial. Your internal mechanism will work according to how you program yourself.

It was very difficult for me to adopt a positive outlook. When I looked at myself in the mirror, I wanted to cover my eyes with my hands. I knew that wasn't me. I didn't want to accept that image and tried to change at least something about myself. Because of the pandemic, absolutely everything was closed in Montreal, including hair salons. The discomfort and unease with myself prompted me to experiment. One day, I couldn't take it anymore and cut my own bangs — with office scissors. I think you can understand the level of desperation I was in.

If you don't accept your appearance, then you need to look for adequate ways to fix the situation. Complaints and weary sighs won't help. o love yourself, you need to do things you're not used to doing. If you're not satisfied with your appearance, physique, or skin quality, you should change your diet, start exercising, or see a doctor — the main thing is not to remain inactive. If you don't like your hairstyle, you can experiment and change it. If you're tired of your old image, try changing your wardrobe. Nothing will change on its own — change is always about working on yourself, experimenting, using your imagination, and stepping outside your comfort zone.

Fig. 5. Ten Steps Towards Self-Love.

In the process of change, some steps may work and some may not. But when you get a good result, it will drive and motivate you to continue changing. It's like the domino effect — once one piece moves, then the movement of the entire structure can't be stopped.

After the conditional acceptance stage came the next one — the stage of finding solutions. But how do you force yourself to act when you feel like you're at rock bottom? I had no resources for action, or even for thinking. But I understood that soon I would have no money left, and I needed something to live on.

You can only change your life by doing what you've never done before. It all starts with your inner state and the simplest habits.

Here's a small exercise: if you brush your teeth with your right hand, try doing it with your left. Give yourself the instruction: "I want to be happy, healthy, successful, and confident." Every time you brush your teeth with your left hand, cultivate this state, try to merge with it. By changing the conditions, you change your feelings, your thinking, you open yourself to new sensations, and then to new solutions. At first, you'll be uncomfortable, but then you'll get used to it, and the resulting state will become the norm for you. New neural connections refresh the brain, making it work differently. The world becomes wider, your perspective on things changes — from a different angle, they acquire new meaning. You need to practice this for a month, and at the end of this period, evaluate: how has your life changed?

When all I wanted was to sit and cry, I had to remind myself that action, however small, could break the cycle. I needed a fresh start, and I found it in physical activity. To clear my mind, I had to challenge my body and restore my spiritual balance.

The driving force that launched the process of change for me was regular running. Jogging became my only escape. With gyms closed and options scarce, I laced up my shoes and stepped into the cold, empty streets, desperate for relief — for movement, for something to lift the weight off my chest.

I counted the days until the doctor allowed me to go for a run. It took about two months to recover after giving birth. Everything happened gradually. I started with regular walking, slowly transitioning to running. I was so heavy and clumsy, like a water-filled balloon that couldn't get off the ground. The most I could manage then was a brisk walk, and even that left me breathless. And yet, it was incredible — the first day I went out to exercise, I felt like a different person.

As I sat in my small apartment, overwhelmed by my circumstances, I realized I had two choices: let despair consume me or take action. Small, deliberate steps could help me reclaim control. I started with running — not just to move my body, but to quiet my mind and restore my spiritual balance. Gradually, running became something special for me. It was a source of energy, motivation, a push for my upcoming transformation.

I ran not just mindlessly, physically, but also mentally — my consciousness raced far ahead. Running awakened not only my body but also my spirit; it became my place, or rather, my action of power, inspiration, and enlightenment. Motivational music, podcasts, and audiobooks that I listened to also contributed to this.

Sports and physical activity are powerful drivers that fuel our lives and inspire transformation.

If you have the opportunity, be sure to engage in sports. It affects not only your physical form but also your inner state. The main thing is not to focus on the pain, but to experience all your emotions.

New neural connections, formed thanks to running, prompted further development. Over time, I added push-ups and squats to my runs. By that point, I was feeling much better — both in body and soul. My strength began to return. It surged within me, spreading warmth and vitality through every part of my body.

I ran and didn't stop anymore. It was during running that I came to a much firmer realization that my life would change, that I would definitely cope.

Develop yourself, even in the most unsuitable conditions. It all starts with a simple run and ends with perfect form and a new spiritual fulfillment.

I knew that a regular job wouldn't cover all my basic needs. You need to think big, so that each subsequent goal surpasses the previous one in magnitude. I felt that I had enough experience to launch a startup. At that moment, I was incredibly inspired by Silicon Valley. The very idea that any idea could be developed to such a colossal scale gave me goosebumps.

Dreams are what make us act. Dream, write down your desires, and clearly formulate your goals. Then you will clearly see what exactly you will have to spend your strength and energy on.

Exercise: "What do I really want?"

Make a list of your desires that have ever crossed your mind. Don't think too hard. Write down the first thing that comes to mind.

When you run out of desires, reread your list, putting next to each item the number of years you allot to achieve it.

Find the goals you want to achieve in a year. Choose the four most important ones.

For each of these four goals, write down the steps you need to take to achieve them.

Now choose your most desired goal. Focus your efforts on it for a year.

Break down the big goal into steps and write down goals for each month.

What can I do for my business? I thought, evaluating the paths for its development. I returned to the idea of taking flower delivery to the international level. But not just opening a new location in a new country, but creating a network like Starbucks or McDonald's. The concept was that in any corner of the world, the customer receives a product created according to a single standard. Wherever we are, a caramel frappuccino remains a caramel frappuccino, just as the 'Milania' bouquet remains 'Milania.'

The idea was very promising, especially during the pandemic. During this period, delivery helped people a lot. I started actively promoting my store. Everything was ready for scaling; everything except one thing — I simply didn't have the strength. My energy was depleted, my physical condition was still dragging me down. To get out, I needed to look further and deeper — to focus on myself, change my thinking, reboot.

Of course, the conditions and circumstances were not favorable to me. There was no tailwind. When I wanted to exercise, my mother, like a warden, would loom over me and say that I wasn't going anywhere until I put my son to bed. I could afford to go out for a maximum of 40 minutes while David was sleeping. As soon as he woke up, my mother would call me and say, "David is awake. You should wrap things up and come home."

Yes, there are no ideal conditions. If you feel like you're swimming against the current, perhaps this is your point of growth.

I didn't have a nanny who could look after the child and not ask me to come back when I was working on my development. I didn't have a housekeeper to do the housework for me. I didn't have a translator, a lawyer, a driver, a personal assistant, or a sponsor. I was practically alone, and even my husband existed in my life only on paper.

Changing Internal Settings

While I was taking care of the baby and barely making ends meet, Michael was having a great time in Ukraine. Betrayal by a loved one is painful, and that pain doesn't go away for a very long time. For some, perhaps never. Before accepting and forgiving, you have to go through shock, denial, anger, and sadness.

I knew he had someone else. It wasn't hard to guess — Michael created a new social media account where he added girls. He didn't add me as a friend. "Tell me how it is, let's break up," I told my husband when we talked on the phone. "Why are you starting all this? We're a family. Everything will be fine," Michael would reply as if nothing was wrong.

But nothing good was happening — my husband was only growing more distant. He was practically uninterested in David, only looking at him a couple of times via video call during the entire period. He didn't even offer extra money for childcare and always justified himself by saying he didn't have any.

However, the facts spoke otherwise. It so happened that statements from his credit card account were sent to my email. What I saw there would easily break any woman: every week — flower shops and lingerie stores, hotel payments in Odessa and Ibiza, restaurant bills for thousands of dollars. Photos from his parties would sometimes appear online (or friends would send them to me), while I was buying diapers for our son with almost the last of my money.

Of course, it was very difficult for me. My husband's betrayal hurt me deeply, but I held on as best I could. I didn't throw tantrums and tried not to waste my energy on переживания (worries/emotional distress). On the contrary — I gathered information to use later in court during the divorce. Restrained, calm, and with a cool head. Otherwise, I would have simply drowned in my emotions and never surfaced.

While my husband was having fun, I spent sleepless nights with the baby, got myself back in shape, and continued to work on my spiritual development. I didn't feel sorry for myself, because the position of a victim of circumstances is the most destructive human feeling. Such a self-image makes us insignificant and helpless. And the main help always comes only from ourselves. I didn't expect anyone to come, feel sorry for me, and solve all my problems. I tried to lift myself out of the abyss through sheer willpower.

I was in a deep depression and reached a state where I wanted to jump out the window. But I had a child, so I simply couldn't become a victim, I had no right. Yes, I needed help, and I understood that well. But help not with pity and sympathy, but rather with mentorship.

At that moment, I remembered that a long time ago, a friend of mine had successfully worked with a psychologist and gotten a positive result. I asked her for the contact information. I had to wait two weeks to see this specialist because she was on vacation. The wait was real torture — it felt like I urgently needed a breath of air, but I was being asked to wait when I was already suffocating.

We all find ourselves in situations where we need outside help. Don't be afraid to talk about your weakness, to admit your mistakes.

At first, I had to go outside for sessions with the psychologist — my mother didn't give me the opportunity to be alone. She felt competition: "Who can give advice better than a mother?" But working with the psychologist really helped me. At first, it was unusual — the specialist just listened and said almost nothing in response. She allowed me to talk, paused, gave guidance, and at the same time carefully recorded the information. After three years of working with her, I realized how important and effective it was. In the future, the psychologist would often return to my past and say: "Masha, do you remember you had such a moment...?"

Working with a psychologist is always a long-term endeavor. It's not an ambulance that will bring you back from the other side in a couple of minutes. It's a gradual and consistent work on yourself that requires concentration, effort, and a desire to change something.

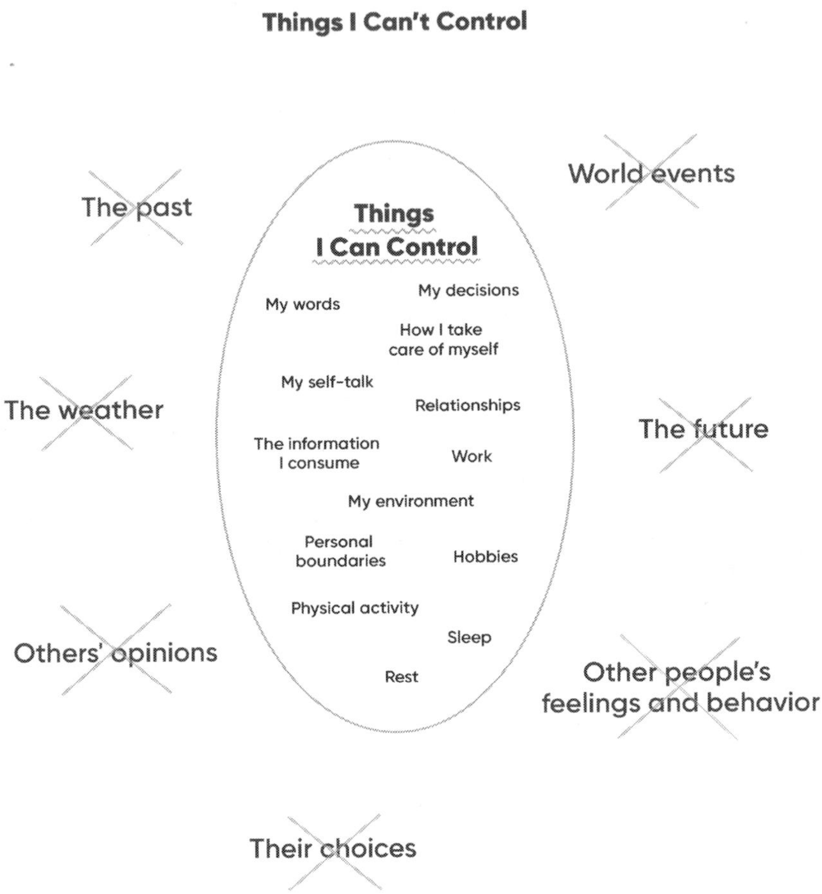

Fig. 6. Control

Gradually, I began to work through my problems. If it weren't for the psychologist, it would have been more difficult for me to cope with this. Of course, the most important thing is our own strength. But when it's running out, it's important that someone tells you how to fix and recharge yourself.

Don't be afraid to ask for help when it's necessary.

The psychologist helped me establish communication with Michael, to build a proper dialogue with him. When I completely ran out of money, he started helping to pay the rent and the car lease. My husband realized that in a critical situation, I would return to Ukraine. His mother lived there, from whom he was still hiding the fact that he had a son. Michael got scared and therefore started taking at least some action.

Rebirth

With a baby in my arms, I slowly started moving towards my dream and began delivering flowers. Just like during my pregnancy, I delivered the flowers myself. The proceeds from their sale went towards buying food.

Next, I started assembling a team. I wanted to create a new platform, and that required programmers. While walking with the stroller, I would occasionally hand it over to my mother and join a Zoom conference. I had to manage everything on the go.

During this period, I seriously focused on my dream. The idea of creating an international network of flower shops inspired and supported me greatly. I was doing what I was good at, and I was sure that everything would work out.

Self-development continued: I read books, listened to podcasts, and watched motivational mentors. My English improved every month, and I gradually got back in shape.

For any woman, male attention is extremely important. As I slowly regained my emotional and physical strength, I decided to try dating sites as a form of self-therapy. This was also a kind of therapy. Dating sites are good because girls receive many compliments. And this is a dose of energy, self-belief, and a boost to self-esteem. My self-confidence started to return, I began to feel much better, and I slowly broke through the ice, like a snowdrop. And on dating sites, I could also look for programmers. I was killing several birds with one stone.

Feminine energy thrives on appreciation and admiration, which helps restore confidence and inner strength. Love yourself and allow others to admire you. Don't be afraid of new acquaintances and be sure to go on dates.

This is how I built my path — alone again, only with my own strength, and again confident that all my dreams would come true. Michael's relatives distanced themselves completely, turning their backs on David and me.

I tried to make contact with them, but they were like cold rocks, against which it seemed completely pointless to struggle. Our little boat drifted further and further away from them into the sea. In this world, we were completely alone — me and my treasure, my child.

Once again, I was convinced that I realized that the only person who could truly help me was myself.

I could only solve my problems myself, and I should only rely on myself. I had no one left but myself.

After David's birth, Michael's relatives visited their grandson only twice. At some point, they said they no longer wanted to communicate with me and the child, and our connection almost completely broke off.

They didn't accept me in our past life, which I saw in regression therapy — history repeated itself. Back then, a son stood between me, my husband, and his family. But now I clearly understood what karmic lessons I had to go through to change the course of events and not repeat these lessons over and over again.

Chapter 12: The Magic Number 17

Working with a psychologist was like a sip of water in the desert. I waited for each session with a desperate thirst — they were vitally important to me. We had two sessions a week, and when money was tight, we'd have one. Some say that there's no better psychologist than a close friend or relative. This isn't true — a professional psychologist is a magnifying glass, allowing you to see all the cracks, all the tiny details within yourself, and put them in their place. No frank conversations with friends can compare to professional help.

I continued to search for answers to my questions. In addition to the psychologist, I incorporated other methods of self-discovery. I needed to get to the truth: where did the failure occur, at what point did I take a wrong turn? I wanted to understand why the last few years had unfolded the way they did and what to expect in the future. Gradually, the picture came together, and clarity slowly began to return. But the details still remained very blurry. To adjust this magnifying glass, I needed to adjust myself. Self-discovery is preceded by a stage of self-development, and accumulating knowledge is the first step on the path to it.

I slowly began to understand what happened between Michael and me. We are two opposite signs: I am a Capricorn, and he is a Cancer. The foundation of our family took place during an eclipse corridor[6]. This is a very energetically powerful period.

[6] An eclipse corridor is the period between a lunar and a solar eclipse. It typically lasts about two weeks.

It is during eclipse corridors that energy undergoes a profound shift and it is extremely important to manage it correctly. Some astrologers believe that during this time, the foundation of fate for the next years is laid.

Michael and I were polar opposites, standing at the farthest ends of a shared axis. Digging deeper, I paid attention to the magic of the numbers associated with our personalities. This was a sign that hinted I needed to go further and led me to the 'Matrix of Destiny.'

In a state of stability, a person thinks that everything is going as it should, that this is their destiny. Talking to the psychologist, I explained that I felt like a cat who had recently given birth to kittens. It was as if I had been driven into a corner, closed off in a confined space. And so, like a scalded cat, I was jumping from side to side — instincts were boiling inside me. I was ready to climb any wall to get out, but I didn't know which one. Personal tragedy, fear, and confusion prompted me to search, awakened a lot of questions in me, and forced me to act.

We all start to move when we feel that things are really bad. It's not easy to admit, but rebirth can only come through suffering. We either endure it and emerge from the situation as a new person, or we break. The choice is ours alone.

If it weren't for the pain I went through, I would hardly have turned to the 'Matrix.' I was lucky — there were always people by my side who experienced this pain with me — my friends. Some of them appeared when I was in trouble and smoothly dissolved in space and time when the trouble passed.

One of my friends sent me clothes from Kyiv from her kid, who was older than David. In addition to material help, she provided me with moral support. We talked a lot about spiritual topics, discussed palmistry, astrology, numerology — she told me about different specialists and their courses. I ignored some of it, but once my friend mentioned the 'Matrix' — she said she had found an interesting and inexpensive consultation.

Out of curiosity, I decided to try it. The consultation turned out to be extremely unsuccessful — its author went over the 'Matrix' very superficially, skimming the surface, leaving the roots deep underground. However, I was hooked by the research method itself — the numbers contained much more information than it seemed at first glance. I wanted to go further and started studying the 'Matrix' on my own.

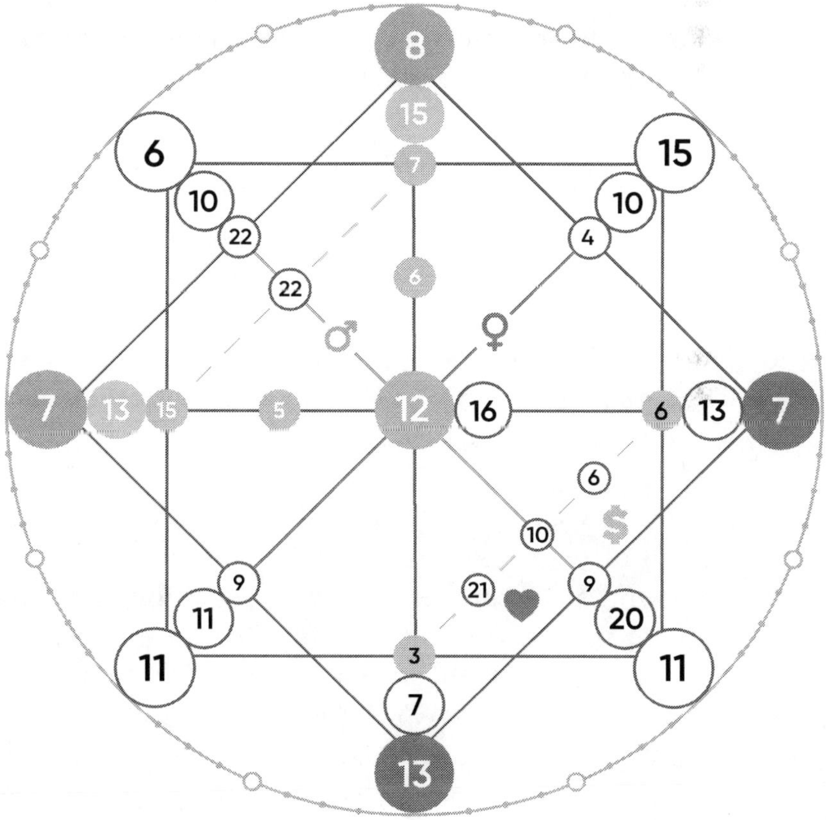

Fig. 7. Compatibility Matrix

Analyzing Michael's and my compatibility matrix, I was amazed at how accurately we lived out our destinies — what was predetermined for us. Only by looking beyond the visible — looking not at the images, but at the numbers — did I finally see clearly. Laying out our matrices, I realized that we were destined to part. The number 16 — 'The Tower,' meaning fall, the energy of destruction — stood between us. It was the number 16 that crossed out Michael's and my relationship.

The number 13, with which we manifested ourselves in the world, was of great importance to our couple. It indicates our joint task of living in this incarnation and speaks of death, rebirth, global transformation. This relationship inevitably had to radically change both of us.

Also, the magic number 17 ('The Star') appeared everywhere in our relationship between my husband and me. Both Michael and I were born on the 17th, and on July 17, 2019, I found out I was pregnant. As I mentioned earlier, our son was also born on the 17th. If you combine Michael's and my energies, it also results in 17. The 17th energy is always a bright creative nature, stardom, and the necessity to manifest and realize one's talents. Our family is essentially a huge whirlwind, a giant clot of manifested energy, multiplied a hundredfold. However, because of the energy of destruction, that is, the number 16, which stood next to 17, this fragile crystal vase was destined to break.

The mission of our union was the birth of David. As soon as I got pregnant, the goal was achieved — and our marriage began to fall apart. We both put a lot of effort into conceiving a child, and lived through this moment together: I overcame a serious illness, and Michael was there all this time. But when the baby was born, his energy divided Michael's and my flow in half, and each of us went our own way. Our common path ended. And I finally found answers to my questions and was able to calm down.

When we begin to understand cause-and-effect relationships, we create order within ourselves. Why is this happening? Why did this happen to me? What can I expect from the future? By putting everything in its place, a person finds solutions. Create order inside, and order is established outside as well.

In my relentless pursuit of the truth, I left no stone unturned. I read, watched, studied, and sought out countless specialists, each adding a new piece to the puzzle.

I needed to understand how the universe works. Every specialist I turned to, whether a numerologist or a hypnologist, cut me like a diamond. But each from their own side. To get a full-fledged diamond, I had to go around dozens of masters.

Don't overlook unconventional tools. The truth often lies hidden in the depths, waiting to be uncovered. To get to it, you need to turn to the very origins. Numbers, planets, energy flows – all of this can tell you more than you think.

I am the owner of my life

Continuing with sports and therapy, I immersed myself in business. I no longer wanted to depend on anyone, to be a victim, to be manipulated. Freedom, in many ways, depends on financial stability. I wanted to return to my former self – independent and self-sufficient. The one who decides how to act, where to be, and with whom.

For the past few years, I have lived not for myself, but for others. I gave up my own pursuits for the sake of family, fulfilled all my husband's requests, and moved to another country with him. The inability to make decisions for myself practically destroyed my personality.

Now, I was determined and uncompromising — I would do what I enjoyed and provide for myself independently.

From my past life, I brought certain skills into this one. Thinking rationally, I understood — I was a mediocre poet, musician, and singer. What did I do best? Build a business, of course.

A serious step towards my rehabilitation as a businesswoman was the opening of an import-export company, through which I began supplying food products. I took the money for the startup from my last remaining resources. While previously I had delivered flowers as a sole proprietor, now I had a corporation. This required a sum that seemed astronomical at the time — $1,000. Plus, it was the end of the year — I had to file a tax return. That was another $300–400 on top. For comparison, my monthly rent was $1,400.

Astrologers called that time period the 'millionaire's aspect' — a very auspicious period for starting a business, which happens once every 200 years. According to them, any business launched at that time was guaranteed success. In my despair, I was ready to believe anything. In the end, the corporation really did take off. Years later, I wanted to close the company, but at the last moment, my accountant dissuaded me. I transferred my existing business to it, and now that company is worth millions.

After a long break, I went back to the gym. Simultaneously, I developed my product supply business and continued delivering bouquets. In between feeding David, I held Zoom meetings, built a platform for a new flower marketplace, and wrote a business plan.

Through my company, I started supplying sanitizers to Ukraine — they were in high demand during the pandemic. I established a good relationship with the owner of the European goods store. He was interested in collaborating on the purchase of bread, butter, and grains — all of which I could import from Ukraine to Canada.

A very important point — as soon as the business started to revive, I delegated my responsibilities. I still had financial difficulties, but, living modestly, without any excesses, I hired an assistant from Ukraine. She worked on European time while I slept on Canadian time: making presentations, signing contracts, handling sales, and shipping goods. I took on the logistics — figuring out how to ship containers and paying the bills. This way, we managed to work 24/5.

Contacts and acquaintances played a decisive role for my business at that time. Since the world was in lockdown, all communication took place online. Romance didn't interest me much — I only scheduled meetings with people who were useful in a business sense. Through new acquaintances, I expanded my network and sought out new specialists.

Eventually, I had enough contacts, and I launched projects with Costco — a company that manages an international chain of wholesale hypermarkets. They had huge volumes of goods, which offered good earning potential. I was only interested in large-scale projects — all the 'small stuff' was left behind forever.

I finally had enough energy for some side projects. For example, I started uploading videos to a YouTube channel and even bought a vlogging lamp. I was drawn to creativity: I wanted to launch a "How to Become a Florist" course and started recording videos on this topic. Another idea for the channel was to interview people who enjoyed their professions. I managed to film the introductions, but the interviews themselves remained in the planning stage.

Over time, I gained numerous admirers, but from the height of my round-the-clock busyness, I simply didn't notice them. I went to my first photoshoot since my son's birth. It revived me like a breath of fresh air and became a remedy for boosting my self-esteem.

I set a certain standard for myself and never dropped below it. I knew my worth and maintained my level. Goals were set, and nothing could stop me. I set clear priorities for myself and chose to focus only on meaningful projects and relationships.

"What are you doing for a living?" young men would ask me online. This question literally made my eye twitch.

But by that time, the need for making new acquaintances had completely disappeared — I had already established all the necessary contacts, the export and import of goods was generating income, and my morale was slowly starting to improve.

Focus on Myself

As I later discovered, my husband had already found a new girlfriend by that point, and his entire family had already met her. I wasn't even aware of this, and even if I had been, it wouldn't have bothered me. I was entirely focused.

It's impossible to help others until you've helped yourself. To save yourself, you need to concentrate on your own rescue and not scatter your energy on actions that are neither beneficial nor meaningful. Confronting Michael would have been precisely such an action – a useless and pointless waste of time and energy.

I took a different path — I focused on self-improvement, did photoshoots, developed my company, held numerous conference calls, and simultaneously cared for my child.

At some point, I felt that the idea of an online platform for the flower shop had stalled; progress was painfully slow.

The path of maximum resistance doesn't always lead to success. You need to distinguish between objective difficulties, which arise in any endeavor, and the stop signs the universe sends. There's no need to pound on a closed door – it's better to spend your energy finding an open one.

Running a business has always been challenging for me, largely because I'm a woman. While good looks generally help women in everyday situations, in business, it's the opposite. At least, that was the case in Ukraine. "Why wasn't I born a man?" I asked myself a million times. If I were a man, the processes I spent an immense amount of time and effort on would have been resolved with a snap of my fingers. In the Ukrainian business world, I wasn't accepted. I had to constantly bang my head against a wall to achieve even the slightest result.

Everything turned out differently in Canada. Equality reigns in this part of the world — both in business and in everyday life. Couples split restaurant bills evenly. But to be on par with men, you need to match them. No one gives you any breaks here. Therefore, I had to navigate and quickly switch between Ukrainian and Canadian partners.

In the end, I shut down the platform that wasn't generating profit and was only consuming my precious time. I parted ways with my business partner, who wasn't contributing anything worthwhile. We separated on a sour note, but I closed that chapter with an iron curtain. Tantrums and showdowns are not my style. When necessary, I say goodbye to people quickly, decisively, and permanently.

Overall, I became much more assertive. While I used to try to please everyone, striving to be agreeable and accommodating, I now acted much more deliberately and calmly. I wasn't going to waste time on people who encroached on my time and resources, and I easily cut out the excess.

What Does It Mean to Be Mindful?

Mindfulness is being present here and now, in the present moment. It helps you respond adequately to events, maintain your immunity and mental health, reduce the risk of cardiovascular diseases, and effectively manage your emotions.

Check how mindful you are. The more checkmarks, the closer you are to the goal.

1. You maintain the hygiene of your body, mind, and the space around you.

2. You don't harm or destroy your body.

3. You carefully filter your environment (people and information).

4. You don't answer meaningless questions.

5. You end conversations when they turn into conflicts.

6. You don't look for someone to blame. You understand that you alone are responsible for your own actions (and inaction).

7. You don't impose your point of view and worldview on others. You don't argue with those who think differently. You allow others to follow their own paths.

8. You love unconditionally, without demanding anything in return.

9. You can look at any life situation from the outside, adopting the perspective of an 'observer.'

10. You perceive any problem as a task that needs to be solved, without panic.

11. You don't rush to solve other people's problems but are ready to help if asked.

12. If your inner child gets carried away, you know how to engage your inner parent in time.

13. You treat everything that comes into your life and leaves it with respect.

The Most Important Secret to Success: The universe began to appreciate me and my new approach to life. At first, it tested me, dumping a pile of unnecessary junk on my head. I didn't accept these handouts because I had clearly formulated in my mind that I would only do what I wanted. I would easily leave behind anything unnecessary.

Now I'm focused on important and promising tasks. I was considering installing a refrigerator in the European store and launching flower sales. While in negotiations, I continued to engage in export and import, accepting barter — for example, advertising products.

One day, I received an offer: someone would wash my car, and in return, I would conduct a photoshoot and create an advertisement. I got eyelash extensions, and as luck would have it, I developed a stye due to stress. With eyes swollen like a weeping princess, I set off to the Rolls-Royce dealership.

My dear friend

I'd never had a sty as big as the one I had that day. Thankfully, I wasn't going on a date, so there was nothing to worry about. Even though I looked like I'd been crying, I felt very confident inside. I had a ton of things to do, and I simply didn't have time to pay attention to some silly sty.

The car wash was located inside the dealership, but it was a separate entity — a contractor handling the entire auto aesthetics and detailing department. An employee took my keys and offered me a tour of the showroom while they washed my car. Utterly exhausted and rushed, I looked at the luxury cars with interest, took a bunch of photos and videos, and, quite satisfied with my visit and clean car, drove home.

The next day, the dealership called and said they'd forgotten to apply the window film. I went back, thinking I'd likely never return again. I was wrong.

By then, my life was already buzzing with new activities and events. I was completely immersed in my affairs — business, my child, and myself. I was developing a website for my food company and creating a vision board, something I continue to do to this day. My focus was solely on myself and my own life. Most importantly, I felt completely fulfilled. There was no longer a need to cling to someone like a leech, expecting them to provide for me, give me gifts and flowers. I could do all of that myself.

After some time, I bought a child's car seat. Although I had assembled cribs and strollers myself, my skills weren't enough for this. Perhaps it was a sign of fate. I remembered the guys who had washed my car and decided to ask them for help.

The owner of the car wash came to my rescue — a private entrepreneur from Mexico with only four employees. Installing the car seat turned out to be extremely difficult, and the owner had to call in the dealership's staff. Several grown men, including the top Rolls-Royce sales manager, surrounded my car, trying to solve this puzzle. While they struggled with the car seat, I took pictures, unaware that the owner of the car wash had already set his sights on me.

Antonio became one of the dozens of men who messaged me. He was the same guy who had taken my keys. e turned out to be not an ordinary employee, as I had initially thought, but an entrepreneur. A medium-height brunette with very pleasant features, which, I confess, I hadn't paid any attention to. In the midst of everything, I hadn't even noticed him — I didn't need love and romance; I was building my life. He, however, looked at me like I was a dazzling star. In Canada, my appearance, my fiery blonde hair, was still something extremely unusual, so I didn't suffer from a lack of attention.

Over time, the tone of our communication shifted to a warm, friendly one. Antonio might ask me to edit a photo for him or give him business advice. He became a sort of hook — at that time, I was interested in everything related to entrepreneurship. One day, my new friend very cautiously and sweetly invited me for coffee. All the cafes were still closed due to restrictions, so hot drinks could only be ordered to go and drunk, for example, in the car.

Antonio drove up to my house in his old Audi. We chatted in English, discussing his small business, and I offered advice on how to improve it. I have an excellent entrepreneurial sense;

I clearly see the prospects and weaknesses of any company. Just like with the factory back then, I immediately scanned all the shortcomings and offered the owner possible solutions.

Antonio became the first man in my life who listened to what I had to say. This was infinitely important and valuable to me. It was precisely what I had sorely lacked in Michael.

A week after another meeting, Antonio told me, "I tried your advice, and it worked out really well." I saw that progress was being made. He started YouTube and TikTok channels and focused on marketing. When I visited him at work, he would take pictures of me — we had a mutually beneficial symbiosis. Antonio tried to ask me out on dates, but like a cat that doesn't want to be picked up, I skillfully slipped away. I kept him at arm's length — he seemed completely out of my league.

One day, Antonio announced that he was moving. He mentioned that his new house had a lot of free space and all the walls were bare. I happened to have a large painting in my apartment that I had created, and it was taking up a lot of space. I offered it to Antonio as a gift. He refused and instead wanted to buy it. So, the painting I created found its place in his home. I was incredibly pleased.

One day after New Year's, I found a beautiful mirror. When I arrived to pick up the new decorative item, I realized it wouldn't fit in my car. Then I remembered that Antonio was moving his belongings to his new apartment that day and had rented a truck. He helped me without hesitation — after my call, he arrived within minutes and later helped me install the mirror. "If you need any help, for example, with something physical, I'll gladly help. Please, just ask," he told me.

I was touched by Antonio's responsiveness, his kindness, sincerity, and decent behavior. But at that time, I was, shall we say, occupied. I had started a relationship with another man. Antonio wasn't my type and wasn't even in my circle of friends. I treated him with gratitude, but rather indifferently. Like in that Allegrova song: "Not my style, not my size."

Meanwhile, Antonio turned out to be very jealous and persistent, sometimes going too far. His feelings for me grew stronger every day. He wouldn't leave me alone, waiting for hours near our lobby. This seriously bothered me. Sometimes I couldn't go home peacefully because I knew there was a trap waiting for me.

One day, Antonio called and said, "Come out, let's have coffee." I refused because we had already settled everything, put everything in its place. "Please, it's very, very important," Antonio insisted and added, "I have something for you." He knew I wouldn't fall for just coffee anymore.

Sighing and rolling my eyes, I put on my down jacket, pulled on my hat, went down into the snowy evening, and got into his car. He greeted me with the words, "You will be my wife." This phrase evoked a mixture of astonishment and laughter in me. But, as they say, he who laughs last laughs best.

"Thanks for the information. Is that all you wanted to tell me?" I asked, losing my patience. "Yes, that's all. But don't think it's just like that, the Akashic Records told me." *Ah, now everything is clear! You should have said that right away.* Except I had no idea what he was talking about. But it became clear that the guy was completely out there, and I needed to read about these Chronicles — I don't like the feeling of not knowing something. Back then, I didn't realize how soon I'd have to lessen my skepticism.

A little later, suburban restaurants opened in Montreal. I agreed to go on a date with Antonio. I understood that his feelings for me had grown to uncontrollable proportions, and I didn't want to hurt him. "Let's just not communicate anymore? Because it's painful for you. And anyway, why do you need all this?" I said to Antonio. After this meeting, he disappeared for a while, and our communication ceased for some time.

At that point, men weren't of much interest to me; they were something of a bonus. I had set certain standards — for example, "I want a huge house with a garden." I wouldn't settle for less. Either that or nothing at all. I would achieve everything myself, and if there was a man by my side — great, a pleasant addition.

Chapter 13: My Bright Angel and Chanel Ballet Flats

In March, when David turned one year old, my grandmother passed away. It was a deeply painful and melancholic period. She was an incredibly important person to me — a role model, a guiding light, and a source of wisdom.

I was her youngest granddaughter, so we had a special relationship. Every summer, I would visit her dacha, wander through her enchanting flower-filled garden, chase lizards, and sway on the swing my grandfather had lovingly built for me.

My time at their house was a joyful and serene time, a fragment of the past reflecting the most sincere and genuine happiness. This house and its inhabitants often come to me in dreams and meditations.

And I wasn't surprised at all when I realized that in the past life I saw during a regression session, my grandmother was also there — a kind nanny with warm hands who replaced my mother, who had passed away early. In this life, she chose to be born as my grandmother to teach her daughter how to be a good mother to me. I think she succeeded in many ways, but for two lifetimes now, my mother and I haven't had the connection we could have. I believe that one day we will both learn. My grandmother will help us again because she never leaves me alone and continues to protect me.

One day, I had a very disturbing dream in which my grandmother came to me. The next day, David, Antonio, and I went to the park. Walking along the path, David became distracted by the trees — we had to stop to call him back. Suddenly, there was a deafening crack — a huge branch fell out of nowhere onto the path. Had we taken ten steps forward, that branch would have fallen directly on us. And at that moment, I remembered my grandmother's warning in my dream. I feel her protective presence constantly surrounding me, guiding me with subtle signs from above.

My grandmother is a white angel; her light and warmth were enough for the whole family. She possessed a firm yet gentle demeanor, and under her nurturing guidance, the house was both filled with love and kept impeccably organized.

He loved her madly and adored her his entire life. Thanks to them, I understood how to behave properly with relatives and how to build relationships with a partner.

My grandmother and I agreed that when she left us, she would come to me in a dream and tell me what it was like on the other side of life. She dreamed of holding her youngest great-grandson in her arms and waited for him for exactly one year and one day. Unfortunately, because of COVID, I couldn't visit her with the baby. My grandmother passed away the day after David's first birthday — March 18th. I miss her very much.

Because of the family loss and COVID restrictions, we couldn't properly celebrate David's birthday. To distract myself, I decided to take him to Quebec. I desperately needed a break — David had reached an age where he was becoming difficult to manage. Exploring the world around him, he became like a wind-up toy — he didn't sit still for a second. My mother had already left Canada by that time, so all the childcare fell on my shoulders.

Shortly before my mother's departure, when David was 10–11 months old, I found a nanny for him. If there's an opportunity to delegate, never miss it. It's better to spend an extra 20 dollars on a nanny and take care of useful things or just get some sleep. By investing in a nanny, I was, in a way, investing in myself. I spent the freed-up time on my business and self-development.

At this point in my life, Antonio reappeared. I told him I was going to another city and that if he wanted to join us, he could. He agreed. However, we agreed beforehand that we would stay in separate rooms and pay for ourselves. I clearly stated my position: "We are friends. If you want to be around, be around, but only as a friend, nothing more." I told Antonio directly that he had no chance of a romantic relationship with me.

At that time, a hotel was the only available option for a getaway. Larger cities were still locked down due to the pandemic. We chose our room very well — it offered majestic and peaceful views. We could see the entire castle, which looked down on the hotel guests with a stern yet peaceful presence. Due to the pandemic, prices had dropped significantly, so we enjoyed all this beauty for very little money.

During this trip, I observed how naturally and joyfully Antonio interacted with David, with an ease and warmth that felt entirely genuine. When I asked him to watch my son for a few minutes, he played with him as if they were close relatives. This was despite the fact that Antonio didn't have much experience with children — he had none of his own.

The connection between Antonio and my son was heartwarming. At that point, I didn't feel a romantic spark with Antonio, as my focus was solely on my own growth and my child. I was self-sufficient and didn't need anyone else. I enjoyed this state of independence and didn't want to lose it. I felt like I had finally returned to my true self.

After the Quebec trip, Antonio and I had a falling out due to his jealousy, and he disappeared again. We didn't communicate for a couple of months.

Summer was approaching, and he contacted me again. During our correspondence, he congratulated me on Mother's Day and asked, "What would you like as a gift?" This question caught me off guard.

I knew Antonio was unlikely to be able to give me what I truly wanted — my wish list was full of extravagant and expensive items. In general, personal matters and responsibilities had consumed me. I was grieving the loss of my grandmother, and my business demanded my constant attention — I was constantly busy. On top of that, I was caring for a one-year-old child without any help. At that time, I had little time or energy for Antonio and his gifts.

Playfully, I said, "Chanel ballet flats," with a hint of irony, fully expecting him to brush it off as a joke. I genuinely wanted them, but I didn't have the extra money for this purchase. I didn't seriously think Antonio would actually buy them for me. To me, his question was just empty words — I didn't expect any action to follow.

"Excellent. Then let's meet at the store in an hour," he replied. At that moment, my inner skepticism towards Antonio diminished slightly. "Could he really be serious?" I thought with a touch of disbelief as I drove to pick up David from daycare.

After picking up my son, we went to the agreed-upon location. I doubted he would actually buy the ballet flats until the very last moment and even offered to split the bill. But my companion was determined, despite the cost of the shoes.

Later, I learned that when Antonio had messaged me about the gift, he had decided it would be his last attempt. If I didn't respond, he would stop pursuing me.

He had reason to be apprehensive. Before the ballet flats incident, there was another awkward situation. He had sent me a gift. When I went down to the lobby to retrieve the package, I found... car keys. The accompanying note explained that Antonio had bought a new car: "These are the spare keys. You can use it whenever you want."

This gesture infuriated me. "Why would I use someone else's car when I have my own?" I thought, annoyed, staring at the keys. Exasperated by such foolishness, I took the package to Antonio's workplace and gave it to the first manager I encountered. "Tell him to stop doing things like this," I said sternly and quickly left the office.

The Chanel ballet flats, like the women's shoes in my father's hallway once had, became a symbol of change. If before them I had my back turned to Antonio, from that second on, I involuntarily began to slowly turn around.

Still, Antonio didn't gain any new status — he remained just a friend. Happy with the purchase, I thanked him, and the three of us went to a restaurant. David's presence didn't bother him — on the contrary, during our trip to Quebec, they had immediately connected and become fast friends. My son enjoyed the company of an adult, and the adult enjoyed the company of a child. Antonio interacted with him sincerely and with genuine curiosity. He wasn't trying to impress me — he simply played with David as if they were father and son. Antonio enjoyed spending time with my son, and David reciprocated wholeheartedly.

By this time, the iron curtain of the lockdown had begun to lift — public places in Canada were starting to reopen. A few days after our trip to the boutique, Antonio suggested we all go to the zoo. There, I took their first photo together — Antonio holding my son in his arms. They made a great team.

Navigating personal life with a small child at home is challenging. Thanks to David, I had a new and very strict criterion for selecting men I was willing to date. If a man was willing to and could pay for a babysitter while we spent time together, we would meet; if not, then no. This was an easy way to discern who was all talk and who had serious intentions and was willing to back up their words with actions.

Antonio made a clever move: he not only paid for a babysitter but stayed with David himself, sending me and the babysitter to a restaurant — in his car. It was a surprisingly thoughtful gesture. I knew what male care was, but Antonio's was particularly strong.

He surprised me more each day. Like any mother with a young child, I treasured my sleep. Antonio took advantage of the situation and decided to help. While I caught up on sleep, he would take my son for walks in the park. Sometimes he would even take David to his workplace. On their first visit to his office, Antonio jokingly introduced David as his son, a gesture that caught me off guard but showed how naturally he had embraced their bond. This both amused and surprised me — we weren't even dating at the time. They spent a lot of time together. My son was happy, and he and Antonio grew closer and closer.

At that time, David didn't know or understand who his real father was. This was a sensitive topic for me, and I wasn't sure how to explain it to such a young child. David's very first words were a poignant question: **"Where is Daddy?"**

In his still-developing mind, there was already an understanding that there should be two parents. However, one figure was missing from our chessboard. It turned out that Antonio was able to fill that role, appearing at the right time and in the right place. He embraced this new role with such ease and authenticity, it felt as though fate had always intended for him to be there.

At a Distance

My friend Lily and I once took a trip to another part of Canada with our two young children. It was an unforgettable vacation. We visited two lakes, Lake Louise and Emerald Lake — a truly breathtaking sight! Magical landscapes of snow-capped mountains set against turquoise waters. The color of these lakes was so vibrant, it was hard to believe they were real. We only had a few precious seconds to snap some photos while our children sat patiently in their strollers. David was 1.2 years old at the time, and Lily's son, Andrew, was 2.3.

Traveling with them wasn't easy. It took considerable effort to reach our destination. Five hours on a plane, followed by several more hours in a rental car navigating challenging mountain roads — all with toddlers in tow. My motto was, "I'm a mom — I can do anything." And I never once regretted my decision — the vivid experiences were more than worth it!

The trip was quite intense. Upon arriving back in Montreal, I felt happy but completely exhausted. All I wanted was some peace and quiet.

Then, as if reading my mind, Antonio reappeared. He suggested a trip out of the city. Under normal circumstances, I probably would have declined. But I was craving relaxation and a chance to clear my head, so a getaway to nature seemed like the perfect solution. I agreed.

Antonio paid for a babysitter, booked a hotel, and we set off in his car. Before this, he had asked me about my monthly expenses. I told him I spent roughly $5,000 a month. He then inquired, "How much money do you think you would need to support a family?" This wasn't a difficult question for me — I had already done the calculations.

"$50,000 a month is what I would need for a family," I explained confidently, breaking down the costs of the lifestyle I envisioned — housing, education, and travel — not as an indulgence but as a well-calculated goal. The moment the words left my mouth, I heard the screech of brakes. Antonio slammed on the brakes, practically stopping the car in the middle of the highway. A wave of indignation crossed his face. He was instantly fired up. "Where on earth did you come up with that number?! " he asked, struggling to contain his voice. "Well, this is it," I thought, nervously shrinking back into my seat. I fully expected him to kick me out of the car right then and there. The speed with which his fiery Mexican temper flared was a little intimidating.

"Look, let me explain," I said calmly, and proceeded to lay everything out for him. "First, I want a big house. Let's say such a house costs $3 million. That translates to $15,000 in monthly mortgage payments. Second, the upkeep on a house like that is also significant. Plus, there's food, clothing, car maintenance, leisure activities, travel, and other expenses. Then there's private school. Assuming I have two children, and private school costs $2,000-$3,000 per child, that's another substantial amount."

Of course, I didn't have those kinds of resources at the time. But there's a difference between having a poor mindset and facing difficulties. I knew my current situation was temporary. I set ambitious goals because I firmly believed I would achieve them. I wasn't about to settle for less or abandon my plans.

It was important for me to be honest and set clear expectations. After my little explanation, Antonio calmed down somewhat.

A couple of hours later, we arrived and went zip-lining. It's an extreme sport — not for the faint of heart. The weather was dismal — pouring rain and thick fog. I couldn't wait to get back to the hotel room and warm up. After zip-lining, we returned to the hotel. I collapsed on the bed and fell asleep instantly.

That evening, we went to a restaurant. At this point, we were still just friends — there was no particular intimacy between us. I maintained a certain distance.

However, he did manage to get close to me — through my son. They became the best of friends, their bond filled with mutual adoration. Antonio's time with David wasn't a ploy to win me over. He genuinely loved my son. Over time, David began referring to Antonio as "Papa," a reflection of the deep bond they had naturally developed.

David instinctively chose Antonio as his father figure, and Antonio embraced this role wholeheartedly, treating him with the unconditional love of a devoted parent.

Relationships Begin with a Contract

Antonio and I lived in separate apartments and only saw each other in neutral territory. One day, he suggested we move in together, and this happened before we had even started dating. Considering there was nothing romantic between us, this proposal sounded rather strange. Of course, my answer was a categorical "no."

Later, weighing all the pros and cons, I started to think: *Yes, I live a very comfortable life in my own world. I love my cozy apartment, where it's just me and my son. And this could go on forever. I could drift in this state for a very, very long time because I'm perfectly comfortable.*

But what if I step outside my comfort zone again? a thought echoed in my head. Change is always an experience. I liked the stability I had worked hard to achieve. But I'm used to moving forward and constantly developing. And since the opportunity arose to drastically change my life, why not?

Important decisions should always be made with a clear head, without emotions. Before deciding on anything, analyze the situation, assess the risks, and weigh each argument.

I understood that if I started living with Antonio, my ex-husband would stop paying for my apartment. In general, by making this decision, I could incur significant losses. I was afraid to leave my comfortable world, especially after my husband's betrayal, and along with that, I was also taking a financial risk.

After some thought, I came to a very simple and, as it seemed to me, brilliant solution — I would sign a contract with Antonio.

What Does it Mean to Love Yourself?

I'm not talking about selfishness or indulging your whims. I'm talking about healthy self-love, which is the foundation of our mental health and healthy relationships with others.

Evaluate how much you love yourself:

1. You take care of your body and health.

2. You maintain safe relationships and social connections.

3. You maintain a work-life balance.

4. You have hobbies, interesting activities that fulfill you.

5. You get enough sleep and allow time for recovery.

6. You fulfill your simple and accessible desires.

7. In your inner dialogue, you support yourself more often than you criticize yourself.

8. If rules or standards cause you pain, harm, or discomfort, you can abandon them.

9. You know how to set personal boundaries and defend them.

10. You allow yourself to safely experience any emotion.

Always choose yourself and never sacrifice yourself. Why would I risk exchanging the life I had carefully built for myself for a leap into the unknown?

I'll lose a lot, but what will I gain? I've already been stabbed in the back once, and it was done by the closest person to me. What if it happens again? I need guarantees, preferably written down in black and white.

Antonio took my arguments reasonably and agreed. Men tend to think in a highly structured manner. Their psychological framework operates differently from that of women, often favoring logic and clarity over emotion.

Many women are afraid that approaching financial matters so directly, formally, and bureaucratically might offend their partner or cause misunderstanding. On the contrary, when everything is clearly written down, a man receives a constructive approach that he understands. It's difficult for them to understand emotions — it's much easier for them to work with organized and clearly formulated information.

Creating the contract was a thorough and thoughtful process. It wasn't about mistrust, but about ensuring mutual understanding and stability, especially with a child involved. We spent a lot of time creating the document and bringing it to a form that would suit both of us. We argued a lot, and sometimes there were disagreements and misunderstandings. But dialogue and the ability to listen to each other saved us.

Open and honest dialogue forms the bedrock of any relationship – romantic or otherwise – laying the groundwork for mutual understanding and growth. If there's dialogue, there's a future; if there's no dialogue, the relationship is doomed.

While drafting the contract, we also began searching for the perfect home — a place that could truly become ours.

By the time we found it, I had signed the contract with Antonio. The notary was visibly taken aback, clearly unaccustomed to seeing such an arrangement.

"Will you really pay all the bills? Even when you're on vacation?"

"Yes, absolutely, without question. I will cover all bills," Antonio nodded so emphatically that the notary could barely keep up with his notes.

"And the electricity?"

"I will pay for everything!" Antonio repeated this phrase about ten times.

The core of the contract stipulated that, in the event of our separation, Antonio would provide financial support for a set period afterward. That is, if we live together for 10 years, my partner would sponsor me for five years after the separation — rent an apartment for me near a kindergarten or school, and provide financial assistance. This was necessary primarily because I was raising a child. I was determined never to find myself in a position again where I had to struggle and exhaust every avenue to provide for myself and my son.

Even before we moved into the house, our relationship had begun to evolve naturally, step by step.

We started spending more time together, going out somewhere as a couple, and going on dates. I saw how Antonio tried for me — he was ready for anything, and his words were always followed by actions.

I understood that there was potential and growth in this man — he didn't just listen to my business advice, he applied it in practice, and quite successfully. With small steps (and they are the foundation of success in business), his business began to expand. He dove into expanding his social media presence, forging new partnerships, and even treated himself to a new car — a reflection of his growing success. I saw him grow as a businessman. His personal qualities radiated an undeniable assurance that he would make an exceptional father and devoted family man.

Thus began a new stage of my life in Montreal. For the first time in a long while, I was no longer alone. I had a partner by my side, someone who brought stability and warmth back into my life. However, I knew that my stay in this city was temporary — just a phase. Circumstances had brought me here.

I've always traveled a lot and looked at different places, thinking about where I would like to live. In my youth, I dreamed of settling in London. Later, I realized it wasn't for me. I couldn't exist in a stone box, even if Buckingham Palace was visible from its windows.

I had already moved to another country once, but only out of necessity — to Canada. I wasn't going to repeat that experience; I would search for my place in the world based on my needs and desires. I realized that this decision required careful thought and deliberation, as I was now choosing not just for myself but for my child as well.

Everything had to be perfect — the climate, the business environment, education for my son, personal comfort, and, most importantly, room for growth.

Personal growth and self-improvement are at the heart of my life, driving everything I strive for.

In absolutely everything – in business, in spiritual life, in relationships – never stand still, always strive for something – that's my essence. I have the same requirements for my partner. It's important that he grows with me – both spiritually and materially.

Like two streams of water racing each other. And if one stream stops and dries up, the other will continue to flow forward — but alone.

Chapter 14: An Unbreakable Bond

I follow my intuition in raising David, though I was also seeking guidance from parenting books.

At the very beginning of motherhood, Masaru Ibuka's book, *After Three It's Too Late*, helped me immensely, and I started putting its techniques into practice. There's a widespread belief that a child can do whatever they want until the age of three and grow like a weed in a field, and only then should one focus on their development. In reality, during the first few years, a child's brain develops so rapidly that the information they encounter during this time remains with them forever. And that's precisely what the author discusses: the seeds you sow in a child before the age of three will determine the fruit they bear.

Before school, I received almost no structured learning — only my grandmother tried to teach me to read, so I wanted things to be different for my son. From an early age, I exposed David to cartoons in various languages, starting with French and Spanish, and even occasionally adding Chinese and Japanese, to nurture his subconscious aptitude for languages and broaden his auditory palette.

He was always bored listening to me read books. I could see his mind working much faster than the text progressed.

To this day, I can't understand whether I truly managed to instill in David the qualities I envisioned during pregnancy, or if I intuitively sensed what he would be like. His character, potential, abilities — my son grew up exactly as I imagined him. Even during pregnancy, I felt that inside me was a quick-witted, intelligent child with leadership qualities who wouldn't let anyone boss him around.

Given my complicated health history, I always wanted my son to grow up adapted to life and the world, not as a hothouse flower, overprotected and unable to do anything independently. And from the very beginning of breastfeeding, David didn't like being hugged and cuddled too much. Of course, sometimes he would be affectionate, like all children, but more often I heard the words, "Mom, go away." He actively explored the world and learned from his mistakes: tripped and fell — next time he'll watch his step more carefully; pinched his finger — then he won't stick it in the door again.

During my pregnancy, I experienced severe mood swings, but I was often laughing when I should have been crying. David was born a cheerful boy. Even at kindergarten, they noted this and told me, "Your son is constantly smiling; we've never seen a child like that." Children have always loved him — he attracts them like a magnet. David had only been attending his new kindergarten for a week, and I was already observing him practically kicking the door open to the classroom, beaming, and the children immediately flocking to him, hugging and kissing him. "David, what are your friends' names?" I'd ask him in the evening. He hadn't memorized them yet, but everyone already knew, loved, and awaited him.

And how he kicked me in the belly, how he thrashed! I expected a boxer, or at least a soccer player. Even during pregnancy, his character was clear to me; he was rebellious — he couldn't wait to come into this world. I couldn't sleep properly, go to the movies, or a concert — the baby simply wouldn't let me lie down or sit still. The only thing that calmed him down was classical music. I would play Mozart on my phone, hold it to my belly, and blissful silence would descend within me. During my eighth month of pregnancy in Kyiv, I constantly attended classical music concerts, and even then, the baby didn't like all the pieces, which he promptly communicated with another kick to my stomach.

When David was born, I continued to play classical music for him, even if I was in the mood for something else. My son continues to cherish classical music, finding joy and inspiration in its timeless melodies. Of course, when he learned to speak, he started asking for popular children's songs — the kind that get stuck in your head so you sing them for a week. But if I switched tracks on the playlist and classical music came on, David always asked me to leave it: "What beautiful music, Mom!" He loves Vivaldi most of all, especially *The Four Seasons*, and also Glinka and Tchaikovsky's *The Nutcracker*.

David has an impeccable sense of pitch. The moment he hears someone singing off-key, he becomes visibly uneasy and insists they stop. Once, without thinking, I gave him a microphone — a child's microphone, but loud enough to regret the purchase that same day. By evening, my ears were ringing — from how loudly and diligently my son was practicing his musical talents.

At the same time, David has a mathematical, engineering mind. He adores technology, robots, construction sets, mechanisms, and various devices. It's no wonder his first word was the universal command, "open!" My son chose the best word for a little explorer because you can open anything: a door, a jar, a box, an app on a phone... I don't think I've heard "open!" as many times in my entire life as I did during those two months when David used practically only that word.

My son is fascinated by exploring the world of gadgets — studying, tinkering, disassembling, and meticulously reassembling them like a budding engineer.

Even when I take him to an amusement park, instead of enjoying the speed and turns of the carousel like all the other children, he examines how it's built. While others happily gaze around, David carefully observes the pistons, connections, motors, cables... Like a little scientist who can't quite speak yet, but in whose head simple, yet very reasonable, algorithms are already being constructed.

"Mom, where does the water in the faucet come from? Why does it only flow when you lift the handle? And where does the hole end, where the water then drains?" A million questions arise, and David, forgetting to wash his hands, tries with all his might to see what's there, in the darkness of the drain. I'd never even thought about it — water is water. But David already has a question about how the toilet tank works: "Mom, what's making that noise? Let's open it!"

By the age of three and a half, David could effortlessly count to twenty in Russian, English, Spanish and French, impressing everyone with his natural curiosity. He developed an interest in numbers on his own. One day in a store, my son was carefully examining price tags and finally asked, "Mom, are these clocks? Why so many?" I explained that these were numbers that indicated the cost of things. When we returned home, we immediately started studying them. This isn't surprising, because Michael has a phenomenal memory and a mathematical mind, as I mentioned at the beginning of the book.

I was deliberate in choosing a partner to father my child, guided by specific values and aspirations.

I'm glad that David came into the world this way, with us. Everything happened as it should have – these are the tasks of our souls.

Regardless of whether we manage to learn our lesson and 'pass the exam' in this life, I will always be grateful to Michael for the best healthy, intelligent son. I recall the image of the coronation that came to me during a regression session — and I recognize David as that stately young man whose head was crowned. And I understand: my son came to me in his second incarnation, and Michael and I are reliving a certain scenario that we didn't live through the last time. Needless to say, today my son and I have many more opportunities for self-development!

Mathematics and classical music are excellent for brain development, but that doesn't necessarily mean David's life will be inextricably linked to them in the future. I believe in recognizing a child's potential and predispositions and gently guiding them in that direction — like a warm, subtle current. The captain of the ship should decide where to turn. It's wonderful that he enjoys something, that something captures his attention and inspires him. In any case, it will help him in life.

I always imagined myself as a hockey mom, and it seemed like the best activity for any boy — sport, endurance, strength, drive...

But David, having tried it, showed no interest in hockey. Now he goes to karate, as well as speech development classes, which help him practice focusing.

Focus is still a bit of a challenge, but the stage beckons him. If there's a stage in a hotel, restaurant, or anywhere else, David is instantly drawn to it. He doesn't understand yet what he wants to do there, but the desire for public performance is already evident. His personality matrix and natal chart agree with me on this.

A child needs to be given the opportunity to develop the skill they are most drawn to. If a child is drawn to music, it's worth getting them musical toys; if they like to draw, buy them brushes and an easel. On the one hand, I give David freedom of action, and on the other, knowing my child's characteristics, I gently guide him on his right path.

It was also always important to me that my child have one kindergarten, one school, one neighborhood, and the same friends. Life had shuffled me around quite a bit through kindergartens and schools all over the city, so I knew perfectly well what it was like, and I didn't want that for my child. For a person, especially a small one, the feeling of home is important — something of their own — familiar and special.

I gave myself five years to determine where and with whom I would settle down, carefully shaping the foundation of our lives. During that time, David and I traveled extensively, and I paid close attention to where he felt happiest and where the environment suited him best.

One sunny afternoon, as we lounged by a sparkling blue pool in Bali, surrounded by a paradise of lush greenery and tranquility, David suddenly announced, "I want to go to Canada." His declaration caught me off guard. How could he long for Canada while basking in a tropical dream? “I want to shovel snow,” he explained with sparkling eyes. His love for snow is unmatched!

As for me, I’m no fan of the cold, so our snow adventures usually end quickly — within five minutes, David notices I’ve already turned into a human icicle. But to my relief, Antonio steps in to fill the gap, indulging David’s snowy enthusiasm. Together, they build snowmen, have playful snowball fights, and even venture onto the slopes for snowboarding or skiing. Watching them share this joy warms me in a way the winter chill cannot.

Five years are almost up, and that very moment is approaching — soon David will start school, so every decision I make becomes not just important, but life-altering. Nothing is more important to me now than the environment my son will be in. What kind of classmates he will have, who their parents are, what kind of homes he will visit.

Unfortunately (or fortunately?), I couldn’t protect David from frequently changing kindergartens and peer groups. But despite everything, he still has that inner sense of home and his own neighborhood. They say frequent changes of place are not good for a small child, but I see the opposite: David feels comfortable in any group, easily integrates into it, adapts to any changes, and is like a fish in water everywhere — no matter what body of water he’s placed in.

One day, his grandmother, Michael’s mother, called him, and my son, taking the phone from me, went to his room to show her his toys. I could hear their conversation perfectly through the closed door.

"Grandma, I go to school," my son boasted, to my surprise.

"Which one? A Russian one?"

"No, my Mexican school. I like it so much!"

"Wow, and what do you do there?"

I couldn’t make out what followed, but my son enthusiastically shared his delights.

In the evening, while we were driving in the car, I couldn't resist and asked, "David, what's this Mexican school you were telling Grandma about on the phone?"

"Mom, what are you talking about? My favorite Mexican school!"

"Son, you've never gone to one."

"I have! Remember in Mexico? There was a pool there, and my friends and I drew."

The ‹Mexican school" turned out to be the kids' club at our hotel. Now I at least know what he envisions as the ideal school.

I understand that David is attached to me, but his personal development is more important to me than my desire for him to always be by my side. Therefore, I'm already gradually preparing my son for separation.

Indian wisdom says: "A child is a guest in your home. Feed them, teach them, and let them go."

Imagine that a stranger, or even an alien, came to you. And you need to tell them about this world, explain everything, teach them the basics. And if it seems that there's a whole life ahead for this, that's not the case at all. We are given a little over 10 years to show a child, through our own lens, what is good and what is bad, how the world works, and how to live in it. And then we nudge them so they can build their own lives.

Honestly, selfishness helps a lot in teaching a child independence. We are all living people, and sometimes I really wanted to sleep in on the weekend, but there was David, who woke up at the crack of dawn and was already demanding food and cartoons. I purposefully gave him instructions, and he quickly memorized where the cereal was, where the milk is, and how to make breakfast from it. Now, sometimes on Sunday mornings, after eating on his own, he brings me the phone so I can turn on something for him to watch. My son doesn't have unrestricted access to the internet, but I've carefully curated a selection of cartoons and programs that offer both entertainment and valuable learning opportunities. And that's it — I can go back to sleep.

I believe you need to make life easier for both yourself and your child. This won't happen if you tie them to yourself and don't give them any independence.

When David can't do something, I don't rush to help him immediately. He gets frustrated, trying to tie his shoelaces, which keep slipping out of his small, clumsy fingers and refuse to form a neat knot with a bow. I don't try to interfere, but just try to support him. I tell him, "You're doing great! You'll get it." And then everything depends on him, and he understands that perfectly.

I see that my son is subtly adopting my outlook on life and its challenges. One day, a client of mine came over and brought David a toy. He couldn't figure out how to turn it on and asked the girl to help him. But she couldn't figure it out either, and then he delivered the motivational phrase: "You'll get it, I believe in you." If only each of us had someone to say that every time we felt discouraged!

Chapter 15:
The Stratification of Reality

I once laughed at Antonio when the Akashic Records told him I would be his wife. Now, I am turning to this tool myself. I approached my first session with a skeptical mindset. I had learned it was possible to communicate with the soul of a deceased person, and my intention was to speak with my grandmother. If they tried to deceive me, I would know immediately. I wouldn't confuse my grandmother with anyone else.

The ceremony was conducted by a Mexican woman with a hereditary gift for reading the Records. It's only recently that we learned about the Records, while in Mexico it's an ancient ritual. Imagine my surprise when the woman spoke to me in my grandmother's words and with her familiar intonations. I felt her presence — her voice, her warmth, and her light filled the entire space, but when the Mexican woman finished speaking, my grandmother disappeared in an instant, as though with a snap of her fingers.

It was strange, a little frightening, but it left no doubt — it wasn't a deception.

One day, Antonio consulted the Records, and what he discovered stunned me. I knew that, strangely enough, he had Scottish blood, but I never connected this fact with the large birthmark on his chest, and I certainly never thought that in a previous incarnation we had known each other. Moreover, we loved each other and almost got married. Yes, that very same paternal commander to whom I was promised in a past life — it was none other than Antonio! I clearly remembered where he was wounded then, and the birthmark was in that exact spot.

Now I believed in Akashic Records, and decided to go for a soul reading session. “The Akashic Records read the general information space: past, present, future, and all possible outcomes of events,” the Mexican woman explained. “They provide the information you need to know right now. Every soul has its own book, and yours says that you can read everything you need from the field yourself. Don’t be afraid, but soon your abilities will begin to open. You will subtly feel people, understand their thoughts, see what they are hiding. But start with plants and animals — it’s a purer channel than a human.”

I thought about it — indeed, every tree that has been growing in the park for decades, or even a century, has seen so much. Every day hundreds of people pass by it, and it remembers even those who are long gone from this earth. “You need to relax more and listen to the meditation on opening the third eye. Feel the ground little by little,” the Mexican woman added.

This information hit me like a ton of bricks. Antonio picked me up to take me to the gym, and on the way, I recounted the entire conversation to him, realizing that the topic frankly frightened me and it was still unclear what to do with all of this.

Finding myself in a modern, stylish gym, I felt like I had woken up from an overly realistic dream. The fear receded in the face of the familiar atmosphere, and after looking around, I headed for the treadmill. No, I need to deal with this once and for all, right now. I immediately turned on the third eye opening meditation and felt... well, I didn’t feel anything. Complete nonsense, it doesn’t work. What third eye? With a clear conscience, I decided to forget about it and about talking to trees.

It was a day off, and we spent it together with Antonio and David. My mother cooked for us, everyone ate the same thing, but only I became so ill that night that I thought I was going to die.

I vomited endlessly, my body ached, all my bones felt like they were being pulled out of me alive. Medicine didn't help because nothing stayed in my stomach. All I did was crawl from the bed to the toilet and back. I was literally turning inside out.

I gathered my strength and decided to take a shower. As soon as the water touched my feverish, goosebump-covered skin, it was as if a radio losing its signal, jumping from one station to another, started playing in my head. I saw how the water flowing down my body was at first a dark thundercloud with plump sides, pouring down on the earth, feeling incredible relief after the leaden heaviness. Then it ran down as an icy stream from the mountaintop to its foot, flowed into a shallow, noisy river, which then carried its waters into another — full-flowing and slow. I heard the voices and laughter of people who came to this river to swim, relax, and fish. And then, against its will, the water was drawn into wide pipes.

I thought I was going crazy. How else could I explain the fact that... water was talking to me? Quickly turning off the tap, I wrapped myself in a bathrobe and shuffled to the bedroom. I tried to sleep, but I could no longer understand where the dream was and where reality was. As soon as I closed my eyes, bloody, realistic scenes unfolded before me. I fell into a nightmare that was indistinguishable from reality. Khrushchev-era buildings, new buildings, fir trees planted in alleys. Torn bodies lying between the houses. A dog dragging a piece of human flesh...

My head and stomach turned cold, the blood drained from my face and hands, and I was overcome with such a wave of weakness that I could barely stand. What did I just see?!

I spent four days in this semi-delirious state, and the only thought close to reality during this time was: no more third eye opening meditations!

After recovering, I tried to forget the terrible visions — anything can be dreamt in such a state.

Soon I flew to New York for the weekend to visit a friend, also from Kyiv. During the day, we walked 15 kilometers around the city, and we decided to watch the sunset in Manhattan, where she lives. We went up to the roof of her building, which offered a gorgeous panoramic view: skyscrapers rose in slender rows, Central Park nestled comfortably in the center as a green rectangle, and the top and spire of the Empire State Building glowed in different colors. Such beauty took my breath away, and so as not to miss a single moment, I quickly took out my phone. A newsfeed notification popped up: Kyiv is being bombed...

I looked up from my screen. Beneath my feet lay New York, shimmering with lights, bustling with life and movement. It didn't align at all with the realization that somewhere across the ocean, my hometown was trembling under explosions. If war had truly begun, why hadn't the whole world stopped? Why did I continue to see this perfect picture before me? There must be a mistake somewhere.

Silently, I showed my friend the notification. Her face changed, and she pulled out her phone, too. Without a word, we both immediately started searching for more news, simultaneously calling and texting everyone who had remained there.

My brain couldn't keep up with the rapid succession of events and tried unsuccessfully to reconcile two images: one peaceful, the other terrifying — but it couldn't. My thoughts jumped around: how good that Mom was currently in Canada, sitting with David. But Dad was in Kyiv, along with my relatives and friends, and simply 3 million people who, just an hour ago, were sleeping in their beds.

Many were still sleeping — I was getting sleepy replies from people who weren't yet aware of what was happening. I woke them up, they called their acquaintances, and maybe this saved someone's life. "Masha, what war? Why would we leave the city?" another sleepy voice answered me through the phone, and my friend added immediately, "I have a massage today, and then I wanted to go to a burger joint."

"What war? Let someone else believe in all these tales, it will all pass us by" — I'd heard this often before, especially from young people. You could understand them, especially those who lived in Donetsk and had been right in the middle of this situation for years. The human psyche is designed in such a way that it can get used to any nightmare and consider it the norm. But I felt it, with my whole being, that it was all true, which is why I called my mom to come stay with me. She was also nervous and said they were sitting on a powder keg.

All night, my friend and I stayed in contact with family and friends in Kyiv, and the next morning, she took me for a walk around New York, because we both needed a distraction. Sightseeing wasn't happening — we were glued to our phones, endlessly scrolling through the newsfeed with new details and horrific footage.

Reality continued to split in two. Standing on a path in Central Park, raising my gaze to the tallest building I had ever seen, I couldn't understand where I was. For the first time in my life, the picture before my eyes felt like an illusion. All that remained was to be an observer, because I couldn't change anything, couldn't help in any way. This soul-wrenching feeling was struggling to break free. It was ready to erupt into a scream, but I fought with all my strength to maintain my composure. What could I do? I was already doing everything I could.

Such situations teach you that sometimes all you can do is go with the flow, trying to notice what the universe is showing you at that time, what it's giving you. Perhaps at this moment, another leap in growth is occurring, because

we are learning to emotionally process a situation we've never encountered before. We are learning to live with the fact that we are walking through a luxurious park while our relatives are hiding from bombs in basements.

At first, I took what was happening very hard. I joined a demonstration in Times Square, helped refugees with paperwork for moving to Canada, donated money to aid victims, actively worked in Telegram channels, and shared important information — I did everything I could.

Soon, news channels were filled with horrific footage in which I recognized destroyed houses, fir tree alleys, and piles of mutilated bodies. These were the towns of Irpin and Bucha, and the first truly candid footage of what was really happening. Eyewitnesses posted one video after another in Telegram channels, and everything inside me went cold with horror.

Irpin was blocked from all sides and bombs fell directly on houses whose residents were left with no way to escape the siege. Craters blackened where buildings once stood, shells tore people apart in the streets. Even after the shelling stopped, Ukrainian troops were forbidden to enter the cities to at least retrieve the bodies, which stray dogs had already begun to drag away.

The survivors were forced to step over the bodies of the dead.

I scrolled through the feed with numb fingers, swallowed tears, and remembered where I had seen all this before. Could it be that the meditation hadn't been in vain after all, and this was a shamanic illness?[7]

[7] Shamanic illness — the awakening of a gift through psychological suffering, accompanied by vivid visions. It is believed that this is how the spirits demand that the future shaman accept their power, while the shaman refuses and resists.

For a long time, I couldn't accept that people voluntarily stayed under the bombs and didn't want to leave, risking not only their own lives but also the lives of their children. Why didn't they run, try to find a solution, but simply stay in their warm, familiar place, which had now ceased to be such? Of course, people had their reasons for staying, but when I heard them, it only intensified my inner conflict. Some justified it with elderly parents, but there were countless cases around the world where families evacuated even

I wholeheartedly wanted to help, but an anxious bell rang inside: people don't want to help themselves, so how can I do it?

Even Dad flatly refused to move in with his brother in the UK. "Where will I go? I'll die in my own bed," he stubbornly repeated. When city services warned that there would be no heating in the winter, this turned out to be the only argument that worked on Dad.

The hope for a positive outcome was very faint, but we still managed to get Dad out — and even with the dog. I arranged for him to travel with people to Germany, to our relatives. From there, my brother picked him up by car, as I was worried about Dad — with his weak heart, flying seemed too risky.

And then I realized — those who truly wanted to leave had already left, thereby changing their lives. If people stayed in Ukraine, it means their souls chose this path for a reason. They were meant to go through this transformation. Some even went to war, and perhaps this was a decision made by their souls, or maybe just their egos. Whatever they explained it by, I believe that fighting for the political position of other people means laying down your life for the interests of others.

I don't evaluate the world through the prism of politics, religion, or ideologies – I rely solely on my own feelings.

I Open Myself to the World

No matter what happened, I kept moving forward, step by step, towards my true self.

As expected, my imposter syndrome became an obstacle. The number nine energy in my numerology chart constantly fuels doubts: I don't know something, I lack experience... It's like looking in a mirror and seeing a distorted reflection. People with this number can study their whole lives and, even with a degree, still believe they're not competent enough, that it's too early to share their knowledge and present themselves to the world as a mentor, because they're still 'nobody' — unlike others.

But at the same time, I also have the number one energy, which is reflected in my soul's purpose. This signifies leadership qualities, a pioneering spirit, and the ability to inspire and lead others. Ones are magicians, capable of transforming their space. I knew all this perfectly well, but I was waiting for someone else to highlight it.

Behind every teacher, there is a teacher – it's an *eternal* system.

Another obstacle for me was the opinion of others. I had to transform from a blonde girl with beautiful photos on her social media page into a different person. For 30 years, I presented one side of myself to the world, and suddenly I needed to take a serious step and open up, show who I really am. I had to show the depth, and the inner qualities hidden beneath a beautiful but superficial image. Not sharing the accumulated baggage of knowledge and experience meant going into the negative for me, so I stepped over my fears.

Criticism, of course, didn't take long to arrive, and I started playing out the worst-case scenarios in my mind. What's the worst that could happen? They gossip behind my back, judge me, and how much time will they spend on it? Half an hour or an hour? Constant discussion and judgment are a sign that you're doing everything right because success doesn't exist without criticism; such is the fate of all public figures.

The opinions of others shouldn't hinder your self-expression – it's important to detach yourself from them.

And then people started telling me, "You're so great, you're not afraid to express yourself, but I'm scared." It turns out many people are afraid to open up, and I can serve as an example for them! As I realized this, my fears gradually subsided.

In Bali, I accidentally found a very young woman who was involved in personality unpacking and personal brand mentoring. I'm not easily convinced, but she had a special energy and a precise understanding of what she was talking about. She charged a fee for promotion that, at the time, seemed substantial to me. For that money, I could have hired someone to manage my social media for several months. I decided that I didn't have to buy the full promotion right away; I could pay for one meeting and see how it felt.

From the very first meeting, the mentor won me over. I accepted the challenge, and we started working. It turned out that I completely failed to see the value of my own experience — the brief I had to fill out opened my eyes to this. To all the questions about what I currently have, I answered by downplaying it. It seemed like there was nothing to say, and none of it mattered to anyone.

Analyzing my life through the prism of the current situation, focusing on who I am now, I seemed to have forgotten what I had been through.

But the past is the baggage you carry with you – your greatest asset.

Everything I once dismissed — my business, emigration, overcoming illness, and difficult relationships — suddenly took on a whole new meaning. It was a bright flash that blinded me for a second and then gave me the opportunity to see what I hadn't noticed before. And I not only have something to tell my mentor about, but also something to write a book about!

If before I had still doubted whether it was worth spending money on such mentoring or whether it would be better to hire an SMM team instead, now all doubts melted away.

The best investment you can ever make is in yourself. When you invest in yourself – in revealing your inner self – you will never lose, you will never fail. Our greatest value is intellect, development, worldview, inner core.

These are the sources from which absolutely all spheres of life begin. And then people, events, and circumstances are attracted and drawn to this energy, to this core. And there's no need to copy anyone — look inside yourself, find the treasure of your unique individuality.

The transformation I dreamed of in Bali finally happened. Three and a half weeks later, I returned to Canada a completely different person. It felt like they opened the door to the real world and handed me a map to navigate it. "That's it, you're on your own," they told me, and I was ready to take on that responsibility.

Information can come from anywhere, but whether to take it or not is up to the individual. Just like when to turn in a dif-

ferent direction and choose a different destiny. Everything depends only on ourselves.

Having started to open up on social media, I thought about what else I could offer people. I had successfully built up Antonio's business, and I had other successful cases with friends and acquaintances, such as helping to develop a factory. In addition, for the last 10 years, I've maintained an active business stance and have constantly been in the entrepreneurial flow. Most of my friends had their own businesses, and we constantly discussed work processes, came up with ideas together, drew up business plans, and helped each other. This became my image and lifestyle, but I didn't want to go into this field directly — I wanted to help people not just achieve financial well-being, but to live happily.

At first, I decided to do this to some extent for charitable purposes, so I offered my services for donations, so that people could send as much as they felt appropriate. My energies show that I have a huge need to constantly help people anyway, whether for money or for free. But the balance of give and take is important, and I didn't want my charity to cause something to be taken away from my clients later on for balance.

There's always a price for any work done, even if it's symbolic, otherwise balance might be restored in unexpected ways. Because the world is like a set of scales, always seeking balance.

Every client I mentored taught me something as well. My first client was a man who had once offered me a job developing his art gallery. I, however, proposed a different kind of development for him. We agreed he would pay when he saw results, but he constantly forgot to complete assignments, always finding excuses. After analyzing the situation, I realized he enjoyed wallowing in it all; even debts and loans suited him. Moreover, he didn't value my work because it was free.

So, I decided to approach mentoring more professionally, knowing how much time and energy I invest in each client and how much each hour would cost me if I invested it in my own business. My approach to mentoring also evolved. Previously, my focus was purely on marketing strategies and metrics. This time, I decided to incorporate not only all my business skills, but also personality matrix analysis.

Clients came immediately: a mother and daughter, owners of an art gallery featuring works by artists from around the world. They didn't understand how to move forward and grow. The mother, an elegant woman in her 60s and a great art connoisseur, was old-school and didn't trust modern technology.

I began by creating personality matrices for them, their partners, and their team members to visually demonstrate each person's capabilities, their compatibility, and how they could support each other. Sometimes, two individuals might be good specialists with excellent potential, but when their matrices combine in a team, there's a destructive explosion — a powerful wind fanning a small fire into an all-consuming inferno.

When I started consulting with these clients, my work flowed. It became immediately clear that the gallery owners needed to delegate social media management and develop a clear operational strategy — a casual approach wouldn't work. I advised them to focus on sales in America, as the European, Russian, and Asian markets were oversaturated. I provided them with strategic and marketing tools. The result was a symbiosis of numerology and business development, unlocking enormous potential.

I realized I enjoy participating in businesses as a crisis manager — entering a project when a company is stagnating or experiencing rapid growth and doing whatever is necessary to help it soar. A fresh perspective and a sense of current trends help me see what can aid development at any given moment.

As I began showcasing my knowledge of personality matrices, I continued to delve deeper into myself, honing my strengths and not focusing on fears. For example, the significant number 17 in my own matrix indicates that I need visibility, public exposure, and that my strength lies in my voice. This doesn't mean everything will come easily — the potential is there, but it needs to be realized.

I started doing live streams, and my mentor challenged me to make a video about my life. Overcoming my reservations, I began sharing my story, which resonated deeply.

No one could have imagined the events hidden behind the beautiful pictures I presented. No one knew that I had overcome cancer and had been left alone in a foreign country without my husband. People wrote to me, "Masha, how is that possible? I've known you for so many years and am only hearing about this now." It's not surprising, as even my ex-husband's relatives only learned about their new family member six months prior.

This honesty proved to be a step towards healing. By telling my story, I cleansed myself, lifted a weight from my soul, and became myself again. Before, I hadn't realized the burden of my secrets and how easy it is to live openly, from the heart.

And then, I finally became indifferent to the opinions of others. Come to think of it, I started prioritizing other people's opinions during my relationship with Michael, when every step, every gesture had to be analyzed through the lens of "what will his relatives say?" I chose to worry about what others thought.

Now, I'm attracting so many amazing people and events, the kind that are hard to find even in ten years of life. This energetic whirlwind has been drawn to me in just one year. In just a year, I've undergone a radical transformation.

Sacred Medicine for Soul Healing

My massage therapist once suggested I try Hawaiian massage – it incorporates many breathing techniques that can allow deeper access to the subconscious. I was having disagreements with Antonio at the time, and something clicked inside me – I had to try it.

Previously, my massage therapist had told me a lot about her experiences with Latin American ceremonies and 'sacred' medicine. I didn't understand why I needed these experiments, but when she mentioned magic mushrooms[8], which I'd heard about from various sources, I wanted to add mushroom tea to the Hawaiian massage.

"You're stressed right now, and to truly relax, it's better to drink this tea. From a scientific point of view, some mushrooms cause hallucinations," the massage therapist explained, pouring boiling water into a small teapot. "But in reality, during this time, the chattering mind switches off, and that inner voice, the one that's constantly communicating with us, answers us, you understand?"

"Yeah," I smiled, turning the still-empty cup in my hands. "That voice has an opinion on everything. Listen, can I drive afterward? Can I leave my car in your parking lot?"

"You can drive. It's just tea with mushrooms; you'll be completely sane, just connected to your subconscious and your flow."

---

[8] The book presents solely the author's personal experience and their perspective on certain areas of life. The author does not encourage readers to use mushrooms or other described methods for any purpose and does not advocate their use. By using the information presented in this publication, you agree that the author of the book is not responsible for any decision you make, or any action you take or do not take, regarding your health based on the information contained herein.

I nodded understandingly. The tea steeped, and a steaming stream flowed into my cup. A herbal aroma spread through the massage room. It was hot, 30–32 degrees Celsius, or even more; this temperature is necessary to fully relax during a Hawaiian massage. Quiet Hawaiian-shamanic music played, candles burned, and everything was conducive to fully immersing myself in the practice and connecting with myself.

When the tea was finished, the massage therapist asked me to lie down on the heated massage table and warned:

"At some point, you might feel nauseous. Try to ignore it and endure. It's just that very switch of consciousness, the one that never shuts off, turning off."

She warmed some massage oil in her hands and began working, guiding my breathing and synchronizing with me. I felt my body fully relax, inch by inch: the tension in my forehead melted away, my jaw unclenched, and my shoulders and spine softened. My arms and legs felt weightless, as if they could float.

Finally, the relaxation reached my brain (although not a muscle, it's the most tense part of the body), and I did feel nauseous. A tunnel seemed to form in front of me, which I had to go through — that's how I would get to my subconscious, I guessed. Multicolored mandalas swirled and merged, like the shifting pieces of a kaleidoscope forming intricate patterns.

I don't know how much time passed, but suddenly, crystal clarity came to my mind. Information began to come to me — open and understandable now, but I would forget it all, lose it, upon returning to my normal state! And even if I didn't forget, my sober mind would deny everything and say that I remembered it wrong and that it was all nonsense. Therefore, I needed to make an effort, open my heavy eyelids, and write everything down, risking losing this wonderful picture in the same instant.

"Give me paper and a pen, please," I asked the massage therapist, hearing my voice as if through a thick layer of water.

Using my phone to take notes felt wrong at that moment. I tried not to lose the state and continued watching what was being shown to me with one eye, while the other followed the scribbles that filled the paper line by line. If only I could just say it all aloud, and a special assistant would write it down for me...

It took all my willpower, and I filled two A4 sheets on both sides with insights. Mostly, they were quite earthly things: who I needed to take on as business partners, how this partnership should look, and what results it would bring me.

Surprisingly, during the session, I felt the presence of my childhood friend Anna's sister. Anna and I hadn't spoken in 15 years, and her sister had died in a car accident shortly before our paths diverged. "Anna needs help," said the sister, whose existence I had already managed to forget.

To my surprise, the very next day, Anna reacted to one of my posts. "Hi! I was just thinking about you," I wrote. "Can we talk? We've kind of lost touch." My friend didn't reply, but a couple of days later, she sent me her new number.

"Everything's fine," Anya replied curtly to my question about how she was doing, and I felt her putting on some familiar social mask.

I still tried to get her talking, recalling mutual acquaintances and funny little things from our past. Anya barely reacted at first, but then gradually began to laugh with me.

"You know, I'm alone with a four-month-old baby," she suddenly revealed.

"Wow, you have a baby? Congratulations! Your parents must be thrilled! Are they helping you?"

Anya came from a wonderful, wealthy family of successful dentists. Her parents doted on Anya's sister, who was 10 years older, and her death was a great shock to them.

"Mom..." Anya hesitated. "After my sister's death, Mom gradually began to lose her sight. It's been 7 years since she went completely blind, and I'm taking care of her. Dad is also very ill, bedridden, and needs a hip replacement. So, as you understand, I'm the one helping them now..."

A quiet sob was heard on the other end of the line. So much for "everything's fine."

You can only help those who are willing to ask for it, and it's incredibly difficult when someone won't even admit to themselves that they're struggling. They close themselves off not just with a mask, but with whole armor, inside which they will eventually break themselves and everything around them.

That's how I first experienced the incredible effect of Hawaiian massage and mushroom tea. I'm aware of cases where people use such means for relaxation and might go to an inappropriate place for that state, like a club. But this tool must be used carefully — without the right setting, it can leave someone emotionally vulnerable.

Just as microbes cling to an open wound, negative energy enters an open channel, trying to take root within a person with tenacious tendrils. And then natural medicine, instead of healing, makes you vulnerable. It cannot be used this way. Medicine for the soul should be taken in the right atmosphere and energy, alongside an experienced guide.

In reality, such a state can be achieved through breathing practices, if a person is sufficiently experienced. But most people simply cannot relax to that extent. t's easy to cleanse the stomach, but the brain... It's not easy to throw off the shackles of fear and the protective reflexes that help us survive. This tough nut cannot simply be cracked — it must open with the help of gentle force, on its own, from within.

I started hosting tea ceremonies, surrounded by people eager to join me on new journeys of self-discovery. As soon as I offered my own lived experience, they immediately agreed, knowing I wouldn't suggest anything that could harm them. Then word of mouth started to work.

Soon I was convinced that 70–80% of people see the same tunnel that I do. For some, it's also filled with mandalas and ornaments, while others encounter various entities.

At the next stage, each person enters a realm that feels entirely unique to them.

For example, one client saw himself in a castle and said that he was alone there, with no one to talk to — this is how the subconscious offers clues. In one of the rooms, he discovered a dragon — his totem animal. Another client of mine flew on a dragon, a third transformed into this mythical creature (which, by the way, is seen quite often).

No matter what the space looks like or who inhabits it, people often describe it as a place that feels deeply familiar, as if they've been there before — even in their dreams. And that's exactly right, because someone might find themselves in a past life, and someone else in a parallel one. It's difficult to imagine, but we simultaneously live through several variations of events, which can unfold differently depending on our decisions. During a mushroom ceremony, a person sometimes sees this fork in the road.

When a client describes the space they've entered, I ask them to describe how they see themselves within it. Regardless of their gender and age in their current incarnation, they might see themselves as a boy, a girl, a wise old man, an animal, even as energy — anything at all.

Then, together, we gradually string beads of answers onto a thread. In our ordinary state, we simply don't see them, but they are always within us, lying on a shelf, waiting for us to finally reach out and take them. We can understand the causes of illnesses — not only our own but also those of our relatives. All cause-and-effect relationships become clear, and scattered links assemble into a chain. Clients have thousands of questions, and they are all different.

I developed my own unique method, which I assembled brick by brick from various techniques and continue to refine every day, combining techniques: matrix, hypnosis, breathing practices, sacred medicine, raising kundalini energy... And all this during a single tea ceremony. I am a guide on this path. I always read the client's matrix beforehand to see how everything functions as a whole, what their soul's purpose is, and which specific clues to look for in the subconscious to begin fulfilling their destiny in this incarnation.

I never cease to be amazed at how unique each case is and how differently the ceremony affects each person depending on their level of preparedness. Some can only look at their lives on a mundane level, while others travel between worlds, saying, "Well? What new level are we opening today?" And some come to me with a look that says, "Well? And what are you going to tell me? They say this completely changes lives. We'll see, we'll see..." Later, that same person hugs me in tears, thanking me for crossing their path.

After the mushroom ceremony, even those who live a mundane, Groundhog Day existence experience a shift in their perception of the world. Vivid colors, sounds, and smells return, as if new receptors appear, or we return to childhood, when the world was magical and full of wonder. Therefore, I recommend that clients take a walk in nature immediately after the ceremony to see it with new eyes. There, they continue to have epiphanies, and everything around them is seen completely differently: every drop of water, every blade of grass, every feather of a bird sitting on a tree — the world opens up in detail from all sides.

Then situations begin to unfold in the most unexpected ways. For example, a client recently wrote to me: "Masha, remember how during the ceremony I got the feeling that my connection with two people hadn't been broken? I was surprised then, because we haven't spoken for three years, what connection could there be? So, one of them unexpectedly contacted me today about a completely trivial matter that we resolved long ago. I even jumped in my chair when I saw who was calling!"

This is how the energetic connection with a person plays out, who most likely didn't understand why they suddenly wanted to call an old acquaintance. It's worth bringing this information out of the subconscious, and the person starts thinking about you. And then chains of interconnections are launched — all that remains is to admire the process.

But most of all, I love working with serious transformations, with situations where there is a concrete before and after, a contrast that is visible to the naked eye. I'm interested in the amplitude of development; not just tweaking the result a little, but triggering incredible changes.

Methods of Self-Discovery and Keys to Understanding Yourself

I sense everything changing in this world, and it's time for us to reflect: why did we come into this life? What talents lie hidden within us, and how can we develop them?

Each of us is born with specific energies and a particular purpose to follow. It's like an avatar with basic settings and potential.

In other words, a person, even one newly arrived in this world, isn't a blank slate upon which anything can be written. Traces of past lives remain, although deciphering these faint impressions can be incredibly challenging. I see each person as a diamond that can be transformed into a sparkling brilliant if it's cut and polished correctly.

To achieve a high-quality cut and not lose anything along the way, it's crucial to deeply understand your true essence, your strengths, and weaknesses.

Each person is beautifully unique; the challenge is to unlock the depths of your own potential and purpose. You can do this through trial and error, or you can use the many tools available for self-discovery.

I always smile when I hear, "I went to an astrologer, a numerologist, a Human Design specialist — they all say the same thing." Of course, specialists will say similar things because they're talking about the same individual, just viewing them through the lens of different methods, each valuable in its own way.

I've examined myself through numerous prisms, but the first was astrology, and it continues to help me. It's a precise, ancient science based on numbers and rigorous methods. Even a skeptic can't deny the Moon's influence on earthly processes, such as ocean tides and the female cycle. Similarly, other celestial bodies impact our lives. Even the lines on our hands mirror our natal chart: the Sun line, Mars line, Girdle of Venus, Ring of Saturn, and so on. If you still doubt astrology's validity, study ancient predictions and compare them to historical events.

It's essential to consult an experienced professional, not someone who's just completed a short course, but someone who has received at least three years of astrological education. Also, don't look for the cheapest option — you only pay for a natal chart once, so it's better to receive all the accurate information upfront.

When I began my self-discovery journey, an astrologer suggested I undergo rectification — calculating the precise birth time based on key life events: illnesses, marriage, childbirth. I was always certain I was born at 7:00 am Kyiv time, as recorded at the hospital. Imagine my surprise when I was given a completely different time — 5:55 am. Apparently, the night shift registered all newborns at the same time before handing over to the next shift.

The most striking insight from my natal chart was discovering my Moon in Scorpio, a placement that signifies both immense challenge and extraordinary power. This placement is as challenging as it is powerful; a person engages in deep introspection, constantly transforms as an individual, burns out, and rises again like a phoenix.

A Moon in Scorpio grants its bearer the ability to become, for example, a psychotherapist working with complex cases or a detective investigating serial killings. Such a person isn't afraid of what would overwhelm a typical psyche and possesses the skill to get to the heart of the matter. Back then, the astrologer told me I would counsel people and likely choose esotericism or psychology, fields to which I have a strong predisposition. I hadn't even considered such a talent. Like a pioneering explorer, I had discovered a new land, and it was up to me to cultivate it.

In 2022, in Cancun, right after my birthday, I ordered a solar return reading[9]. It's a useful tool for understanding which periods are best for focusing on specific matters, such as family or changing a child's preschool. This time, the stars revealed that I would gradually approach my life's work throughout the follow-

[9] An individualized personal horoscope, calculated for the upcoming year, starting from the person's birth date. (This is often referred to as a Solar Return.)

ing year. Still unsure what this meant, I enrolled in design school, as the astrologer had also noted my unconventional worldview. He described it as incredibly beautiful and different from how others perceive things. Although I enjoy drawing and do so intuitively, my studies revealed that I couldn't pursue design as a career. Besides creating beautiful images, it requires precise calculations, accurate measurements, meticulous attention to detail, and even monotony. That's definitely not for me.

But it's important to try, to experience, to test the waters, and to be certain that something isn't a good fit. It's not enough to simply say, It's not enough to say, 'This isn't for me' — you need to dig deeper and understand why. For example, someone might dislike mathematics, but that doesn't mean they won't enjoy accounting. Yes, it also involves numbers, but the calculations are different, and there's also the aspect of order and structure — perhaps that's precisely what they need? By trying, we can gain a clearer and deeper understanding of ourselves, fine-tune the strings of our soul, and discover our reference points.

What I can do every day is work with people. I'm fascinated by studying personality structures, understanding how people think, and finding the cause-and-effect relationships behind their experiences. I love exploring these connections, unraveling one thread at a time until the full picture becomes clear.

I also appreciate astrology because it can answer the question of which environment, which place, is suitable for a person to live in. Astrological characteristics directly influence how we feel in certain geographical locations: where we can learn best, where our business performance will be higher, where we'll become parents, and so on.

It occurred to me one day that if someone asked me which places on the planet I associate myself with, I would answer: California, Bali, Italy. Italy represents delicious food, aesthetics in the details, design solutions, life as art, *dolce far niente*. California embodies a frenetic pace of inspiration, urbanization, a concentration of great minds of our generation, and has everything: oceans, greenery, cacti, snow... Bali evokes subtle sensitivity, unity with nature, flowers, jungles, waterfalls, freedom. These are places where I feel comfortable. So why did I spend so much time living in cold Canada, which felt like a cage?

The planets in my natal chart give me a lot of water, but water always freezes at low temperatures. My body floods with fluid, which turns to ice and paralyzes my whole system. Now I've found an explanation for why I can't do anything in a cold climate; I don't even want to leave the house, everything is a struggle, and even the simplest actions become a serious ordeal.

Water is also an element that can both adapt and take any form, as well as break through a dam, overflowing its banks and flooding everything around. Knowing my subtle peculiarities, I already understand where my water can flow freely, and where I should redirect it to obtain an endless circulation of energy, my own personal source of inspiration.

The world is simple and understandable; it's people who tend to complicate everything. Imagine being a cactus meant to thrive in the desert, but constantly trying to survive in the freezing Arctic. It just doesn't work. But why, if a different path is destined for you?

I consult with professional astrologers. For instance, as I mentioned in Chapter 12, I timed the opening of my first company in Canada to align with a 'millionaire's aspect' — an astrologically auspicious period for financial success.

Now I have three astrologers whom I can consult with the same question. If all three confirm the correctness of the decision I'm leaning towards, then I'll make it. If there are discrepancies, I'll look for other clues.

It's important to rely on various sources and not make decisions based on the opinion of just one person.

You can consult specialists who use different methods. For example, Human Design is fascinating because it reveals a person's strengths, weaknesses, and how they interact with the world around them. But one of my favorite tools that allows me to help people is the Destiny Matrix, or Personality Matrix, as I like to call it. With it, I can easily see a person, read their manifestation in the world, look not at the program itself, but at its code — that is, at the very root, the very foundation.

I came to the Matrix gradually, first encountering it through an unsuccessful consultation. Then I tried to understand the calculations myself. Of course, I started by calculating the matrices of all my relatives and friends, immediately drawing parallels with real character traits and events, since I am primarily a practitioner, not a theorist. If a theory can't be applied to real life, it holds little value for me. Thanks to this, I easily memorized the properties of each energy in the Matrix, which I now associate with real people. No textbook can compare with experience, when you've looked at hundreds of matrices and know how a particular set of energies functions in specific people.

For example, my dad has the 19th energy — the Sun, abundance, the millionaire's arcana, gifts from life. The more such a person gives their sunbeams with a generous soul, the more they shine and radiate to this world, demanding nothing in return, the more they receive from the world in response. Those with the 19th energy thrive when they embrace generosity and abundance, avoiding stinginess or obsessing over discounts. My dad, however, at some point started behaving this way because of the situation with my cousin (my mother's nephew borrowed a significant amount from him to start a business and never returned it) and because he didn't want to take money from us. The 19th energy should also never be lent — this is like giving away all your energy and expecting it to return multiplied. Having started to live the 19th energy in the negative, Dad got sick, and everything snowballed. At the same time, the other energies no longer mattered, faded into the background, and didn't help to pull the situation out, because the main driving axis was broken.

I have the 8th energy in my center — it signifies the balance of the spiritual and material worlds. And it's true: the deeper I develop spiritually, the more successful I grow materially. I have no contradiction between these spheres. I can't cheat, come up with illegal schemes, or avoid paying taxes — my main energy requires everything to be legal.

After exploring the matrices of those around me, I began analyzing how potential partnerships might unfold. Sometimes I saw that I shouldn't have any dealings with this person, but I still went ahead with the interaction. Later, situations inevitably arose from which it was clearly evident: the Matrix hadn't deceived me. It's a compass that shows the direction.

I potentially know the fate of a car whose total number adds up to 13, 15, or 16, and therefore I try not to get into one. A favorable total number for a car is 5 or 7. 15, however, is the energy of the devil, beautiful, alluring, but destructive. It offers something tempting, but a person can always refuse it if they are at the necessary level of awareness. The 15th of each month carries temptations — it's a day to stay mindful and cautious.

So what is the Personality Matrix? To tell you more about this amazing tool, I would need a whole book, but I want to give you at least a general idea... All calculations in the Personality Matrix are based on the date of birth, which is the code embedded from the beginning and driving us forward. Neither the time nor the place of birth is important for the calculation. So what can you see in the end?

Imagine a clock face. The minute hand runs along it, leading the hour hand. In the Matrix, this is the central energy: the main one that drives a person and can be lived both positively and negatively.

An important zone of the Personality Matrix is the soul's task, which a person must fulfill in this incarnation. Most likely, it will be difficult, and this is what you will constantly stumble over. For me, it's the 22nd energy – the archetype of the free spirit, symbolizing lightness and constant renewal. As a Capricorn who values stability and structure, starting over from scratch feels incredibly challenging. But if I don't go into reset myself, I will be forcibly reset, and in such a way that it won't seem like much: they'll give me a serious illness, take away a loved one, leave me alone in a foreign country, send me to an alluring but foreign and unfamiliar island... Thus, every time I learn something new and conquer new heights, I fulfill my soul's task.

When I compile a person's Matrix, I don't just give them a characteristic, but I tell them what can be changed, how to go from negative to positive, and what tools to use for this. The Matrix highlights, for example, which energies are in balance or imbalance and helps you better feel your potential.

One of my clients worked as a restaurant administrator for a long time, constantly grappling with whether it was the right career path for her. The job felt like a suitcase without a handle: difficult to carry, yet hard to let go. When I examined her numerology chart (matrix), I saw incredible potential in the beauty industry and asked, "Have you ever considered opening a beauty salon?" She was surprised and admitted she had been contemplating training in permanent makeup or eyelash extensions. "Exactly! That's your calling!" I confirmed. Now she owns her own beauty salon and actively manages its social media presence, fully aligned with her energies.

The dominant energy in her chart was a 6, indicating an interest in aesthetics, beauty, and, most importantly, self-love. In most cases, when someone with this energy pursues a leadership role, they tend to manage businesses like flower shops, art galleries, or beauty salons. Moreover, they choose their field specifically out of self-love. For example, a woman might value stylish hair, manicured nails, and a fresh complexion but realize how much she spends on these services and the inconvenience of visiting different salons across town. The natural solution presents itself: open her own salon, bringing together the specific treatments and specialists she desires.

Besides revealing inherent energies, a numerology chart can offer insights into building relationships, determining compatible partners, forecasting the year ahead, identifying promising business ventures, and advising against others. You can even create a chart for a specific country to understand its current phase, stage of development, and whether it aligns with your current needs.

In the five years I've been working with numerology charts, I've found answers to all my questions. Numbers are the building blocks of the universe — everything is based on mathematics and sacred geometry[10]. My soul has found peace. I've learned how to stay in a state of flow and align myself with the rhythms of the universe. I'm certain that a vast, beautiful, and unexplored world still lies before me, but my life has already gained new, sparkling facets.

I'm aware of my strengths and what I can rely on. Instead of taking shots in the dark, constantly wondering if something will work or not, I take steps that will lead me to my desired outcome with 100% certainty. I no longer have time to waste on the superfluous and unnecessary.

---

[10] Sacred geometry, in this context, refers to the arrangement of key points within a person's numerology chart, forming geometric shapes (quadrilaterals). These shapes symbolize the individual's innate predispositions and the ancestral information passed down through their lineage. Each point and line within the chart holds a specific meaning. It's possible to adjust these parameters, thereby influencing one's life and transforming negative manifestations into positive ones.

Fig. 8. Sacred Geometry

Understanding yourself significantly shortens the path to fulfillment.

I believe it's crucial for children choosing their career paths to understand their own numerology charts. By recognizing their potential and understanding their way of thinking, they can forge their own paths instead of having parents or teachers dictate them.

I remember when our class was divided into science/math and humanities tracks. This was decided by the teachers, without considering that a child might possess entirely different hidden potential. Often, difficulties with a subject aren't due to a lack of aptitude, but rather other factors, such as a poor connection with the teacher. Some students have equally developed left and right brain hemispheres, creating a balance between the two. How can such a child be placed in a class that prioritizes one over the other?

Many self-discovery methods, including astrology, have emphasized the importance of this hemispheric balance in my own life. I'm capable of both artistic expression and successful business management. Perhaps this explains why I see the world differently. The most surprising confirmation came when I hand wrote something and initially felt dismayed by how messy my handwriting had become. Only moments later did I realize I had unconsciously written with my left hand, which I never use.

I've always known I was different, that I had my own unique plans and dreams, and I never compared them to others'. Others, however, constantly measured themselves against me, and that was their problem. They were trying to create another copy, when only the original holds value.

The original is *you*. Each individual is unique. The only requirement is to know yourself.

Understanding yourself and your purpose is especially vital now, as we steadily move into the age of robots. Soon there will be no cashiers in stores, no bank tellers, and no other similar professions where people are often mismatched with their roles. As robots take over routine tasks, many will finally have the freedom to pursue their true passions— make some art, play jazz, or teach children mathematics. They'll be able to authentically express themselves in the world, as encoded within their personal matrix, doing what resonates deeply within their souls.

Ask yourself:

- What are my strengths and weaknesses?
- Do I understand my purpose?
- Who am I, and what am I here to do?

Believe me, you're not here simply to raise children or work a routine job. You're not here to mold yourself to someone else's expectations or build their dreams. Each of us must find our own core. You can do this through any method — it doesn't matter which entrance you use, as long as you eventually find that door.

Chapter 16: Signs, Symbols, Dreams

As time went by, changes in circumstances helped me heal and move forward. But to attract something new into my life, I needed to shift my internal energy. I was in Bali — an island

I had dreamed of moving to while pregnant with David. It was here that I achieved my that I found my energetic renewal

I no longer needed to worry about meeting basic needs – my business had grown enough to provide comfort for my entire family. My psychological state had normalized. I was living with a loving and devoted man. Yet, I understood there was a significant imbalance within me. I felt like I had hit a ceiling. All my needs were met — I had successfully built Maslow's entire pyramid. Finances, success, self-realization, security for myself and my child... All my goals had been achieved, and... I didn't understand what to strive for next, where to grow further.

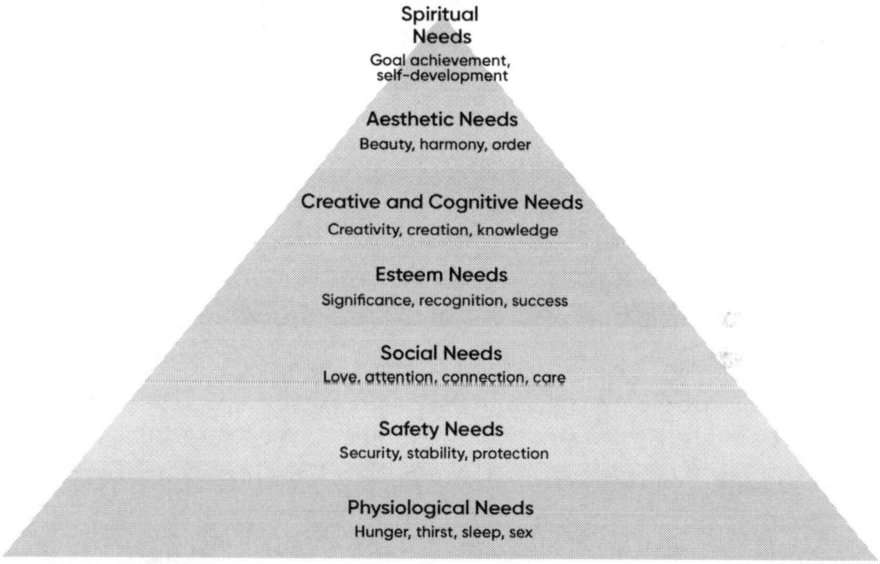

Fig. 9. Maslow's Pyramid

This oversaturation turned destructive: arguments with Antonio, obsessive thoughts, and a complete lack of self-understanding. I felt like we were diverging — he was walking straight ahead, while I was striving upwards. A powerful surge of energy built up inside me, desperate to find an outlet. I felt like I was being carried somewhere, but I didn't know in which direction to channel my inner flow.

This had happened to me a year earlier, when I first went to Bali. Understanding David's strong attachment to Antonio, I wanted to make our potential separation as painless as possible for my son. He needed to detach from his stepfather in a pleasant environment. I tried to imagine life through the eyes of a two-year-old — what could make him let go of everything else? And where I myself could completely shift my focus, because at that time, I was in a very bad place.

Looking at Antonio, I saw that he had reached the limit of his dreams. He was so comfortable and content that he had become stagnant. I, on the other hand, was being pulled forward and upward with an irresistible force; I couldn't even discern the direction. And if I didn't know where I was going, how could I drag someone else along with me? I was restless and unable to concentrate, searching for a way beyond the confines and not finding it. Maybe I had imagined everything, and he simply wasn't the right man for me? If I ended this relationship, would something change?

In such a state, a woman is prone to destructive behavior, starting arguments out of nowhere, inventing grievances, accusing her partner of not giving her enough attention. In reality, she needs to find herself. I constantly see this with my clients. Destruction often occurs precisely in a state of abundance, and the woman immediately blames the man. A plant grows so much that it starts to break through the boundaries of its pot.

If a woman doesn't start to understand herself and succumbs to destructive energy, she can ruin the relationship and dismantle, brick by brick, the once perfectly constructed Maslow's pyramid.

Fortunately, I managed to understand: I needed to stop flying upwards and start moving in the opposite direction. To dig deep, look within myself, search for answers somewhere in the depths of my soul, not externally.

All this time, Bali had been flickering at the edge of my consciousness. The island called to me, remaining a saving oasis in case I reached a critical point. What if this was it?

Carefully sharing the idea of living in Bali with David for a while with Antonio, I received a good-natured chuckle in response: "I can just see you riding a motorbike, decked out in your designer brands and diamonds, with David clinging on behind like a monkey." Antonio didn't fully believe I would go through with it. And even to me, it sounded crazy.

Soon, I realized there was no point in resisting; it was better to look for ways to achieve my goal. There are no unsolvable problems – there are only goals.

I began searching for the most suitable solutions: tickets, accommodation, and, of course, a qualified nanny for David whom I could trust, so I would have enough time to focus on myself. Armed with a list of criteria, I read reviews and suddenly realized: I found her! After a phone call, the nanny and I immediately agreed on everything, and I became even more confident that she was an excellent candidate.

It took David and me almost three days to reach our cherished destination. Montreal — Vancouver, Vancouver — Hong Kong, Hong Kong — Denpasar, and finally, the magical island was beneath my feet. Despite the terrible fatigue, as soon as my foot touched this land, I felt an energetic charge. I couldn't get enough of it. It felt like drinking water and still wanting more — a captivating energy I couldn't get enough of.

Bali is an island that has to accept you. There are people whose 'batteries' don't seem to connect with this powerful charger, and all sorts of misfortunes begin to befall them. Our connection with the island happened at first sight, with the first breath of air. I immediately felt an internal reboot begin; exhausted and drained, I was as if connected to a power bank; my power supply vibrated and charged. The burden I had been carrying for the past few years gradually began to lift from my shoulders.

I spent most of the day with David, and only when I felt an unbearable need to be alone did I call the nanny. I practiced yoga, meditated, went for massages, strolled through the market admiring the amazing souvenirs, dedicated time to connecting with nature and self-discovery, and interacted with people. I liked that they were so diverse here that it was impossible to tell who you were facing: a billionaire or a hippie — the desire to stand out with brands or other attributes of a wealthy life disappeared here on its own.

I was surrounded by incredible people, the likes of whom you won't find anywhere else! They always smile, they are happy with you and with the present day; everything is wonderful for them because today they have this life, food, the sun above their heads, and the ocean waves at their feet. Being among such people makes you want to be present in the moment and enjoy life.

As I looked at the locals, thanking the Universe for everything they had, I desperately wanted them to always remain this way, untouched by money and the growing popularity of tourism. The island will remain, as will the incredible beauty of its nature, but if this incredible energy of love, gratitude, and acceptance leaves Bali...

Life on the island was very different from my life in Canada. Everything was contrasted. A week ago, I was staying in one of the most expensive hotels in the world, and, today, I was riding a scooter through rice paddies. And in this contrast, I experienced immense pleasure: emotions, adrenaline, a zest for life.

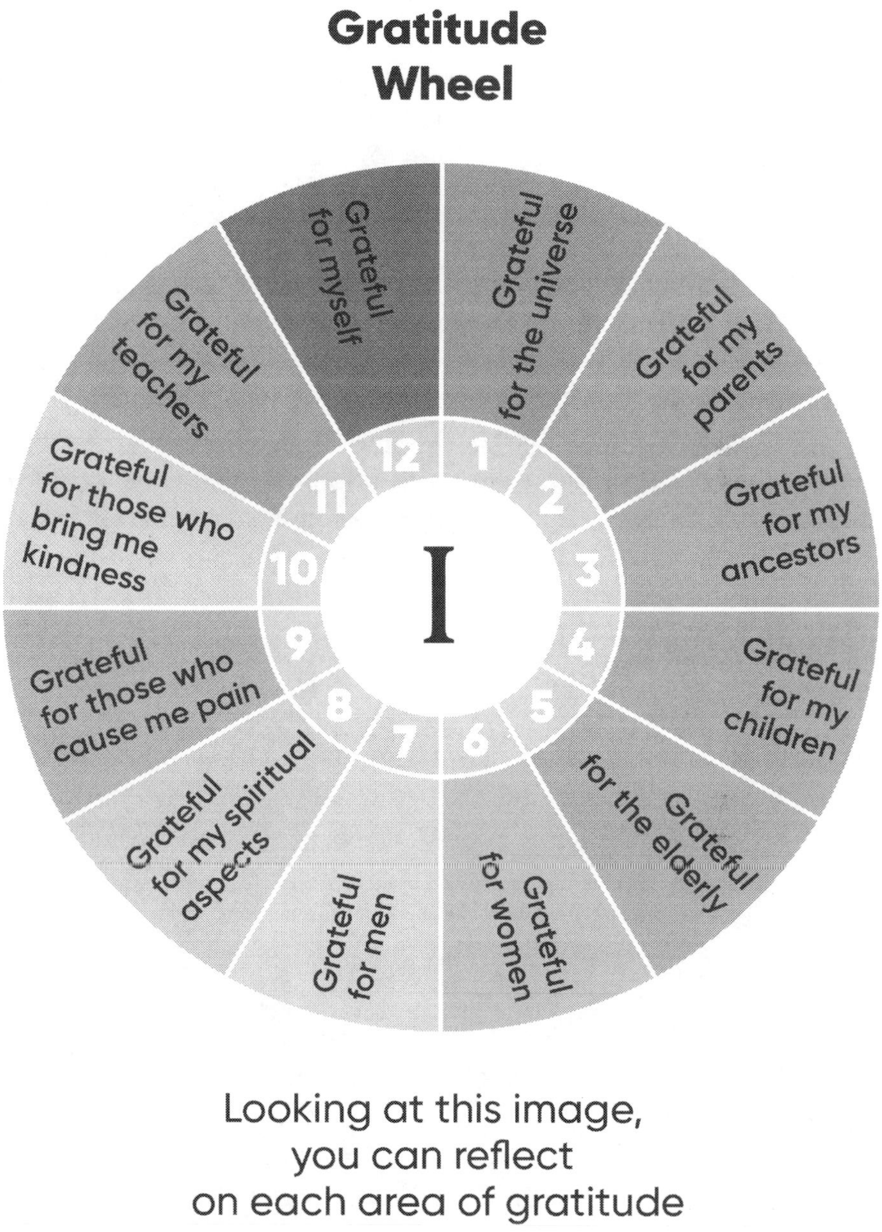

Fig. 10. Wheel of Gratitude

I sought spirituality in Bali, dreaming of going as deep within myself as possible and being filled with new energy. My acquaintances were shocked when they learned that I hadn't swum in the ocean once in almost a month. But I came here with a different purpose, having decided from the outset that I would say "yes" to life in every way. But it turned out that my willingness wasn't enough.

More than anything, I was drawn to the idea of experiencing ayahuasca. I had tried four times to attend a ceremony before Bali, but something always went wrong. On the island, where every other person seemed to have tried it, I couldn't find ayahuasca anywhere! Having already resigned myself to the fact that it wasn't the right time or place again, I received information that ayahuasca was unnecessary for me because my channel was already open.

Although I was clearly aware that I was in the right place at the right time, I still proceeded very cautiously at first. Like a cat brought into a new home, I carefully studied the world around me, afraid to scare away the magic. Until one wonderful moment, and I became a part of it.

The Flower Ceremony of Soul Cleansing

During my last few days in Bali, as my return to Canada loomed, a sense of disappointment started creeping in. Yes, I had rested, recharged, and reset, but the miracle I'd hoped for hadn't happened. I still didn't know where I was headed or how to live my life moving forward. Then, unexpectedly, while chatting with an employee at a massage salon, I received an intriguing offer.

"Would you like to experience a flower ceremony of soul cleansing?"

"Yes, what is it?" I replied, habitually agreeing before fully understanding. After all, I had come here to say "yes."

The woman handed me a small instruction sheet, which I barely comprehended, but it looked beautiful and enticing. It even mentioned a photographer.

Still unsure of what to expect, the next day (the day before my departure from Bali), I set off. It turned out the location was inaccessible by car, so I hailed a motorbike taxi. Across fields, meadows, and rice paddies, the driver swiftly delivered me to my destination... and stopped in front of a small hut. I was about to ask him to take me back when the door opened, and well-dressed, contented-looking people of European descent emerged.

The scent of incense wafted through the open doorway, and the people were engaged in animated conversation, smiling broadly and seemingly radiating a magical light. I dismissed the taxi driver and stepped inside.

A kind, smiling woman poured me some tea, and I settled in on the cushions, cradling the cup in my hands and curiously observing the hut, which was beautifully adorned with flowers. A small fountain gurgled softly, spirals of smoke rose from burning incense sticks, and fluffy cats weaved between the legs of women dressed in colorful clothes.

When I finished my tea, I was invited to undergo a soul reading ceremony and directed towards a door. Behind it, I discovered a dark, square room with wooden walls and floors, adorned with stones, photographs, Buddha statues, and, of course, armfuls of flowers. A white canopy draped from the ceiling, reaching the floor like a tent, and within its folds, in the lotus position, sat an elderly woman in white robes. She beckoned me with her hand, and I approached, feeling as if I had stepped into the movie "Eat, Pray, Love."

Unsure of what to say or ask, I offered a greeting, but before I could add anything else, the woman spoke.

"You have incredibly vast, bright energy," the woman began, her sharp, piercing gaze scanning me. You have the potential to become a mentor whose influence reaches far and wide. You already possess all the knowledge, and you must share it. Listen to your soul, not your mind. People need what you can give to this world. This is your purpose, and there is nothing more important for you."

Chills ran down my spine. I was completely bewildered by what was happening. "You will come to me again, but you will be completely different," the woman smiled, not giving me a chance to recover. "But how soon our meeting will take place depends on you. If you start opening up now, you will come quickly. But if you don't accept yourself, your path may be long and agonizing."

"What if I don't know what to share, or I don't want to do it?" I cautiously inquired.

"Then you will lose everything you have, everything that has been given to you and that you cherish most. Your entire life and mission are tied to helping people find their way. And remember: you need to speak not one-on-one with individual people, but to a wide audience."

I didn't know what to do with this information. My Maslow's hierarchy of needs was fulfilled to the last detail; I gave advice to friends and acquaintances, gradually developing frameworks. But the prospect of broadcasting myself to the masses still seemed unattainable.

Meanwhile, the shaman continued: "You have the gift of seeing the fork in the road of events and options, and through this, changing people's destinies by suggesting which path to choose. You can also change your own destiny, so whoever predicts anything for you will miss the mark. You will subsequently take different actions — and the future will change again."

I wanted to ask how I should then interpret her prophecy, but I immediately realized that the woman was only listing what I had come into this world with, not predicting the future. It remained my responsibility, my choice, my path.

After our conversation, the flower ceremony itself began, Melukat — a sacred Balinese ritual intended to cleanse the body, mind, and spirit, rid one of negativity, and fill one with new energy.

I changed into a swimsuit, as instructed on the sheet I had been given. The women offered to tie a large, multicolored scarf over it, the shade of which I chose myself. Large, fragrant buds were woven into my hair, and a garland of flowers was placed around my neck. I tasted a special dish made of rice with petals, and then I returned to the shaman, carrying a basket full of flowers on my head. A photographer documented the entire process.

I felt as though I was immersed in a vibrant, colorful, swirling vortex. I was doused with flower-infused water, symbolizing purity, truth, and an endless flow. The shaman and her assistant sang a beautiful prayer — words I didn't understand, but they seemed to penetrate deep within me. "Scream," the shaman commanded, and I released a deep, raw cry, channeling all the pain and exhaustion inside me.

"The more you follow your mission, the more rewards you will receive from life," the shaman said before I left the hut, not yet knowing that I would return in just a year.

I felt that I had finally recovered morally, physically, and energetically... and rediscovered myself. It turned out that I didn't need to become anyone else – I just needed to become myself again.

Loss

Then an event occurred that triggered the most crucial period of my development and formation. From that time on, the person I am now gradually emerged.

My dad became seriously ill. His serious health problems began five years earlier when my mother's nephew failed to repay a loan. Dad often lent money with interest, and, of course, there were instances when debts weren't repaid. This time, what truly devastated him was that it was a relative, a family member, one of his own, who had done this. Moreover, this money had been set aside for his "bright future and peaceful old age."

Later, I looked at my cousin's astrological chart: it showed the typical numbers (manifesting in their negative values) characteristic of charlatans, gamblers, and people who don't worry about anything in their lives. And they get away with everything! Dad couldn't even speak ill of him but was forced to sue. He won the case, and my cousin was forbidden from leaving the country until he repaid the money, but he still managed to escape and settle in America as if nothing had happened.

At that time in my life, I was planning a trip to California for a few months. I had long planned to live there, to explore, as it seemed like the perfect place for me. But things kept falling apart — it was as if doors were slamming shut in front of me, one after another. Three days after another landlord refused to rent me an apartment, Dad was hospitalized. I immediately returned my tickets to America and rushed to Kyiv.

At that point, Dad had already suffered three heart attacks. The first thing I saw with horror, upon arriving in Kyiv and going to see him, was that the central city hospital no longer had experienced, qualified doctors. Interns and students were conducting examinations and consultations. They showed me his test results and explained that they themselves didn't understand how, with such indicators and such a damaged heart, a person could still be alive. Only Dad's will to live kept him going — he was optimistic then and had no intention of dying.

I found another hospital for Dad and transferred him there. He quickly got back on his feet and started walking slowly. During the diagnosis, it turned out that a week earlier, while already hospitalized, Dad had suffered a stroke, but no one had even noticed. 60% of his brain was affected, and the doctors threw up their hands, just as perplexed about how he managed to joke in such a condition when he shouldn't even be able to speak. There were no other typical consequences of the stroke — no changes in facial expressions or limited mobility.

Of course, Dad no longer communicated with us as he used to, but he was absolutely himself. He just became rude and sharp in his remarks — as if he had turned into a sharp stone. It pained me to see him like this, but I continued to visit him. Perhaps Dad behaved this way because it was unbearable for him to feel helpless and in need of special care. He didn't like to depend on others, wouldn't let us buy his medications or pay for a nurse; he paid for everything himself.

I remember Dad constantly asking me to watch the old Soviet film, *Winter Evening in Gagra*, with him. I didn't recall him ever liking this movie and didn't understand what he was trying to tell me and why it was so important to him at that moment. I was constantly busy, rushing all over Kyiv, searching for competent doctors for him. But I did promise him that we'd watch the movie sometime.

On my next visit to the hospital, I took Dad for a walk. He wouldn't have had the strength to go down to the courtyard, and the doctors wouldn't allow it anyway, so I usually took his arm, and we slowly walked back and forth along the corridor of the ward.

"Dad, you're doing so well, walking on your own," I squeezed his elbow and leaned my shoulder against his for a second. He muttered something unintelligible, and for some reason, a feeling washed over me that this was the last time we would see each other like this. No, not our last meeting, but the last... earthly, physical one.

I wanted to leave quickly, as if someone invisible was pushing me towards the exit. Dad quickly tired and wanted to return to his room. I offered to sit with him, but a new roommate was just moving in, and another patient was fast asleep — I was clearly superfluous. We hastily said goodbye, and I went home with a peaceful heart. Imagine, I made it all up! Dad was recovering, which meant we would see each other again.

I had things to do — David and Antonio were waiting for me. My son had never been without me for so long, and we had a long-planned trip to Mexico for a friend's wedding, so I had to return to Montreal. Dad knew about our trip and, with the enthusiasm of an avid traveler, asked in detail which cities we would visit and what we planned to see in the country. When he started walking, I realized I could leave with a light heart.

To pass the time on the flight, I put on *Winter Evening in Gagra*. It turned out to be a film about the complex relationship between a career-driven man and his daughter, who didn't invite him to her wedding and calls her stepfather "Dad." Dying in the hospital at the end of the film, the main character remembers a time when he took his daughter on vacation to Gagra and says he would give the rest of his life to return to that time.

I still didn't understand what Dad was trying to tell me by recommending this film. "I wanted to know how to build our relationship further," he explained vaguely when we spoke after my arrival. "We have a wonderful, warm relationship, Dad," I reassured him. "I flew to you from the other side of the world, across the ocean." Our relationship had long been established, but clearly, from Dad's side, it was an attempt to get even closer.

A few days later, Mom called and told me that Dad's condition had deteriorated sharply. He went to the bathroom, fell, and hit his head, and because he was taking blood thinners, he suffered a brain hemorrhage that couldn't be stopped. Dad was taken to intensive care, where he fell into a coma. He was breathing on his own, without machines, but he wasn't regaining consciousness. The doctors suggested trepanation, but in such a critical condition, it was simply inhumane.

Meanwhile, we had already arrived in Mexico, and one morning at breakfast, I absentmindedly watched Antonio and David, laughing cheerfully, putting omelets on their plates. My phone vibrated on the table, and I saw with alarm that it was a video call from my brother. What could have happened?

"Hi, I wanted to ask your opinion," my brother began anxiously. "For some reason, they've disconnected Dad from the heart monitors. They're not really saying anything. Here, look." He showed me Dad lying peacefully on the bed. There were no sensors on his chest or arms. I assumed he was recovering, otherwise, what was the point?

"Wait a few minutes, please," I asked, stepping into the elevator. "I'll go up to the room, and we can talk calmly."

Once on the right floor, I ran to the room, feeling on the edge of reality and another world. Opening the door, I called my brother back. "I'm here, with you," I breathed into the receiver.

"Good, Masha. But I think Dad's not breathing anymore..."

On my phone's display, there were two clocks — the one showing Kyiv time displayed 17:17.

Signs Again

Later, Mom vividly described how hard my brother took the news. Dad was his everything, his whole universe, and it pained me to even imagine my forty-year-old brother rushing to his bedside, shaking his shoulders, crying like a child, and begging him to get up. All of that would come later.

For now, I stood in an expensive, beautiful, stylishly furnished room overlooking the ocean, but none of it mattered anymore. I mindlessly watched the snow-white seagulls soar above the turquoise-blue water. Their wings barely moved, catching the currents of the warm breeze. I, too, froze like a seagull, allowing the currents of life to carry me. I wanted to cry, but everything inside was so frozen that the tears seemed to have turned into sharp icicles, unable to break free. A song that Dad loved, "I am Free" performed by Valery Kipelov, began playing in my head. Now it seemed to have taken on a new meaning.

I felt something similar when my grandmother passed away. We had honestly and openly talked about death. "Grandma, when you get there, will you come to me?" I used to ask. She promised... and she came.

The night after David's first birthday, I woke up as if someone had shaken me. I gasped and opened my eyes, not understanding what had woken me. In the empty, dark room, I felt my grandmother's presence, and at that moment, I understood that she was no longer with us. Grabbing my phone, I read a message from my mom, confirming what I already knew. My grandmother was 94 years old. Her last task, her last goal in life — to hold her youngest great-grandson, my child, in her arms — was never achieved.

And now here I was, in the middle of a hotel room, searching with my soul for my dad's soul. I wished he would come too, like Grandma. It was so beautiful outside the window and so empty inside me...

Suddenly, like a light cloud, a thought drifted through: Dad had seemingly arranged for me to be in a warm, beautiful place on such a difficult day because if I had stayed in gray Montreal, it would have been much harder for me to cope with this loss. Dad loved to travel in style; we had seen so much together, and now it was as if he had made his final decision — to leave me while I was near the ocean, which would gently embrace me with its waves and whisper words of comfort in my ear. I accepted his choice. I always respected Dad's decisions.

There was another reason why I could cope with the loss more easily — now I was beginning to read the universe more deeply, to see signs, to receive hints. Had this happened five years ago, I would have only grieved, mourned how Dad could leave me like this — that is, I would have experienced his death from a place of selfishness. But now I felt Dad's departure differently. Despite the pain, I was ready to perceive information on a different level, and the signs were not long in coming.

It was November 13th, an eclipse in Scorpio. 13 is the number of death, transformation, and Scorpio in this position divides the world into before and after, forcing a person to decide whether they are ready to radically change their life to move to a completely different level or whether it's easier for them to leave. A corridor with only two paths: to the world of the dead and to the world of the living. I knew that if Dad survived this eclipse, everything would be fine. But he decided otherwise — and Scorpio took him. And today was also the birthday of that same cousin who hadn't repaid Dad's debt. Coincidences, coincidences...

I suddenly remembered how much had already happened to me in Mexico, on every trip! On the one hand, these were powerful transformational moments, on the other, I didn't want to fly there anymore.

Mexico is famous for a cult in which death is not just the end of life, but a real, powerful goddess named Santa Muerte. She is revered, gifts are brought to her, and people ask her for help. For Santa Muerte, all people are equal, and she gives everyone the opportunity to live their life as they want and for exactly as long as they are meant to. In November, Mexicans celebrate the Day of the Dead, bringing flowers and treats to the altars of their ancestors. For us, these unusual traditions of a foreign culture sometimes seem eerie, and for me, after several incidents, Mexico has become firmly associated with illness and death.

The first time I was here, one-year-old David's temperature spiked to 42 degrees Celsius in the middle of the night. I hugged my burning child, not knowing what to do. Antonio and I had had a big fight before that, but we immediately forgot our disagreements and went to the hospital.

The next time we were in Mexico, Antonio's dad had a heart attack that caused his death. And just yesterday, I came out of the water and saw a crowd of people near my sunbed, shouting and waving their arms. It turned out that a man was running along the beach and had a heart attack — he collapsed not just anywhere, but next to my sunbed. While they were trying to resuscitate him, an ambulance arrived and took him away. I don't know what kind of planetary collisions these are and what I have to do with them, but I'm never setting foot in Mexico again.

Help came from an unexpected source — Michael took full responsibility for Dad's funeral in Kyiv. I couldn't have imagined that he would ever become so close to my family again, and I am very grateful to him for everything he did for us then.

On the day of the cremation, Michael sent me a few screenshots. One showed the hearse driver's number, ending in 1717, and the other showed the number of the person in charge of the funeral services — also 1717. These numbers seemed to haunt me, highlighting what to pay attention to and how to react to the situation.

It was around 5 a. m., and we were soon due to fly from Cancun to Mexico City. Antonio and David were asleep, and I quietly slipped out of bed and went out onto the balcony with my phone. I called Mom. She said she would call me back in five minutes because they were just entering the crematorium.

I waited twice as long and started calling myself; Mom, my brother, Michael — they were all unavailable, as if they were in some kind of Bermuda Triangle. Probably no signal inside. I was distraught — not only could I not see Dad off on his final journey, but I couldn't even be in touch with those who were with him now. I felt lonely and cut off from my family, and time stretched to infinity.

Half an hour later, Mom called back and confirmed that their phones had no signal. It turned out that for some reason they were let inside 15 minutes early, and then the gates were closed, and those who arrived later couldn't come in to say goodbye, even though it was scheduled for a specific time. It was as if Dad didn't want these people to see him in that state, including me. I was grateful that life had given me the chance to say goodbye to Dad while he was still alive, and in my memory, he remained alive.

An hour later, we packed up and left for the airport. "There's a traffic jam ahead, according to the navigator," the taxi driver warned. "Seems like something happened." Soon, police cars, fire trucks, and ambulances began flying past us at high speed, sirens wailing. A giant column of smoke appeared on the horizon, rising into the sky. "Wow, the market's on fire," the taxi driver said, glancing at his phone the whole time. We got stuck in a traffic jam for hours, and I watched the rising smoke, mesmerized. Dad, are you sending me signs?

Dad did manage to say goodbye to me on the third day, appearing in an incredibly vivid dream. I dreamt that he, David, and I were riding in a subway car. My son and I were on one side, Dad on the other, and he was in the same condition as he had been for the past couple of years — he had difficulty walking and was leaning on a cane. Dad was wearing a red jacket and brown pants.

We reached the station where we had to change to the next train. We needed one line, and Dad another. I led David to the elevator that would take us to the platform above. Dad didn't come with us, and I said goodbye — calmly, easily, as if we would see each other tomorrow. "See you," he replied and kissed me, then David, in turn. I pressed the elevator button, turned around, and saw Dad's limping silhouette with his cane and rings of cigarette smoke dissolving into the crowd. It was as if our lifelines had intersected in this incarnation for the last time, to temporarily diverge.

The dream, as vivid as reality, full of living details, left a distinct aftertaste: we are all not here forever, and my soul's task is not yet complete. My mission is not yet over. I need a little more time to be useful on this planet.

Dad and I will definitely meet again, because we have met before. In a past life, I felt his care, warmth, and paternal attention, which I lacked so much then. He loved a lonely little girl with all his heart, even though he was only her father's advisor[11]. In this life, I intuitively recognized Dad's soul and always felt that this was a person dear to me, not only by blood.

---

[11] See the story in the prologue.

We can come to Earth in different bodies, but the soul remains the same. That's why sometimes, when we meet someone, we get a sense of déjà vu: it's as if we've already met and have known each other for a long time, but from where? When? It couldn't have happened! Such feelings suggest that we recognize a soul we've encountered in a past life.

I experienced the single day we spent in Mexico City as a strange, surreal vision.

We checked into one of the city's oldest hotels, which oppressed me with its heavy, dark wood interiors. Chandeliers resembling those of a medieval castle hung overhead, and portraits of celebrities adorned the lobby walls — they had once stayed here, and the fact that they were all now dead struck me painfully. After barely glancing into the dining room, I rushed out, suggesting to Antonio that we find a restaurant. The room resembled a mournful mausoleum rather than a place where people peacefully converse over dinner. The entire hotel felt permeated with an atmosphere of death — I wanted to hide from it, like an animal fleeing a predator, but there was simply nowhere to go. The image of death pursued me everywhere.

Honestly, I lost my appetite completely, and we decided to visit the planned sights, heading to the Mayan Culture Museum. Of course, I knew approximately what I would see there, but I wasn't prepared for such a quantity of death-themed exhibits. Ritual masks, bone necklaces, skulls... I lost my sense of reality and moved as if in a dream because it was simply impossible to believe what was happening around me. It wasn't me walking through the gloomy halls and listening to the guide talk about ripped-out human hearts. It wasn't me bending over another chilling exhibit... The real me is there, in Kyiv, next to my mother and brother, and we are grieving our loss together.

Walking around the city didn't help me to distract myself either. Skulls and images of death with a scythe stared at me with empty eyes from every souvenir shop, from shop windows, and even from the tattoo of a guy who passed by. For Mexicans, this is a familiar aesthetic and significant symbolism, but for me... My father was buried just yesterday, and I'm on the other side of the world, surrounded by death everywhere. It was literally in every cup of coffee, in every alley, in every image.

In the evening, exhausted, we finally went to a restaurant, and while waiting for our order, I turned my head and saw a huge billboard with the inscription "17.1717." Looking through the saved screenshots Michael had sent again, I felt that the number 17 somehow connected me to my family, to my lineage, and that it was very important, although I hadn't fully understood what it meant to me yet.

Since then, this combination of numbers has become an earthly hint for me that I'm going in the right direction. If I need to make a decision and I see the numbers 1717, I always take this sign as a "yes." As a hint from Dad.

How to Accept the Death of a Loved One

Dad came into this incarnation with enormous potential and the code of a millionaire in his matrix. There were times when he lived quite comfortably and was never deprived of female attention. But then he took a different path.

Before complaining about life and fate, you need to understand that these are the consequences of our thoughts, actions, and steps. Everything can be changed.

Sometimes I think Dad could have held on for a couple more months, but he didn't voluntarily go into transformation, so it was his time to leave his physical body. He dwelled on the past, lived in it, without looking to the future at all. Dad, of course, made plans — for example, he wanted to have surgery on his leg, but when I asked him what would come after, he couldn't answer. That is, these were mechanical goals, emptiness, a list where all the items were already checked off.

Life is given to us exactly until the moment it is filled with meaning. If it's just existence, a routine day after day, and a person doesn't bring benefit to themselves or others – they are simply a consumer of space. To understand if there is real meaning in life, you can ask yourself from time to time: How, being present on this planet, occupying space on it, do I make the lives of other people better? Do I help anyone, and if so, how?

The soul's task, which was embedded in Dad's birth code, was the continuation of the family line and the preservation of family foundations. Based on his energies, connection to his roots, a traditional vision of family, and investments in family were important to him. Being a charismatic person, Dad ultimately focused more on expressing himself in this world than on his soul's task.

Moreover, even in his numbers, there was dissonance, and other energies brought Dad loneliness and seclusion. Mom didn't want to communicate with him, my brother and I moved away, and as a result, he was left alone. Pride prevented Dad from showing that he needed anyone — he always demonstrated complete self-sufficiency and independence.

By the end of his life, Dad had ruined his body to such an extent that he shortened his own life. It was not out of weakness, but out of strength, as if he consciously decided how long he would live. Knowing how to change his life, he didn't do it, which means this was his soul's path, which must be accepted and respected.

For my brother and me, Dad had unshakeable authority simply by right of his birth. He never punished us, yet one word from him was enough for us to understand everything instantly.

After Dad's death, I felt 'grown-up' – a woman in terms of maturity. It was as if the mischievous little girl who lived inside me had left with him. Dad was the only man to whom I yielded, bowing my head. His word was law to me.

Loved ones are always near

Everything on this earth has its allotted time. Coffee should be drunk immediately, otherwise it gets cold. The human body lives up to 100 years, sometimes up to 68, as in the case of my dad. Everything on this earth is designed in a certain way, so nothing is eternal, and there is a constant circulation and renewal.

With Dad's passing, I felt that there was no longer any need to limit myself in anything. It was as if he had held me back, constantly repeating, "We need to save money. Why spend so much when you can find it cheaper? You're always showing off."

If someone gave me a ride in an expensive car, I always asked to be dropped off far from home and pretended I came by metro to avoid Dad's comments.

When I was being courted and admirers showered me with huge bouquets, Dad would help me arrange them, saying, "You're like Pugacheva after a concert."

Or, for example, if I refused food, Dad always asked, "You're not going to eat? Then why did you go to the restaurant?"

When it came to travel, he might say something like, "Well, Egypt is not your level, you need Dubai."

It all seemed to be said jokingly, but the subtext was: "Why do you need all this?" So I tried not to show off my lifestyle, downplaying my self-worth.

When I rented an expensive apartment in the center of Kyiv near Dad, in a new building, with a concierge and underground parking, Dad never commented on it, never said how well I had done. He praised very carefully in general. He never called me "his princess," never said I was the most beautiful, never exalted me — as if he didn't want me to get conceited and go down the wrong path. Dad always bet on my intellectual abilities, he could praise me for my deeds, for example, for my business successes. So it became ingrained in me — when I receive compliments about my appearance, I don't attach much importance to them.

Dad could jokingly slap me on the bottom and laugh, "Oh, Manya, look at the tuches you've grown."

This and other Hebrew words were constantly in his vocabulary. I never took offense at him. If Dad said it, then the "tuches" really is worth paying attention to and going on a diet for a week.

Dad simply adored Jewish jokes and every day he dug up three new ones somewhere. I couldn't understand where he got them from, but he always shared every new one with me. He would call and tell me and I would listen half-heartedly, busy with my own affairs.

"Did you understand what it was about? Did you understand the essence of the phrase, Manya?" he would always clarify at the end.

He spoke about everyone with light irony and playfulness, and he had a nickname for each of my girlfriends, mostly based on where they lived.

"Your girls are all the same, I can't remember them," Dad would explain when I once again listed the names of "the one from Troyeshchyna" and "this one from Fastiv."

With Dad's passing, it became easier for me to talk about the esoteric part of my life, because his opinion always constrained me. Now, his kind and radiant soul perceives life without distortion from a pure, spiritual vantage point where judgment doesn't exist.

I know my potential and my capabilities. I no longer care about the opinions of others. I've stopped stretching myself thin to suit the convenience of others. I had decided to dedicate my time and energy to those who truly value and resonate with it. I felt that every day is important, and I will take only the best from life in its best manifestation — experience the best emotions, surround myself with the best people, and help only those who are in need and ask for it themselves.

It feels as though I'm gathering unstoppable energy, ready to take flight, like a turbine and acceleration in an airplane before takeoff. I absolutely don't care if someone judges me. I'm no longer worried about what people will say about me. It's as if I've released the beautiful steed I was hiding in the stable — all my power, all my potential, now ready to be shown to the world in all its glory. I have my own values not imposed by society. I walk my own path with steadfast focus and resilience.

I have my own sincere vision of the world and an understanding of how I can help people and humanity as a whole — by giving not a fish, but a fishing rod. I see this as my purpose, my mission.

Surprisingly, I feel that Dad is constantly by my side as my personal assistant and guardian angel, someone who I can ask a question to if I need guidance. He also had his limitations — a physical body and a task for this life. Where he is now, in his current state, he has no need to worry about me or to control me. He knows more, remembers more, sees more. We interact, and I feel him near, as well as my grandmother — they both send answers to my questions. Dad is always in my dreams. It's as if I have gained powerful support and I believe that everything will work out for me.

Dad and Grandma never allowed me to cry for myself, but here I am, an incredibly sentimental person, only smiling, remembering Dad and Grandma.

When a lump still rises in my throat and tears well up in my eyes, I hear their voices inside, gently saying, "Why grieve? We are here, with you, even closer than we could have been in life." Besides, I cried all I could, because Dad had a stroke, heart attacks, and severe Covid. I said goodbye to him at least three times, and the fourth time he was really gone.

After Dad's death, I constantly listened to Michael Newton's book "Journey of Souls," for the remaining two weeks of the trip. It made me feel like I was closer to him, and it brought me a sense of peace. We will all meet there again. When the soul departs, there is no bad or good ending for it. Even if a person commits suicide, they simply did not complete their task. They will return as many times as necessary.

I often think of life as a multi-level computer game: if you don't pass a level, you're brought back to the start until you've learned the necessary lessons to move forward.

I don't look at death from the position of the ego. It is an act of suffering that I can no longer talk to my relatives or hug them. I managed to feel how hard it is for an ancient, wise soul to exist in a worn-out body that suffered daily from pain and how happy and inspired it is when it is finally released from this planet. My love for them is greater than for myself, so I can only rejoice that they are now light and free.

I feel Dad's presence in every moment, as though he's just beyond the veil, watching over me. I feel an overwhelming sense of peace, harmony, and balance within me.

I am where I should be, doing what I should be doing. I have embarked on the path of my realization and have gone even deeper into spirituality. I practice hypnosis, accompany clients in their different states, and intuitively feel the subtle worlds. I didn't want to reveal this depth of mine to others – I thought that no one needed it, no one was interested. But it simply wasn't time yet.

Everyone on this planet has their own mission, as well as mentors, with whom we make agreements there in advance. When we incarnate in a physical body, they give our soul clues. Our task is to learn to hear and understand them. After all, how often do we act, guided by logic, while everything inside screams "no"?

When you look at life, don't just see it as a set of random events; see cause-and-effect relationships, notice and read the signs that the Universe sends you. It's like deciphering the code of being, gradually, symbol by symbol, weaving them into a common ornament. This way, life is instantly filled with meaning and the original beauty of the divine plan.

Chapter 17: Return to the Enchanted Island

A year after my encounter with the shaman, I found myself back in Bali, the place I had dreamed of visiting with my father. I imagined how much he would have enjoyed lounging at a villa with a cocktail, gazing at the same scenery every day.

Now, Dad could see everything all at once and be everywhere at the same time, wherever he wants to be... he's freer than he's ever been.

This time, I was accompanied by my assistant, Elena, and a group of participants who had come for my first retreat. Being in a place I loved with the feeling of excitement for my first program was such a meaningful milestone for me.

As I looked at the attendees, I recognized the pain and emptiness they carried, having once felt something similar myself. Exhausted by the meaninglessness and monotony of life, the participants seemed to seek refuge in my guidance. Now it was their turn to undergo a transformation and it would be easier for them than it had been for me — they had a guide to illuminate all the potholes and bumps along the way.

No one guided me. I had to find my own path and face my mistakes on my own. Now, I am their guide, their mentor. Their transformations would occur under my guidance, but I would also allow them to make mistakes, because it's natural and necessary.

Some participants arrived with their children, and I had planned everything in advance to ensure their comfort too.

I planned where we would stay, when we would eat and sleep, who would cook for us and what the menu would be, and what the children would do.

Even though I had scheduled activities for each day, there were moments when I trusted the flow and made decisions based on the participants' moods. For example, when they needed to be alone with themselves to process newly discovered insights, there would be other activities for the other participants to experience. It's impossible to create a universal program for everyone, as each person has their own energy and unique potential. I found an individual approach for each of them and made sure they knew that their feelings were taken into account each step of the way.

Bali revealed itself to me in new colors. It remained a special place meant for healing, but I felt with all my heart and soul that I had returned as a different person. I now possessed a powerful energy. I was no longer tentatively feeling my way along the path, but walking boldly and leading others behind me. Could I have even imagined a year ago that participants would travel to me from Canada, Japan, and Australia?

If this path weren't mine, I wouldn't have been able to achieve such results.

Truth always comes to light.

One day, we visited the shaman I already knew to undergo a flower ceremony for the purification of the soul. I was the first to enter for the soul reading, quietly greeting her with a hoarse voice — I had lost it the night before.

I doubt the shaman recognized me, as she sees so many people every day, but she still spoke to me as though she was a dear friend.

"You're spreading your energy too thin. Focus on mentoring and delegate the rest," she said with confidence. "You've even lost your voice because you're draining your energy in the wrong direction. You need to speak."

At the end, the shaman unexpectedly asked if I had a partner. I nodded hesitantly.

"Don't abandon your work, but this year you need to focus on your partner and his success. Allow him to be the emperor and then you will sit on the throne beside him. Right now, you are an empress yourself, capable of solving anything. But if you pause for a bit, you will move to another country together, and you will have a family."

I left the shaman perplexed. Why should I suddenly stop? The shaman's words, at that moment, had no connection to reality, no meaning for me. I thought that if she had been right last year, this year she missed the mark. It happens to everyone.

For all ten days of the retreat, we spent our time playing Lila, burning incense, and practicing yoga at dawn during low tide. We gravitated only toward plant-based food, and all our senses sharpened and started functioning differently: tastes became more pleasant, smells more vibrant, touches more tangible, sounds and images acquired new tones and shades.

I saw the light spark in the participants' eyes, as if it had revived their long-dormant souls. They had arrived on the island drained, like squeezed lemons, and now they soared upwards like beautiful butterflies. My participants radiated love, filled with renewed energy and a thirst for life; they were ready to unlock their potential and express themselves.

The culmination of this trip, which both I and the participants prepared for with special care, was the sacred healing tea ceremony — a cornerstone of my signature program.

Anticipating the ceremony, we sped on motorbikes, returning from the ocean coast to the villa through endless rice fields. The sweet tropical wind caressed our faces; we felt completely free, moving forward toward new discoveries, knowledge, and our purpose.

I had an important mission: to program the opening channels of the retreat participants. This requires knowing the person's goals and objectives and what kind of information they need to receive. The formula that connects to the open channel is like an address entered into a navigator — it is unique for everyone. Just like the state of being — it is very individual and unique for each person.

For the first part of the retreat, I rented a two-story villa with a thatched roof and beige-gray interiors. In the courtyard, a turquoise pool shimmered in the setting sun, and a turtle swam slowly along its bottom, rhythmically moving its paws. The pool was surrounded by a cozy lawn with soft grass and trees laden with ripening mangoes. Full contact with nature, complete merging with the environment — the most primal, true state of being — was what I was hoping the members of the retreat would feel.

It was a full moon — a special day when energy replenishment is incredibly effective. After the beautiful tea ceremony ended, I led the participants into the garden. By that time, a huge full moon had risen, flooding the sprawling branches of palm trees with silver light and painting a silvery path on the water.

Every blade of grass was visible in its bright glow, as if we were in some parallel world or on another planet. Soothing Balinese melodies with gentle chimes flowed in the background. The warm flames of candles danced on their wicks, warming the soul and drawing us in.

I was in a state of inspiring unity with the participants, guiding the process and sensing each one's immersion into their own subconscious. And then it struck me: we are not just part of nature — we are nature itself. And all we really need is simply to be it. I laid on the ground and felt in harmony with it, listening to the rustling grass and the swaying palms in the wind, inhaling the pungent night scents, and watching the distant stars twinkle overhead.

Follow your natural, primal force – this is the only law worth living by.

After the retreat ended and all the participants had left, I stepped into the garden exhausted yet inspired, opened my laptop, and, immersed in memories, began outlining the first strokes of my book.

It's Not Over Yet

After that full moon ceremony, my connection to nature and the people around me deepened and I started noticing even more signs that I'd been changed.

Albino animals began to appear everywhere I looked: cats, pigeons, even snakes. I remembered the shaman advising me to wear white clothing, a suggestion later echoed by the guides I encountered during deep hypnosis.

The other retreat participants continued to share their epiphanies with me for a long time afterward. These insights dramatically changed their lives within just a few months, sparking countless new processes and initiatives. I understood their excitement, having undergone a massive transformation myself.

Although I had always remained grounded and valued material well-being, the balance I had found between the spiritual and material realms began to bear fruit.

New channels of knowledge gradually opened up to me. I became more self-assured, learned to read the energy of spaces, and could even perceive the life paths of others.

When you discover yourself and your foundation, everything in life becomes so much easier. There's no longer a need for diaries filled with wishes and gratitude, or for a constant focus on meditation and quieting the mind. You're able to envision exactly what you want and can start the work to make that goal a reality.

When you've walked through your darkest darkness, you become the light.

People often share their deepest secrets with me — not only close friends, but sometimes complete strangers. An exchange of energy occurs between us, transmitted through eye contact, words, and the very space we share. Often, they cry after telling me their deepest desires and I offer them the comfort of knowing that they are not judged.

Conclusion

It all began with Antonio's question: "I see your career rapidly taking off, and I sense you don't want more children. Is that true?"

Antonio was right and hiding it would have been unfair to him. One child was indeed enough for me.

At that moment, we decided our paths were diverging because our priorities had grown apart.

My career was flourishing and I felt what I was doing resonated with people, helping them. I needed to move forward, learn new things, and continue sharing my accumulated experience. My growth was continuous — information flowed through me like a filter and I shared its distilled essence with those who were willing to listen. I was at a new stage of life, ascending toward another peak. I had my interests and ambitions and Antonio had his.

The second thing that ignited my passion was the upcoming move to Los Angeles. When I first saw the city from the airplane window, I immediately felt its vibrant, beating heart. It was like a living, breathing organism — multifaceted, with darkness and light, black and white. This multidimensionality — its sheer scale captivated me. I felt that Los Angeles's atmosphere suited me perfectly, and it would be good for David too.

At the time, all the circumstances seemed to be pushing me forward, saying, "Your mission in Canada is complete; you can pack your bags." As a conservative zodiac sign, I always strive for stability, but sometimes life makes it abundantly clear that it's time for a change.

The energies currently prevailing in the world teach us to live in the flow and make decisions based on intuition. So, I try to set aside my rational thinking and trust the Universe more. Relaxing in a storm is incredibly difficult, but you have to lie back on the water and it will carry you to the shore where you're meant to be. My shore turned out to be Los Angeles.

Antonio and I decided to divide the company and our responsibilities. He returned to Canada and I focused on paperwork and issues related to the move and running a business in America. I felt grounded, knowing I could grow and follow my path. I became free, finally spreading my wings and realizing I could rely on myself to provide a comfortable life for David and me in Los Angeles. Ahead lay an even more exciting, inspiring, and captivating journey that seemed like a well-trodden path from others that had made their way from where I was.

Soon, I too left Los Angeles and, despite the jet lag, I scheduled a tea ceremony with a client the very next morning — straight from the ship to the ball, so to speak. I prepared everything calmly and unhurriedly. I still had about half an hour before the meeting.

Perhaps these were the first thirty minutes in recent memory where I escaped the whirlwind of events and found myself alone in silence. And then it suddenly hit me: I'd been so busy, I hadn't checked my cycle in a while.

In my app's calendar, the previous month was highlighted in red — of course! I hadn't marked my period, which is always as regular as clockwork. I tried to remember when it last occurred — I couldn't have been so detached from reality as to forget something so significant.

The urge to just let it be never left, and I purchased a test.

A couple of minutes later, after staring in shock at the two lines gradually growing darker on the positive pregnancy test, I began to understand the true meaning of the shaman's words in Bali: about the empress and her emperor.

My head swam, my vision blurred, and my newly spread wings desperately tried to catch the wind, which had so suddenly changed direction, but I could feel my descent begin...